COFFEE, TEA OR ME?

THE HIGH-FLYING NATIONAL BESTSELLER!

"A MANUAL FOR LIVING A LIFETIME IN A COUPLE OF YEARS... This airborne **Fanny Hill** is a frank, authentic-sounding diary of the happiness of pursuit by flying females. Surely 20-year-old young women never learned so much so quickly as they do in the jet age!"

—**Collegiate Journalist**

"A PULL-NO-PUNCHES ACCOUNT OF AERIAL AND BOUDOIR DOINGS, amusing and outspoken... Has the industry chuckling and guessing names!"

—**Aviation News**

"GIVES THE LOWDOWN ON STEWARDESSES—what they do in training, in the air and on the ground between flights... Reads like a footnote to **Human Sexual Response!**"

—**Look**

Coffee Tea or Me?

THE UNINHIBITED MEMOIRS OF TWO AIRLINE STEWARDESSES

Trudy Baker and Rachel Jones

Illustrated by Bill Wenzel

*This low-priced Bantam Book
has been completely reset in a type face
designed for easy reading, and was printed
from new plates. It contains the complete
text of the original hard-cover edition.*
NOT ONE WORD HAS BEEN OMITTED.

COFFEE, TEA OR ME?
*A Bantam Book / published by arrangement with
Bartholomew House Ltd.*

PRINTING HISTORY
Bartholomew House Ltd. edition published October 1967
2nd printing .... December 1967
3rd printing ...... January 1968

Bantam edition published November 1968
2nd printing....November 1968	6th printing....November 1968
3rd printing....November 1968	7th printing....November 1968
4th printing....November 1968	8th printing....November 1968
5th printing....November 1968	9th printing....December 1968

10th printing ..... January 1969
11th printing
12th printing
13th printing
14th printing
15th printing
16th printing
17th printing
18th printing
19th printing
20th printing

Covers and inside drawings by Bill Wenzel.

© *1967 by Bartholomew House Ltd.
All rights reserved under International and Pan American conventions. No part of this book may be reproduced in any form, by mimeograph or any other means, without permission. For information address: Bartholomew House Ltd., a division of Bartell Media Corporation, 205 East 42nd Street, New York, N.Y. 10017.*

Published simultaneously in the United States and Canada

Bantam Books are published by Bantam Books, Inc., a subsidiary of Grosset & Dunlap, Inc. Its trade-mark, consisting of the words "Bantam Books" and the portrayal of a bantam, is registered in the United States Patent Office and in other countries. Marca Registrada. Bantam Books, Inc., 271 Madison Avenue, New York, N.Y. 10016.

PRINTED IN THE UNITED STATES OF AMERICA

Chapters

	Foreword	1
I	"Is This Your First Flight, Too?"	5
II	"Let's Run Away and Be Stewardesses"	25
III	"Big Momma Is Watching"	35
IV	"You're Nothing but a Stew-Bum, George"	57
V	"Can We Fit Eight in This Apartment?"	75
VI	"This Is Your Captain Speaking"	95
VII	"You Must See So Many Interesting Places, My Dear"	107
VIII	"You Must Meet So Many Interesting Men, My Dear"	115
IX	"The Radar Is Built In"	135
X	"They Looked So Normal"	143
XI	"You Ought To Be in Pictures, Sweetie"	155
XII	"Wow! We're Going To Work a Press Trip!"	161
XIII	"Please, Not Another Press Trip"	175
XIV	"There's Another Drunk in 3A"	189
XV	"Baby-Sitters of the Sky"	201
XVI	"Even Your Best Friend Won't Tell You"	207

XVII	"Have a Merry Mistress"	215
XVIII	"The Saga of Sandy"	231
XIX	"What's a Nice Girl Like You Doing in a Plane Like This?"	241
XX	"Should We Strike?"	271
XXI	"A Layover Is Not What You Think"	283
XXII	"An Unhappy Landing"	291
XXIII	"We'll Give It One More Year, Okay?"	305

Acknowledgment

So many thanks to Don Bain, writer and friend, who's flown enough to know how funny it really can be. Without him, *Coffee, Tea or Me?* would still be nothing more than the punchline of an old airline joke.

Foreword

Rachel and I think alike. That's both a blessing and a curse.

You'd never know it by looking at us. Rachel is a tall, rangy blonde with a wide-open face, brown eyes and a breezy personality. She's a go-getter, the one in the crowd who's always ready with the prod for action.

I'm a couple of inches shorter than Rachel. My eyes are black, my hair a dark brown and I was first in line at the dimple factory. I also smile a lot, even when the news is bad.

We met at stewardess school, roomed together and immediately felt that rare and wonderful rapport that lights up when two people get along beautifully. We fly together, live together, hold each other's hands through blighted romances, tell each other of new-found loves, laugh together at today's mad, mod world and, from time to time, get in trouble together.

In many ways, all stewardesses have a common bond. Rachel and I were both from small towns and anxious to take a fling at the big, bad world. That's true of most girls flying today.

Stewardessing is the ideal job for girls looking to travel and see other places, make many new and varied friends, feel at home in hundreds of strange cities and get paid for these things to boot.

Yes, it is true that a stewardess is a built-in baby sitter, flying waitress and congenial hostess, no matter what troubles befall her. The troubles can be endless: a mix-up on meals, a shortage of liquor, engine difficulties, other mechanical quirks, male pinchers, female whiners, vomiting children, two-timing stewardesses who steal your man and, once in awhile, a plane that takes a good friend to a fiery death.

But we accept all this. The bitter with the sweet, and there's so much that is sweet about being an airline stewardess.

Our lives are different. Airline crews are a close group of people. We work together. We live together. Airline crews stay at the same hotels and layovers. But that doesn't mean it's sex, sex, sex all the time. It can be if

COFFEE, TEA OR ME?

you want it that way, and some do. We all like a little of it. But most of us are also discreet about our private lives, which simply puts us in a class with almost every other young girl tasting life and what it can offer.

One last defensive word before we spring you loose on *Coffee, Tea or Me?* A stewardess is a girl. She wears a uniform and works at thirty-thousand feet. But above all she is a girl, female and subject to all the whims and desires of all females.

One of our desires is that you know more about us, our lives, loves and laughter. That's why we put together our similar minds and wrote this book. Smoking is permitted, and seat belts are at your discretion.

Welcome!

CHAPTER I

"Is This Your First Flight, Too?"

It rained very hard the day we made our first flight as stewardesses. We should have recognized it as an omen of things to come. At the time, it just seemed wet. We should have realized that our first flight couldn't be like anyone else's first flight.

Our brand-new, custom-tailored, form-fitting, wrinkle-proof, Paris-inspired uniforms became soaked in the dash from our apartment house lobby in the east 70's of Manhattan to the cab at the corner. The doorman, a portly fellow known for his red face and his ever-present brown paper bag, had taken over twenty minutes to get us that cab, which cut drastically into the hour we'd allowed ourselves to reach Kennedy Airport.

"Damn, damn, damn," Rachel muttered loudly as she settled in the far corner of the back seat and surveyed her light blue skirt, now blotched dark blue. "Damn!"

"You goils ain't gonna be flyin' today." Our cab driver was Maxwell Solomon, Hack Number 30756M.

We looked at each other briefly before crowing back at Mr. Solomon in unison. "Why?"

"You kiddin'? You wouldn't get me up in no airplane in this here weather. No, sir. Not me."

We told him we'd checked with operations before leaving and they'd told us flights were departing, although incoming flights had been cancelled. We told him a big airliner never takes off unless everything is very safe and sure. We told him the weather was only local, probably, and that once you're off the ground, you fly far above the rain and wind.

"No, sir, not me. Anybody flies in this here weather is nuts or sick or somethin'."

We *were* sick. It started right then and there and never left us for the rest of the day. Mr. Solomon was right. Mr. Solomon also asked us for our telephone numbers because he'd kind of heard stewardesses were a real fun-loving bunch of girls and he knew a great place in Coney Island where there was this sensational rock 'n' roll band.

"Whatta ya say, goils? I'll take the botha ya, only later, like, well, you know, like later onea ya can split and go home."

COFFEE, TEA OR ME?

The natural inclination to tell him off was tempered by memories of recent lectures at stewardess school where we were told (a) everyone is a potential customer of the airline, and (b) courtesy always pays off in sound public relations and future revenue.

"Drop dead," Rachel said with a smile.

"OK, goils, just askin'. Can't blame a guy for that. Right? Especially not witha coupla stews." He clicked his tongue against his teeth, winked at us in the rear-view mirror, and drove a little faster. The large overhead sign indicating one mile to Kennedy Airport passed at 12:01 P.M. We were already late reporting in for our first flight.

We paid the big tab, tipped small, smiled graciously and entered our terminal at JFK through the pneumatic doors. Inside, the lobby was a mob of people milling around the ticket counters. Valiantly dragging our blue suitcases and handbags, we stumbled through the door leading to Flight Operations. There were as many people in ops as in the lobby. Or maybe it just seemed as many because of the solid wall of blue uniforms. We dropped our luggage and were heading for the sign-in book at Crew Scheduling when a female voice stopped us in our tracks.

"Rachel! Trudy!" There was no doubt about that voice. We turned to see the flashing white teeth, flaming red hair and remarkable upthrust bosom of Betty O'Riley, better known to her classmates at stewardess college as Betty Big Boobs. Betty bounced and jiggled over to us, her smile as programmed and precise as a roadway neon sign. Suddenly she frowned and pouted her lips. "Y'all look so scared and lost, honeys."

Then she smiled. "Nothin' to be scared of."

Then she frowned. "They probably cancelled your flight, anyway."

Then she smiled bigger than ever, "Mine's been cancelled 'causa weather in Atlanta." She kept smiling this time and whispered, looking around to insure privacy, "But ah'm goin' to dinner with the captain. He models for cigarette commercials, sometimes."

COFFEE, TEA OR ME?

She giggled furiously, the bosom in violent action. "Ah'm gonna love it to death here."

She turned and hurried through the crowd toward a gray-templed pilot lounging against the wall, a cigarette professionally held between his lips. Her bosom made contact with at least a dozen male elbows on her short trip through the crowd and her fanny, sufficiently oversize to counterbalance the excess weight in front, waved like a stormtossed rudder.

We signed in hurriedly with the stewardess dispatcher, a thin, quiet fellow with large glasses and eyes that never made contact with ours. He looked down at our trip number and said, "You girls are awful late. Better hurry down to the gate."

We took his advice and pushed back through the crowd toward the door. Betty O'Riley was leaning against the wall with her captain, both of them right off the back cover of *Life*. I don't think he ever smoked that cigarette. He remained in perpetual rehearsal should J. Walter Thompson call. Betty, smiling at us, sort of flexed everything at once. We just passed by.

Our flight was to depart from Gate 16. We hurried under the signs directing passengers to the higher numbered gates. Suddenly, Rachel stopped, beat her fists against her thighs: "Damn, damn, damn." In our rush we'd left our luggage and purses back at operations. We spun around in formation and ran back up the endless corridor, people turning to watch as we passed. We grabbed the forgotten items, received another automatic smile from Betty, noticed her captain was now trying it with a cigar, and ran back through the door and up the corridor. It was now 12:30, just a half hour to flight time. We were twenty minutes late.

The departure lounge at Gate 16 was from a De Mille epic. Two ramp agents stood firmly behind their fortress of the ticket counter, their faces mirroring their determination to keep things in order according to the book. (Why would all these people want to go to Cleveland, we wondered?)

COFFEE, TEA OR ME?

We walked up to the ramp agents and announced we were the stewardesses for the flight. One of them never bothered to look at us. The other, a chubby red-head with acne, just glanced, curled his lip and went back to checking in the passengers. It was obvious we weren't supposed to check in with the ramp agents. We remembered our keys, one of which was supposed to fit the steel door leading from the gate's lounge area to the aircraft's parking ramp. Unfortunately, the confusion at the terminal that day necessitated parking the 727 at a gate without the enclosed jetway tunnel. After some fumbling, we opened the door and went down the stairway. We reached the door at the bottom, threw it open, and were greeted with a blast of blowing rain.

"Damn, damn, *damn*."

We ran across the parking ramp and tripped up the portable stairs to the front entrance of the airplane. At the top, safely inside from the rain, stood another stewardess. She partially blocked the entrance, and we had to push past her to reach the dry cabin. We splattered her pretty good.

"Sorry about that," I said with a friendly smile.

"Where have you been?" she countered.

Both of us began chattering about our cab driver, the rain, the baggage in operations and any other reason we could think of.

She cut us off in mid-sentence. "Forget it. Just do a fast job of picking up this cruddy bird. The passengers will be boarding any minute."

We followed her orders without hesitation. After a minute of picking up cigarette butts, paper cups, magazines and Kleenex, I made the mistake of asking, "How come the cabin cleaners didn't work on this airplane?"

I was glad I asked. It brought forth from our senior stew an actual chuckle.

"Boy, oh boy, oh boy," she said with a resigned shaking of her head. "Cabin cleaners? They *have* worked on this bird. Don't you know you've always got to clean up after the cleaners? What they don't teach you in school these days."

COFFEE, TEA OR ME?

We *were* taught about the cabin cleaners in stewardess school. We were taught that this dedicated group of men worked hard to provide our passengers with the cleanest, neatest and most pleasant airplanes anywhere in the free world.

"Buncha pigs," Rachel muttered under her breath as she retracted a crushed cigarette package from between the cushions of a seat. "Damn pigs."

And then the passengers started coming aboard. First came two ramp agents carrying a wheel chair between them. In the chair was a little old lady covered with a large sheet of plastic to keep the rain off. When the chair was safely inside, we removed the plastic and helped her into a seat by the window.

"I don't want to be by the window," she said.

We moved her to the aisle seat.

"I think it would be safer in the front," she said.

We moved her to the front.

"Is this a really safe place?" she asked.

"Yes, ma'am."

"Good." Always treat a first-class passenger right.

Next was a disheveled young mother with four children, the youngest about one and the oldest about four. She carried two of the kids, a ramp agent carried another, and the eldest ran ahead of everyone and jumped into a seat by the window in the first-class section.

"Billy," the mother bellowed. "Back here."

He didn't move. She deposited her two human packages in seats, ran past the ramp agent who valiantly tried to ward off his parcel's attempts to tear off his glasses, and grabbed Billy by the collar.

"I told you to be good. I told you you wouldn't have ice cream, candy, toys, soda, cake or cookies for a year if you weren't good on the airplane."

He started crying and I felt a strange face and voice, mine, might help. I leaned over the seat and said, "I'll give you a pilot's ring if you do what your mother says."

"He'll do what he's told without bribes," mother snapped. She pulled harder on his collar and he finally capitulated, crying all the way back to the others. The ramp agent had placed his ward down in a seat, but she was now in the process of getting up for a romp down the aisle.

Rachel smiled at the mother. "They sure are cute kids," she said with a surprising note of sincerity. "I love kids."

The pre-boards in place, the rest of the passengers started filing on, each soaked despite the big black umbrellas supplied by the agents at the terminal door. Our senior stew was up front in the cockpit with the crew and we stationed ourselves near the door to greet the passengers as they came on board. We asked to see each ticket until some man yelled from the steps that he was getting soaked. Obviously, we ought to let them come aboard before checking tickets. We finally just waved them through with a smile and cheery "hello."

We also threw in little quips like, "Welcome aboard." "Glad you could come today." "Some weather, huh?" "My, you're wet." "Watch out for that umbrella." "Please close the umbrella before entering the aircraft." "Aaaaaaaaaaah," as an umbrella spoke gouged Rachel's arm.

One young man, much too collegiate for his thirty years, came through the door with a large package under his arm. He handed it to me.

"Here, tiger, take good care of it, will you. I've got a lot of money tied up in that piece of hi-fi equipment. You should see my *rig* . . . tiger."

The next man, shaking the water from his head like a dog in from the rain, asked, "Is this the Rochester flight?"

"No sir, it isn't. This goes to Cleveland."

"Cleveland?" he shouted with rage. "Cleveland? I don't want to go to Cleveland. I'm going to Rochester."

"We're sorry, sir, but this is the Cleveland flight."

"Preposterous. I want to talk to your manager. Where is he?"

"Sir, please stand aside until all the passengers have boarded. We'll get you back to your Rochester flight."

COFFEE, TEA OR ME?

"I'll raise hell with someone about this. You just see."

"Yes sir."

Everyone finally seated, and our Rochester-bound man back in the terminal demanding the president, we closed the heavy door, looked at each other, and walked to the front of the tourist section, the section always awarded the junior stewardesses. Our senior stew came out of the cockpit and headed to the buffet situated between the tourist and first-class sections. We followed her into the tiny galley. This seemed to annoy her. She pulled the drape across and glared at us.

"Get out there and check for heavy items in the overhead racks. And check their seat belts. Make sure no one is smoking. Ask that mother if you can do something for her. And get everyone's name on the chart. And please get off my back. I'm not going to take your hand every step of the way."

We twisted around to leave the cramped quarters when she asked, "Which one of you got the razor?"

"The what?"

"The razor. The razor for the passengers to use. You're supposed to get it from operations before coming aboard. I suppose you forgot to sign the briefing book, too. And to get the enroute weather. What the deuce have I ended up with today? Six years of flying for this cruddy airline and I end up with inefficient virgins. You'd better get with it, girls. Or you won't be with it . . . much longer."

We went out in the aisle and surveyed the long columns of faces. We walked to the rear section and looked again.

"I've never seen so many occiputs * in my life," I whispered to Rachel.

The three jet engines in the tail started whining as we went back up the aisle. We looked in everyone's lap to check seat belts but some passengers had coats in their laps and we couldn't be sure. It just would have been too personal to peek.

---

* I once dated a medical student who told me the back of the head was called an occiput. He taught me a lot of anatomical terms.

13

COFFEE, TEA OR ME?

One man stopped Rachel and admitted his seat belt wasn't fastened.

"I don't know how," he confessed.

Rachel leaped to the chance to be of service.

"Let me show you," she said. She reached down under his legs to find the ends, found them, and started fumbling with the mechanism. He loved it. She began to realize that any idiot could fasten a seat belt.

She completed the job. "How's that, sir?"

"Beautiful," he answered. "Thank you, Miss . . . ?"

"Don't take that belt off, sir. Have a pleasant flight."

I found an attaché case in the overhead rack.

"Sorry, sir, but you'll have to take that brief case down," I said in a friendly tone.

"Where will I put it?" he grunted.

"Under your seat, sir."

"It won't fit."

"Oh, I think it will, sir. You just try."

"All right. Get it for me."

"Yes, sir."

It was heavy. I stretched on my toes to reach it and managed to slide it over the lip of the rack. It was soaking wet, and a tiny rivulet of water ran onto the head of a soldier sitting directly beneath.

"Sorry, sir," I told the soldier. He enjoyed being called "sir."

"Careful of that," the owner of the brief case barked.

"Yes, sir." The stretching pulled my blouse, supposedly pull-proof, from my skirt, and my bare belly stood an inch from the soldier's nose. He actually touched his nose to my belly-button. It tickled.

I managed to bring the case down to safety just as the plane began pulling away from the ramp. I lost my balance and dropped the heavy case into its owner's lap.

"You idiot," he snarled. I apologized.

I apologized to the soldier, too, but he didn't seem to want one.

Rachel was beginning to take names on the other side of the cabin and I took the second sheet and started on

COFFEE, TEA OR ME?

my side. The first man I went to sat rigidly in his seat, his knuckles white as he grasped the sides of the chair.

"Your name and destination, sir?"

He panicked. "I thought we were going to Cleveland."

"That's right, sir. Only Cleveland. Just give me your name, sir."

"Carlson. C-a-r-l-s-o-n."

"Thank you, sir." I went on to the next.

"Your name, sir."

He quickly slurred off what sounded like Icklensale.

"Would you spell that for me, sir?"

He didn't like being asked to spell his name. He just said it again, only faster.

"I-c-k-l-e-n-sale?" I tried.

"E-k-l-o-s-h-a-l-e," he corrected with a deep sigh.

"Thank you, sir." His look was mean.

We were half-way through taking names when the captain's voice came over the PA system.

"Ah, ladies and gentlemen, ah welcome aboard Flight 81 to Cleveland. Ah, due to the, ah, bad weather conditions that I guess you've all noticed (chuckle), ah, we're going to have to, ah, wait a little while in line for take-off position . . . ah . . ."

He seemed to want to say something else but didn't . . . or couldn't. The senior stew took up where he left off from her microphone in the buffet area.

"Welcome aboard Flight 81 to Cleveland, Ohio. My name is Miss Lewis. Working with me for your comfort today will be Miss Baker and Miss Jones. We're sorry for the delay in leaving Kennedy today, but weather conditions have cancelled incoming flights and slowed up the departure of other flights. Once off the ground, we expect our flying time to Cleveland to be one hour and eight minutes. We'll be cruising at an altitude of 26,000 feet. If there's anything we can do to make your flight more comfortable, please don't hesitate to call on us. Thank you, and have a pleasant flight."

We went through the oxygen mask routine and resumed taking names. I was almost finished with my side of the airplane when I felt a tap on my rear end. I turned to see Mr. George Kelman, whose name I had just taken. He was an attractive young man with neat brown hair, an expensive suit and an outgoing smile. He beckoned me with his index finger. I leaned closer as he started to talk, the whine of the jet engines making hearing difficult. All that airline advertising talk about their super-quiet jets ran through my mind.

"Yes, sir?"

He leaned closer, too. "This is your first flight, isn't it?"

How did he know? "Yes sir, it is."

"I know. What I wanted to ask you was whether you'd have dinner with me in Cleveland tonight?"

I was stunned. We'd been told many times, of course, that many men would ask us for dates. In fact, we *hoped* many men would ask us for dates. Why else be a flying waitress? But so soon? With the rain and all? I thought quickly, trying to remember what the manual said about dating passengers. It didn't say anything that I could remember.

"Sorry sir, but we're not allowed to accept dates with male passengers."

"How about females?" He laughed easily and with warmth.

I giggled. "Oh sir, that's silly."

"Seriously, how about it?"

"I can't. We don't even stay in Cleveland overnight. Well, unless we're weathered in there."

"Don't worry about that. I'll come back with you and we'll have dinner in New York."

Now I was totally confused.

"Well, you see, I have to go back to work now and I have my girl friend with me and . . ."

"Great. We'll have dinner in Cleveland or New York or wherever you say. All three of us."

I began to panic.

"Well, I'll ask her. Oh, but then you'll want one of us to go home later, like in Coney Island. Right?" Now he was flustered.

"Anything you say, ma'm." He was sweet. I liked him.

COFFEE, TEA OR ME?

But I suddenly sensed that despite the noise of the engines, the other passengers in the immediate area were listening intently. I turned from him and went on with my job of getting names. I looked back at him. He had returned to reading his copy of *Forbes,* a magazine I'd never looked into but one that undoubtedly had something to do with money.

I asked Rachel if we could date passengers.

"You bet, honey," she replied. "It's called a fringe benefit."

Names taken, seat belts fastened and mother-with-four-children relatively settled down and quiet, our captain swung the 727 onto the runway, gave it full-throttle and we started gaining speed for take-off. Rachel and I sat together in our jump seats, tightly belted in, and thought of Maxwell Solomon and his philosophy on flying in today's weather. The more the 727 shuddered as it gained momentum, the more we thought of Maxwell Solomon, now safely in his cab headed for Coney Island with a more receptive fare. And then we felt the slight sensation of being away from the concrete runway, free from the friction of rubber on that runway, and free of that maximum moment of strain before becoming airborne. Outside, a marshmallow blanket of gray, colorless and without substance seemed to buoy up the mass of airplane.

The captain was making his first climbing turn when our senior stew, Miss Lewis, unbuckled her seat belt and motioned for us to follow her into the galley. We stepped inside, grabbing onto anything to maintain our balance in the turbulent turns. Miss Lewis again pulled the drape across the galley entrance.

"OK, let's get moving. I ought to let you fall on your faces all alone. But I'm responsible for the flight and I don't want to see you screw up the back end." She looked at Rachel. "You . . . get back there and take drink orders. They pay in the rear, you know. We've only got to Cleveland to serve all the meals and booze. You're squared away on meal service X-17-B, aren't you?"

"Sure," we said. What meal service *was* X-17-B?

COFFEE, TEA OR ME?

"OK. Get those drink orders, put their trays in place and hustle."

"Right," Rachel answered and departed the galley.

"Help me get this food set up." Miss Lewis was a stern girl, I decided. In fact, she terrified me, especially when I realized I didn't remember a thing about airplanes, passengers, food, drinks or being a stewardess in general. I watched closely and followed her every movement, taking the fruit cups from the cold storage compartments, placing the little plastic bag of salt, pepper, knives and forks on the trays after finding them in the same cold storage compartments, taking the Salisbury steak from the hot storage compartments and the rolls from the same place.

Rachel came back with the drink orders written on a small slip of paper. "I'd better get the drinks out there fast, before dinner, huh?" she asked Miss Lewis.

"Are you kidding?" Miss Lewis snapped as she slapped a piece of butter on each roll plate. "Give them the whole mess at once—booze, food, dessert and coffee. Put the booze bottles on the tray and get them to the right people. Come on, get with it."

"Why don't they just serve sandwiches on these short flights?" I asked.

"Ooooooh, what did I do to deserve this?" wailed Miss Lewis.

We grabbed trays and headed up the aisle, no further questions asked.

"I ordered bourbon," said the man with the attaché case under his seat.

"Where's the soda for my Scotch?" drawled the soldier.

"Could I have a rare one, please?"

"I didn't get a napkin."

"The plane sounds funny. Are we all right?" This came from the little old lady.

"How high are we?"

"How fast are we going?"

"Say, tiger, what are we flying over now?"

"It's stuffy in here. Can we open a window?"

"Where are those free packages of cigarettes?"

"Would you feed the two children in back of me," said

COFFEE, TEA OR ME?

our flying mother of four, her voice more a command than a question.

It was bedlam. Total. We eventually matched the right people with the right drinks, managed to shovel a few spoonfuls of mashed potatoes into the kids' mouths, turned down at least six requests for more than the allowed two drinks, and only spilled one glass of water on a passenger.

Everyone finally had his meal tray in front of him, and we actually inhaled our first free breath since take-off. We hadn't quite exhaled it when the aircraft hit a pocket of severe turbulence, sending it into a sheer and rapid descent of at least two hundred feet. The aircraft went down and the meal trays stayed up where they were, at least until nature grabbed hold of them and sent them smashing against the fixed trays that were on their way back up with the airplane. Their contact was violent, the result a cabin smeared from ceiling to floor with coffee, bourbon, gravy, butter, potatoes, fruit cocktail and apple pan dowdy. The turbulence also deposited the two of us on the floor after first reaching the ceiling during the drop. There were yips of surprise, cries of disgust and wails of panic. We just let out a solid "ommph," and picked ourselves up. Food was on everything, including the heads of many of the passengers.

The turbulence continued as we made our way up the side to help the passengers. The plane, buffeted with severe shocks, dipped and swayed in an irregular pattern. The cabin was saturated with anger and fear, and we tried our best to calm those who were frightened and sooth those who were angry. George Kelman grabbed my arm as I rushed by with a towel to help a man wipe gravy from his face. George whispered to me, but with firmness, "Relax, sweetie. Everything's going to be OK." His smile and calm voice were welcome.

"Thanks," I said.

"Dinner?"

"Let's talk when we get to Cleveland. OK?"

"OK." Again, that smile.

We went about cleaning up the passengers and the

COFFEE, TEA OR ME?

cabin the best we could, all under the watchful eye of Miss Lewis. We had to admit later that this senior stew really did know how to keep calm in the midst of chaos. But it didn't make us like her any better.

We thought we were finally about to get the best of the clean-up chore when the first passenger reached for his "barf bag." He made it in time but the second one didn't.

I was delivering my last towel to the little old lady when a middle-aged gentleman leaped from his seat and ran for the bathroom. Rachel stopped him in mid-aisle.

"You can't leave your seat, sir. The seat belt sign is on." He was carrying his little bag.

"I've got to," he mumbled, his words slurred and garbled.

"You can't," she said again, actually pushing him back toward his seat. "This turbulence is severe and you cannot leave your seat for anything."

He looked like he wanted to cry. "Please," he pleaded. "My teeth," indicating the bag clutched tightly in his hand.

"Oh, no," Rachel exclaimed.

"Yes," he lamented, his face screwed up to keep back the tears.

Rachel looked down at the bag and drew a deep breath. "Give it to me," she said quickly, grabbing the bag from his hand and running toward the lavatory. He watched her enter the lav and then sat meekly in his seat. She emerged five minutes later with his teeth wrapped in Kleenex. He took them from her and turned to the window to hide his embarrassment.

We were approaching the Cleveland area and the captain had informed the passengers of this fact when the light from one of the bathrooms flashed on the signal panel in the buffet. Rachel went to the door of the lav to see what was the problem. Neither of us knew anyone had gotten up from his seat.

"What's wrong in there?" she asked.

"I'm stuck," was the reply from within.

Rachel stood outside the lav door and smiled. I came from the buffet to join her.

COFFEE, TEA OR ME?

"What's wrong in there?" I asked my flying partner.

"It's a woman. Says she's stuck."

"Stuck?"

"What's stuck?"

Rachel started to giggle.

"You mean her fundament?" I offered.*

"Her what?"

"Forget it."

The voice again sounded through the locked bathroom door. "Please help me. I'm stuck."

I started giggling, too. There was nothing else to do. But we knew we'd better do something.

"Can we come in?" I asked.

There was a long moment of decision.

"Yes. Alone."

I entered. She definitely was stuck, a victim of the mechanism's strong suction force. It was a freak accident, and it had to happen on our first flight.

Rachel went and told Miss Lewis, who seemed to consider the problem a ruthless and premeditated plot to make her trip even more difficult. After Rachel and I tried various techniques to free the passenger, Miss Lewis went forward to summon the flight engineer who, along with his responsibilities for the major mechanical equipment on the plane, was also responsible for all minor cabin failures. He came out of the cockpit, a long, gaunt man with excess nose, sunken eyes and veined cheeks. He continuously sniffed. He walked right into the lav, a flashlight in his hand.

"Howdy," he drawled to the woman.

"Oh, my God," she moaned.

The flight engineer stood still in deep thought for a few minutes before speaking.

"Shucks, ma'm, I don't reckon we can do anything 'til we hit Cleveland. Reckon all we can do would be pull, and that's sure to smart a bit."

"Oh, please don't pull," she begged.

"I'll tell the captain 'bout this here predicament and

---

* Another term from my medical school ex-beau. It means buttocks.

COFFEE, TEA OR ME?

see if he's got any suggestions. Meantime, you just sit tight."

He chuckled at this pun of his and snorted with great gusto. His Adam's Apple bobbed up and down like a yo-yo. He swallowed hard and returned to the cockpit.

We smiled down at the woman and suggested she take his advice—sit tight—and have a drink. The idea appealed to her and she smiled back.

"Bourbon on the rocks, please," she ordered.

"Coming up." I gave her a double.

We landed at Cleveland after a bouncy and bumpy approach and taxied to the gate assigned to our flight. We suggested to the woman in the lav that she have another drink until all the passengers deplaned. The captain had radioed ahead, and a crew of mechanics were ready to perform whatever mechanical surgery would prove necessary. We brought her a second double bourbon and went about the task of telling the passengers goodbye. Some of them, their suits spotted with food stains and their hair dampened with fruit cocktail juice, were in no need for jovial farewells.

One man, who wore a shiny black suit, a white shirt with high-roll collar and a slick, white-on-white tie, asked Rachel if she'd spend the night with him in retribution for the massive food stains on his clothing. She declined.

We stayed around after all the passengers departed to see how the mechanics would handle the plight of the woman in the water closet. They managed, after much loosening of bolts and dismantling of equipment, to free her from her oval trap. When she stood up, her knees buckled under her. The mechanics figured it was from shock. Rachel and I knew it was the two double bourbons. She regained her footing and wove her way unsteadily off the plane. I think she was too bombed to know she was in Cleveland. We heard later that the airline gave her a lifetime pass. I've often wondered if she had the nerve to use it.

Later, Rachel and I marched to operations where, for some naïve reason, we expected to receive the highest decoration for valor, service and dedication the airline could bestow on an employee. After all, our first flight had been above and beyond the ordinary; as far as we were concerned, we had performed with extraordinary skill and fortitude. But the only official word we received was from our captain. He came over to us in ops and said, "I'm reporting you both to your supervisor for discourteous attitudes and infraction of stated and longstanding rules."

We were stunned. He turned on his heel and strode away, his hat at a cocky angle on his head. Miss Lewis sat nearby filling out the procedure forms for the flight.

"Did you hear that?" we protested. "What are we being reported for?"

Miss Lewis looked up from her paperwork and chewed the inside of her cheek.

"It's very simple, girls. You never even bothered to introduce yourselves to the captain at ops in New York before the flight. And you should know that's rule number one in crew courtesy. I don't blame him at all." She turned back to her papers. "Always meet your captain, girls."

"Damn, damn, damn," Rachel chanted as we walked away. "Damn."

"I can't believe it," I moaned. "I really can't believe it."

We opened the door from operations and walked into the lobby.

"Hi girls." We turned to see George Kelman standing near the door.

"Rachel, this is George. George, Rachel."

"Dinner?"

"I told you we have to fly back to New York."

"And I told you I'd go back with you. Anyway, I've already checked and you're not flying back to anywhere tonight. Kennedy is still closed and expects to be until tomorrow. You're staying at the Sheraton-Cleveland, downtown, and they'll call you there about your next trip. In the meantime, you've got to eat and it's all on me."

We wanted to ask how he knew all these things but didn't bother to ask. We didn't even bother to look in our

COFFEE, TEA OR ME?

manuals about procedures relating to passengers and dating them. We just took his arm, one on each side, and walked toward the line of waiting cabs.

"God bless you, Mr. Kelman," Rachel said.

"My pleasure," he smiled, holding open the door of the waiting taxi. "All of Cleveland's night life awaits us."

CHAPTER II

"Let's Run Away and Be Stewardesses"

Rachel and I didn't know each other before meeting at stewardess school. But our backgrounds were similar, and so were our motivations for becoming stewardesses. For that matter, our motivations parallel those of most girls flying today. And the stewardess recruiters know this. They know all about us when we're young and eager for a taste of glamour and travel, especially those of us living in small towns with bright dreams of running away to the big city.

I first thought about being a stewardess after reading an occupational brief published by Chronicle Guidance Publications. This little piece of propaganda cost me a quarter for the privilege of reading about a career as an "airplane hostess (Stewardess) 2-25-37." It was published in 1958 and contains the following point:

> *In the case of the job of hostess, the main advantage is the opportunity to travel and see new places. The main disadvantage is being away from home at least a third of the time.*

And therein lies the prime motivation to become a stewardess. Amarillo, Texas, my home town, is pleasant but small. At least it used to be. But by the time I was a senior in high school, I knew I wanted the big time—Dallas, Chicago, even New York, I simply had outgrown Waddy Week.

I was born in Amarillo in 1942. It was a nice place to grow up. But excitement did not head the visitor attractions page in the Chamber of Commerce booklet. The new feature at the biggest movie house was an event to be attended, preferably in full dress.

My beau since junior high school was Henry, a bright young man who actually did enjoy getting dressed to the teeth for the new feature and pizza. And I was always his date at these "premières." Henry was headed for state medical school and started learning all the terms of anatomy during his senior year in high school. We used to sit for hours on his front porch while he taught me the terms and quizzed me on my retention.

Everytime Henry would teach me another term, such as

popliteal (back of the knee), he'd leer a little and say, "Now I'll teach you in Braille." Then he'd groan, laugh with a hint of the juvenile lecher, and touch my popliteal, or whatever was the lesson for the evening.

I thought it was funny at first. But after running through over a hundred terms and hearing him say with each one, "Now I'll teach you in Braille," I got pretty fed up with the whole deal. Except there weren't many boys I liked in Amarillo.

So, I'd giggle, fence him off just a little bit after he got in a few touches, and try to enjoy the whole thing for what it was worth.

Still, I eventually found myself hating Henry and his medical come-on. My hatred lasted until he went away for his first year of medical school and then, after looking around at what was left, I found myself missing Henry. I'd find myself saying anatomical terms over and over in my mind, each one bringing back the thought of his touch. I actually yearned to hear him say, "Now I'll teach you in Braille."

Henry and I pledged to remain true to each other for the next twelve years or so, until he became a famous doctor. My parents wanted me to wait for Henry more than anything else they could think of. They would have liked a doctor in the family. Well, I waited for a couple of months. Then one day wandering along the main street I spotted something in the window of Sison's Drug, Food and Stationery Store. It was a poster, a big one, that carried the bold, blue headline—*BE GLAMOROUS—BE A STEWARDESS!* And there she was, a chic blonde girl all decked out in a classy, form-fitting blue uniform, a smile as wide as Main Street. At the bottom of the sign was the information that a member of the stewardess corps would be at the high school gymnasium Monday afternoon at 4 P.M. Interested girls could speak with her and find out about a career as a glamorous member of this elite group of young ladies.

I didn't tell a soul I was going to talk to her. I knew my parents would be furious that I even entertained the thought. And I was equally certain that all other parents

COFFEE, TEA OR ME?

in town would take the same attitude with their daughters. In fact, I expected to be the only one to actually stop and see that glamorous blonde on the poster in Sison's. It was my chance to escape, as Carolyn Jones did, and Cyd Charisse, to become big movie stars. I wasn't reaching for stardom, as they did. I just wanted to swing a little more than I was destined to in Amarillo.

But I was wrong. Everybody wanted to swing. The whole female element of the senior class was at the gymnasium at 4 P.M. on Monday.

Seated behind a makeshift desk were two people, obviously not from Amarillo. One was a young man, about twenty-five, wearing what I considered the epitome of big city, urban male clothing. His suit was a conservative gray, with a vest, and a deep, maroon-striped tie bowed out just so from his button-down collar. His hair was neat and clung closely to his head.

Beside him was a stewardess, a brunette, with a smile every bit as wide as the poster girl. She was chatting with a few of my classmates, and when she spoke, her head cocked pertly to one side and her eyes made all sorts of movements enhancing her words.

Behind them stood a portable blackboard supplied by the school. On it was a montage of posters, some to do with being a stewardess but most dealing with exotic destinations. No matter where you looked, the words *travel* and *glamour* caught your eye. It was the same with the piles of literature on the desk in front of them. I walked forward and picked up one each of the four pamphlets being offered.

The young man smiled at me. So did the brunette stewardess. And I smiled at them, a little too much of a smile, but I decided on that very spot in the gymnasium that I wanted to be a stewardess. And smiling was without a doubt more important than anything else where an airline was concerned. My mouth started hurting and I went back to a seat.

I had just sat down when Mrs. Coolie walked into the gymnasium. Mrs. Coolie, widowed for over thirty years, doubled as history teacher and guidance counselor. She

COFFEE, TEA OR ME?

did know her history. But her guidance usually directed all of us to a state college where we could learn something to bring back to Amarillo.

She didn't look at all pleased having this wild, wicked airline gang at her school corrupting her girls. She wore flat, black shoes with laces. Her hair was pulled back tight in a bun and contrasted harshly with the soft, free hair-do of the stewardess.

"All right, girls. Everyone take a seat now." Mrs. Coolie never needed benefit of microphone.

We were all seated and Mrs. Coolie began pacing in front of the table. She chewed her mouth as she paced, her hands behind her back. Then, secure in some thought, she turned to us and spoke.

"You've all come here today to hear what it would be like to travel all over this nation of ours and live in many different places. I suppose this is a dream that many young, impressionable girls have once or twice in their growing up. Yes, travel does have its appeal. I've traveled, as you all know. (The only trip I knew of was a teacher's conference in Oklahoma City.) And I've found that other places never, never . . . never have what you've left behind in your own particular place of origin. But, you each will make this choice. And those few of you who may decide to leave Amarillo and . . . yes, even Texas, will at least have benefit of a firm and solid foundation in the great history of your state. I found this fact secure in my travels. Well, as part of our continuing effort to present to you people from various careers, we today feature the airlines. And these people are here to say some things about going away and working for their airline. I give them to you now."

We applauded. Mrs. Coolie liked it as she strode to the sidelines.

The young man stood up and smiled at us. We smiled back.

"Good afternoon, girls. And thank you for coming. I appreciate that warm introduction from *your* Mrs. Coolie. Actually, we almost didn't make it here as planned. We've been conducting these meetings all over the country and were in Hollywood yesterday. It looked like the weather wouldn't allow us to reach Amarillo today so . . . well, we just stayed around the pool and watched the actors and actresses stroll by."

Everyone laughed.

"But, I'm certainly glad we *did* have a chance to see and meet each of you. You all look like you'd make fine stewardesses for the airline."

I wanted to ask which actors they saw strolling by. But I thought better of it. I wanted to ask if they'd seen Marlon Brando, my favorite. And I wanted to sign up at that moment before they got away and headed back for Hollywood.

The meeting progressed for about a half hour. The young man introduced the stewardess (I never got her name), and she told us about what she did as a stewardess and where she went and what she did when she wasn't flying. It sounded like a real-live Cinderella story. She lived in Boston where, she commented casually, there were so many college men. She said she always went to Europe on her vacations because she could fly on other airlines for almost nothing. In fact, she even said she never really knew what living could be all about until she decided to become a stewardess.

"I suppose I'll never want to stop flying," she said with a reflective sigh. "Unless, of course, I decide to accept the marriage offers of those college men in Boston."

We all laughed with her. Except for Mrs. Coolie, who sat rigid in her chair, her black shoes planted firmly on the hardwood floor, her hands firmly on her knees. It was obvious she wanted the airline gang out of her gymnasium.

The meeting ended and we were invited to stay around and ask questions. The only distressing thing about the meeting was the fact you had to be at least twenty years old to become a stewardess. But these two representatives from the airline had accomplished their given task. They had successfully piqued my interest, not only in flying but in their particular airline. I came forward to pick up a preliminary application form that the young man said would simply give them basic information on us. Then, when we became of age and went to Dallas to apply and be interviewed, they'd already know certain things about us. I went forward for those forms despite the hard stare of Mrs. Coolie, grabbed them, and returned to my chair. Then, after placing them in my purse, I went back to the desk and thanked the young man for coming.

"I hope we see you in Dallas very soon," he said.

"You will," I answered.

I walked quickly from the school gymnasium and ran through the hallway to the outdoors. I burst through the doorway and, once free of the musty, institutional smell of the building, breathed deeply. I was going to be a stewardess, live in Boston, date all those college men and lounge around a Hollywood pool watching Marlon Brando do swan dives from the high board.

"Whatta ya say, Trudy?" It was the quarterback of our football team standing with a couple of other football players.

Suddenly, he seemed like a third grade kid wanting to carry my books home from school. I practiced my new smile on him, cocked my head pertly, and walked away with a new-found air of confidence and well-being. It was goodbye Amarillo and hello Hollywood. Or something like that.

* * *

Rachel grew up in Louisville very much as I did in a happy family with lots of friends and all the usual high school fun. By the time she was a senior she was getting restless. She didn't want to stay a small town girl with a small town job. She'd looked over all the local boys and found none exciting enough to give her the life she wanted. She watched an older sister marry and settle down into a narrow, contented groove. Rachel knew that wasn't for her. What could she do? How could she get away? Good old Eddie who would some day inherit his father's hardware store wanted to marry her. Her parents thought it would be lovely if she married good old Eddie.

COFFEE, TEA OR ME?

The young couple could build a ranch house out toward the new end of town, join the club, play golf. Wouldn't that be nice?

Ugh, was all Rachel could say to that arrangement and her dimples disappeared under a deep frown. One day she saw an ad in the local newspaper. Airline recruiters were coming to town to inverview potential stewardesses. Rachel was the first girl in line when they arrived. They hired her right on the spot—a great tribute to her looks and her school record. Usually when a girl is interviewed, there follows a long screening process before she is signed.

Rachel told me once about the scene at home when she broke the news to her folks. It was rough going for quite a while. Her parents didn't want her to leave home. They didn't want her to fly. If she must have a career, why not nursing? She could study that right at home. Well, the harder they tugged, the wilder she fought to get away. Don't underestimate Rachel. She made it.

We arrived on the same day at stewardess school to attend class number 14-45, a six-week course of basic training under the watchful guidance of "Big Momma," a stylish Mrs. Coolie in drag. It was under her wing that we became stewardesses, a fact of her life that she probably regrets to this day.

CHAPTER III

"Big Momma Is Watching"

COFFEE, TEA OR ME?

Rachel and I spent the next hour lying on our beds and talking about why we wanted to become stewardesses. We talked about the glamour of flying away to strange places. We talked about being away from home and the men we'd meet because we were living away from home. We expounded on the challenge of serving a nation's traveling public . . . and about the men who made up the bulk of this public.

I started to tell my story about Henry and his Braille line when the door opened and in walked the third member of our cozy little room. She was taller than we thought you could be to become a stewardess, thin, and dressed in what had to be a $400 suit. Her hair was out of *Glamour,* and she struck one of those ridiculous, awkward go-go poses the models all love to use these days.

"Hellooooooo," she said with a nasal whine, her hand professionally on her hip.

"Hi," we chirped back. "I'm Trudy and this is Rachel."

"Delighted, I'm sure." There was no way to like this girl, with her phony voice and gestures.

She looked slowly around the room and turned to the smiling girl guide who had brought her to the door. "I'm afraid I just don't understand. I assumed a private accommodation."

"I'm sorry, Cynthia," the guide replied, "but there are no private rooms at the school. You'll share a room with four other girls. These are two of your roommates."

"Roommates? How quaint."

"Well," Rachel said with a sweep of her hand, "it's not much but we'll all manage, I guess."

"It's absolutely vulgar," was Cynthia's reaction. "I think I'll nap."

She started to unbutton her suit jacket and then suddenly realized we were in the room. It seemed difficult for her to comprehend we were still standing there as she undressed. We just ignored her and flopped back on our beds. She got down to her slip and placed her pale, skinny frame on the bed furthest from ours. She fell asleep and snored loudly.

38

We arrived at stewardess school on a beautiful spring day. Winter would obviously not be back, and the cool, wet air gave us an even greater expectation of good things to come.

We entered through a narrow gate manned by an elderly gentleman, obviously retired from another line of work, who looked at our letters of admission and waved us through.

The grounds were exquisite. Flowers and shrubs were beginning to show some color against the scrim of beige buildings, each in excellent repair and no taller than two stories. And surrounding the entire grounds was a high, formidable electric fence.

Our luggage was left at the gate for later delivery to Room 16, the one we'd been assigned in our letters of welcome. It was a coincidence meeting each other at the airport as we waited for the limousine from the school. The driver was a wizened, old gentleman who smiled a lot, said nothing and drove erratically. It became obvious as we walked over the grounds toward the dormitory building that the advanced ages of the gatekeeper and driver was no coincidence. The gardeners, handymen and kitchen help were all in the Medicare class.

"Maybe they just look old," Rachel offered.

"No, they're old," I said, "and that electric thing around the grounds is an electric chastity belt."

I was right on both counts. There would be no virginity lost here if the airline had anything to say about it.

We were greeted in the dormitory lounge by a pleasant young girl who walked us to the second floor and showed us to Room 16. It was tastefully decorated and at first glance seemed large enough for the two of us. A second glanced ruined that illusion.

"Five beds?" we asked in chorus.

"Yes. Five of you will share this room," confirmed our guide.

"That'll be nice," Rachel said.

"Wonderful," I agreed dubiously.

"You'll love it," our guide said with a strong note of finality. "The bathrooms are down the hall."

COFFEE, TEA OR ME?

Cynthia had been asleep about fifteen minutes when the door opened again and in walked Betty O'Riley. She was undoubtedly the sexiest girl we'd ever seen. She was made up of a series of soft, full curves, each straining to break through her shocking pink dress. We introduced ourselves over the noise of Cynthia's snoring and within minutes, Betty had stripped down to nothing and had climbed between the sheets of the fourth bed.

"Ah always sleep in the nude," she said with a naughty wink. "Hope y'all don't mind."

"She might," Rachel said, pointing to Cynthia on her bed.

"She looks like a boy sleepin' there. There's not much to her, is there?"

"I think she's very rich," I offered.

"Ah hope so," said Betty. "It's her only chance."

The fifth member of our room didn't show up until after dinner. We managed to wake Cynthia, who declined dinner, so the three of us walked to the cafeteria building. There were more than a hundred girls seated at long formica tables. Little old men cleared away the trays and little old men served the food behind the long, spotless counter where all the food was displayed.

The food was good, very good. And there was lots of it, including a massive dessert tray at the center of each table containing a wide assortment of creamy, sweet pastry. Betty cleaned her plate and finished off three pieces of pastry. Cynthia, who eventually arrived, managed to finish two asparagus tips and a cup of tea. We were drinking our coffee when all eyes turned to the front of the cafeteria where a woman, perhaps thirty-five, stepped up on a raised platform and adjusted a microphone to her height.

"Good evening, girls," she said before a loud screech of feedback drowned her out. An old man, presumably an electrician, rushed forward and did something to get rid of the noise.

"As I was saying, good evening." Everyone scraped a chair in response.

"I'm sorry I wasn't here to personally greet each and

COFFEE, TEA OR ME?

every one of you this afternoon, but I was detained on other matters. As you know, tomorrow morning will mark the beginning of your six weeks of study here at the school. I believe your schedule indicates a meeting at 9 A.M. in the auditorium, which happens to be the cafeteria you're in right now."

It did look more like an auditorium than a cafeteria.

"I hope you've enjoyed your dinner and I look forward to seeing each of you in the morning. Until then, have a pleasant evening. Lights out at ten, you know."

Betty went, "yuuuk," at the announcement of the curfew time. Cynthia just gagged on a piece of asparagus.

"Well, what'll we do until ten o'clock?" Rachel asked.

"I'm going to sleep." Cynthia walked away from us.

"Ah'd like to go to a nightclub."

"There's no time, Betty."

"There's always time, kids. Always time."

We ended up walking to the entrance gate and watching the old gatekeeper survey the strip of cleared land along the electric fence, like a scout in a frontier film. And the visions came of old war movies on TV where the POW's race for the fence and throw themselves across it as a human bridge for their fleeting buddies. Had a vote been taken at the time, there's no doubt Cynthia would have been chosen for the human sacrifice. The thought of her frail frame sprawled over the electric fence was vivid and satisfying.

"It's 9:45," Rachel warned as we strolled past an enormous swimming pool we had found behind a high hedge. "We'd better get back."

We turned to leave when the sound of a car's screeching tires brought our attention back to the front entrance. A shiny Ford convertible was visible through the dust its skidding halt had created, and a radio was going full blast with a singer lamenting a lost love. The old doorman leaped up from his chair and yelled to the car's driver.

"Hey, git that car outta here and take that damn-fool music with ya."

The door of the car opened and a young man wearing

jeans and long sideburns got out and approached the door.

"Are we too late?" he asked with a twang.

"Too late for playin' that damn-fool music."

"No, too late for my girl to get in. She's supposed to start school here tomorrow."

The old man didn't believe. "Where is she? You got a letter?"

The boy turned back to the car and yelled, "Hey, Sally Lu. Come on out here."

There was a pause and then the other door of the car opened. Out of it stepped a pretty little blonde with all the obvious physical signs of a recent necking session. She came forward to her boyfriend's side.

"Sally Lu, show the man your letter."

The girl fished in the pockets of her jeans and handed the doorman a piece of paper. He studied it under the single light and shook his head at the couple.

"This ain't no way to start school, young lady. No sir. Big Momma . . . I mean, Miss Gruel sure ain't gonna like you buzzin' in here in the middle 'a night . . . 'specially not with no young fella with ya and all fulla lipstick like he is. No sir. You better git right on inside. You got one minute 'fore ten."

The young man grabbed Sally Lu and held her in a long and lingering embrace. They parted with great difficulty and he ran to the car to drag out her suitcase. He handed it to the doorman and she started to cry.

"I'll pick you up at six tomorra night, Sally Lu."

"Don't you come back here any night at six," the doorman warned. "Not for a week, anyhow." His final words were cut off in a cloud of swirling rubber and dust.

"Where do I go?" Sally Lu asked the doorman.

Rachel leaped in with the answer. "Hi. I'm Rachel Jones. And we've got to run. What room are you in?"

"I think it's sixteen."

She joined us and we ran full-speed upstairs stopping only once for Sally Lu to wipe her tears with a soiled Kleenex.

We'd just reached our room when suddenly the entire

building went black. Then, just as suddenly, three giant searchlights popped on and began scanning the front and sides of the dorm. We were met at the door by our guide of that afternoon. Her stewardess smile was gone. In its place was a thin, grim lip-line, and her arms were crossed over her breast.

"This is no way to start six weeks of training. Do it again and you'll never know the joy of being a stewardess."

We tried to explain about Sally Lu but our guide simply pointed to the stairs. We climbed them and entered Room 16.

Cynthia was asleep on her bed, the covers pulled tightly under her chin. She had dragged a dresser from the wall and placed it in front of her bed, a mahogany fortress never to be scaled.

"That's Cynthia," we told Sally Lu.

She cried.

"That's your bed over there."

She cried harder now, her sobs out of control. The noise of her crying brought Cynthia to a fast rise, the covers still clutched tightly under her chin.

"What is this all about?" she demanded.

"Sally Lu is our other roommate," we explained.

"Well, can you manage to control your emotions, Miss Sally Blue, or whatever your name is?" Cynthia was haughty at that moment, but also looked afraid we'd launch a full-scale attack on her fortress.

To add to Cynthia's woes, the door flew open and an old Mexican came in with Sally Lu's bag.

"Get out of here, you . . . you . . . you horrible thing," Cynthia screamed at him. He froze in his tracks and then noticed Betty O'Riley who was reaching behind for the hook on her bra. As she popped it open, the Mexican wheeled and fled the room, never bothering to close the door.

"Shut that door," Cynthia yelled at me. I was up to here at this point with Cynthia Monroe.

Betty, minus bra, walked over and closed it. She seemed to gush all over the room, and the sight of her hardened Cynthia's face into shock. She quickly turned to the wall.

The only light in the room was cast by the searchlights as they moved back and forth across the front of the dorm. We managed to get undressed, find our respective beds and fall into them. It seemed pointless even trying to locate the bathrooms. We all fell asleep to the quiet sobbing of Sally Lu. Cynthia snored.

* * *

The bathroom was a madhouse the following morning. There were girls everywhere trying to get ready for the big meeting at nine. Cynthia must have gotten up at six because she wasn't to be found in the room or the bathroom.

Breakfast was delicious. We stuffed ourselves and then went outside to allow the staff to clean up the cafeteria and convert it to an auditorium.

At precisely nine, we were all seated at the tables again, a pile of books, papers, charts and a large box of cosmetics in front of each chair. We were looking through the material when the speaker of the night before again stepped onto the raised platform and adjusted the microphone.

"Good morning, girls." Feedback again, only louder. The old man ran to fix it.

The problem corrected, she continued. "Whenever I hear that dreadful noise, it reminds me how quiet our new jet aircraft really are." She added a big laugh at the end.

The eleven girls seated at a long table near the platform all laughed with careful, studied laughs. We watched them for the rest of the meeting and noticed they did everything in syncopation—smile, frown, shake head up and down, etc. We played the game and laughed right along with everyone.

"Well, let me see. I saw some of you last night during the dinner hour. My name is Miss Gruel and I'm the director of the stewardess school."

COFFEE, TEA OR ME?

"That's Big Momma, like the doorman said last night," Rachel whispered.

Gruel went on, "I welcome you on behalf of the airline, its management and board of directors. And, of course, your sisters of the skies, your fellow-stewardesses.

"You're about to begin a glorious and glamorous career as hostesses of the air. Each of you has indicated to us during preliminary interviews high aptitude for this most demanding and rewarding of careers. We begin this six-week course of instruction with the highest hope that each of you will make a definite contribution to our airline's already promising future. It will not be easy. These six weeks have been carefully prepared to demand the most of each individual. But with fortitude, desire and hard work, you'll all be greeting friends and parents on that very special occasion—graduation! In the welcoming booklet you find on the tables, you'll see a very specific and detailed list of rules and regulations that will govern you during your stay here. I don't feel I have to say more than to state even the slightest infraction of any rule will result in your immediate dismissal from school. Work hard, girls, and the future of aviation and service will be yours to enjoy."

She obviously appreciated the thunderous ovation we gave her, much as Mrs. Coolie did back in Amarillo. She tried to appear humble as she strode off the platform, but it was no use.

Each of the eleven girls at the long table now came forward and told us about her areas of instruction. They had all been stewardesses at one time or another and hadn't lost their smiles. After an hour and a half of speeches, we were allowed to break for coffee, orange juice and Danish pastry. I was biting into a butternut Danish when Betty O'Riley, wearing a very tight sweater and skirt, asked me, "What does infraction mean?"

"It means breaking the rules," I informed her.

"Wow. Y'll mean all those rules in the book?"

"Guess so."

"We'll be climbing the walls before six weeks are up."

"Just don't climb the electric fence," Rachel threw in.

COFFEE, TEA OR ME?

"They must use something, huh?" Betty continued with her questions.

"What do you mean, 'use something'?"

"Y'all know," Betty explained, "some sort of chemical that makes you forget about sex . . . Y'all know what I mean . . . Something to take away that tingle when you think about boys. That kind of thing."

"Salt Peter?" Rachel asked.

"No, silly, that's for boys, Ah think. Anyway, all these places use *somethin'*. Frankly, ah hope they do. Ah never stop tingling."

We didn't doubt her for a minute.

Sally Lu hadn't said a word since we met her at the gate last night. She seemed to take a liking to Rachel and said to her, as we were returning to our seats for part two of the meeting, "It says in the book that we can't leave the grounds for a whole week. That's awful. Warren, my boyfriend, will break the door down. It's awful."

Rachel was afraid she'd cry again.

"Don't worry about it, Sally Lu. Maybe you can throw kisses from the window."

"I hope so," Sally Lu sighed, seemingly relieved by this piece of encouragement.

After lunch, another feast topped off with chocolate ice cream, whipped cream and pecans, we had our first meeting on make-up, hair styling and general grooming.

The class was conducted by a faggy looking man with long, wavy hair and a twitch in his left eye. He sketched facial outlines on the blackboard while a sharp looking girl in a stewardess uniform welcomed us to the classroom.

"Welcome to your first class in how to look more beautiful, radiant and charming. I'm Miss Lucas and with me is Mister André, a well-known hair stylist and make-up expert. When Mister André is through with you, your own family won't know you're the same girl they knew when you left to become a stewardess."

Mister André picked on Cynthia first, much to her delight. He pointed out how nicely her hair style complimented her facial structure to which she replied, "It

COFFEE, TEA OR ME?

should. My stylist is very highly paid." We all felt a little waifish by comparison.

The next girl he called to the front of the room was Betty. Gay or not, he couldn't keep his eyes off her forty-inch chest. It was at this precise moment that Betty got her nickname. Rachel leaned over to me and whispered, "She's got to have the biggest set of boobs I've ever seen. And we know they're all for real." Cynthia read a book while Betty was up front.

Mister André told me my face was oblong, and Rachel was handed the sad news she was moonfaced. Cynthia was termed classic, and Sally Lu was actually called ordinary, sort of middle-America. We decided that Mister André's face was definitely early-fag. And his long, lacquered fingernails didn't clash with this diagnosis.

They really worked us in stewardess school. The training was no joke. To graduate you have to pass the FAA test—that's the Federal Aviation Agency—and the test is a long written affair that requires you to know everything there is to know about all the planes the company flies. First we went over those planes inch by inch in classrooms, using textbooks and charts. We had to know where the emergency exits are, how to use them, how much fuel the plane carries, how the galley works, what equipment to use in emergencies and where it is. We had to know all of this and much more for four different types of planes.

Training started every day at 8 in the morning. We were up at 6:30. The commotion in the bathroom was unbelievable as we all rushed to shower and fix our hair. We had to be dressed fit to kill every morning, our fingernails absolutely perfect, our faces made up. After a week of classroom work, they took us aboard the jets out back. A dozen times a day we climbed aboard and worked in one area and then another—the cockpit, the galley, the lavatories.

We had special over-water practice so that we would know all about the life vests, the rafts and the emergency equipment. One day they took us all to a nearby lake and put us in life rafts—those big, yellow inflated rafts that

COFFEE, TEA OR ME?

bob around on the surface. There were about six of us and a supervisor on each raft and six rafts drifting around on the water. At first we paid strict attention because we knew this was important. It might some day be a matter of life and death. Naturally Rachel and I had managed to get on the same raft. By this time all the girls knew, look out for Rachel and Trudy—anything can happen. Well, we floated pretty close to the next raft and right there at arm's length I saw the little cork that you pull to let the air out of the raft. Rachel read my mind, "No!" she said. But I knew she really wanted me to do it.

I looked over at the other raft and waited for the supervisor to turn her head. Rachel, bless her, put out her hand and paddled us a little closer, all the time saying "No, no!" I reached over, pulled the cork and SWWSSHHH that raft went flat, all the girls fell into the water, spluttering and coughing and that supervisor with her wet hair in her face shouted, "Which one of you did it—Trudy or Rachel? It had to be one of you."

* * *

Later on they took us out on actual flights and pulled all kinds of stunts on us. They cut the engines to see if we'd panic. The first time they did that to me, the captain came on the P.A. and said, "The right engine has cut out and so has the left one. You'll notice we're over water." Then he handed me the mike. I guess I was supposed to say something cheerful to the passengers so in my heartiest voice I said, "OK, folks, we're going to swim."

I think they had a conference that night to decide whether to expel me or not. I hung on. But many of the girls didn't make it. During the six weeks they dropped twenty-three out of the forty-five who started with our class and that is about normal. Sometimes they throw you out for breaking the rules or not studying, but mostly because you don't prove to have a stewardess personality —you don't really like people. That's the key to it. You have to like people and be willing to serve them day and night and take care of their needs and demands. When we made our trial flights, they filled the planes with the worst

SOB's they could find. They were there to test us. A man on an aisle seat would say, through clenched teeth, "I did not order this damned steak rare. I want it well done." You bring it back to him well done and he says, "This is the worst airline I've ever seen. I order a cup of coffee and I get a glass of milk. Where do they find such stupid girls?"

Not only are you forbidden to blow up, but they watch even for a vexed expression on your face. They want to be real sure that you can take the worst a passenger can dish out and that you'll stay friendly and even kid him and say, "You're right—I'm with you."

About the third week the grind let up a little. We could go out at night and they raised the curfew to 11 P.M. On weekends there was a continual party around the pool. Fellows came over from an Air Force base nearby and captains and officers working for the airline stopped by to look over the newest crop of stews. We made friends quickly and easily.

Of course, Sally Lu, being from the town, spent every night with Warren, her hot-rodding beau. She confided one night to Rachel that Warren had gotten her pregnant three times, but each time he took her to a friend who was going through medical school who, in turn, took care of Sally Lu. We all agreed upon hearing the story that Sally Lu could not be thought of as an exceptionally bright girl.

They would race back to the school every night just before ten, and she'd throw him kisses through the fence while he cursed at the gatekeeper. One night, as he was yelling at the old man, his arm accidentally touched the electric fence. It knocked him down but he got up again.

"Maybe it made him sterile," Rachel said hopefully as Sally Lu told the story to us that night. Sally Lu cried half the night.

"How stupid can you be?" Rachel exploded at her one night in the room. "Why don't you stay away from him until you're married, or take the pill?"

"Well, I always ask Warren to stop a little sooner but

COFFEE, TEA OR ME?

he never does. Poor Warren. I guess it's pretty hard when you're a fella." Then she cried.

On Thursday, just four days before graduation, Sally Lu burst into the room and announced, "Warren wants to treat all of you to a Coke for bein' so nice to his girl. Isn't that just so sweet of him?" Betty, Trudy and I decided to go with them. Cynthia declined and remained slumped at her desk browsing through a copy of *Women's Wear Daily* that her mother sent her.

We piled into Warren's car for the drive to a local drive-in, where girls sit in their fathers' cars while boys cruise around the parking lot in their fathers' cars. Usually they never hook up. But the parade is always fun to watch. The place was called Ma's Root Beer Stand, a fifteen minute drive from the school but accomplished in ten by Warren. We sat sipping our drinks while Sally Lu shared a big orangeade in the front seat with Warren, their two straws sucking up the syrupy soda in between kisses on the ear and light touches of the thigh.

"Why don't you two get married?" Rachel asked, the root beer going to her head.

"Soon's I git my own gas station," Warren proudly answered as he gunned the running motor for emphasis.

"That's why I decided to be a stewardess," Sally Lu said giddily as she played with the hair coming through Warren's shirt front. "Soon as he has his own station, I'll stop flyin' and we'll get married. Right, hon?"

"You betcha," he grunted. "Unless she goes and meets some fancy dude on one a' them airplanes." He laughed off the comment but his look indicated he would slit her throat if she did.

Sally Lu nudged him, and kissed his ear.

We left Ma's at 10:15, in plenty of time to get back before curfew, especially with Warren driving. He shot away from the parking lot and headed along a dirt road that was a new shortcut he'd found. Totally desolate, it wound around the perimeter of the school grounds. We were directly behind the campus when Warren's drive shaft popped or broke or snapped or did something that brought us to a rattling halt.

COFFEE, TEA OR ME?

After much swearing by Warren, we decided to try to walk back in hope of beating the curfew. We were sure losers because it looked as though a car hadn't been over that road for a year, but anything was better than sitting there all night.

"Come on," we prodded as Warren held Sally Lu tight against the front fender and smothered her with kisses.

They broke and we took off at a slight trot. We soon slowed to a walk and had progressed about fifteen minutes when we spotted a car ahead, parked under an oak tree. The sight of it gave us a momentary feeling of glee. But that feeling lasted only six seconds. Then, the car took on a menacing shape. Maybe a madman was there waiting for the girls he saw walking down the road. Maybe there was a dead body.

"I wish Warren was with us," Sally Lu moaned as we gathered behind a tree perhaps seventy feet from the car.

"Look, maybe it's just somebody necking, or admiring the moon, or something." Good old Rachel, steady as a rock in all situations.

Silence reigned until Rachel again spoke up. "Look, we're late already. And we have to pass that car to get back to the gate. I'll slip up quietly and see what's up. If everything is OK, we'll pass. If it looks like a nut or something, you can all weep over the great sacrifice I made for you."

"If he's good lookin', yell." That was Betty.

Rachel stalked the car like someone out of a James Bond movie. She stooped low as she came up behind the vehicle and then raised her head to look in the rear window. She stayed there looking for over a minute. Then, she turned and came back in a low run.

"You'll never believe it," she panted. "Never!"

"What's up?"

"You'll never believe it," she repeated. "It's Big Momma. Gruel. With a man."

"You're putting us on."

"No, I'm not. And you know who I think it is? I think it's that man who delivers meat to the cafeteria."

"Gruel with the meatman?"

"I think so."

"He's kinda good lookin'," Betty recalled.

"He's not," I said.

"Ah wanna see," Betty insisted.

"I don't think we should," Sally Lu protested.

"Come on. You've got to see it to believe it."

It was a ridiculous thing to do. All Gruel had to do was catch us and we could kiss our wings goodbye. But then again, and the thought ran through all our minds, Gruel would be hard-pressed to make any fuss. We were within ten feet when we heard Gruel's voice. It had taken on a little girl quality, a far cry from the studied tones she used in the classroom.

"Alan," she squealed, "don't do that."

"Shhhhhhhh, Louisa," a gravel voice replied. "It's dark and I'm reading your lovely figure in . . . whatta ya call it? Braille."

I wanted to throw up. The whole world must use that cornball line. And I almost spent a lifetime hearing it.

"Ah wonder if he's wearing his apron," Betty muttered.

We stood there in the darkness, barely breathing. Then we circled the car and reached the front door. When the doorman called in our late arrival we received a stern scolding from the dorm advisor.

"You'll have to answer to Gruel in the morning."

The thought was almost appealing. We got into bed and Betty said, "Ah was last in line when we sneaked past the car. Ah saw them climbin' into the back seat."

Miss Gruel looked tired the next morning as she lectured us on the terrible thing we'd done in breaking curfew. Our broken car story didn't hold much weight with her, but it probably did save us from being kicked out of school.

We didn't see Gruel again until the final class on conduct and personal habits. This was, by reputation, Big Momma's favorite class. She always taught it herself.

Her lecture was brutal. It ran on for an hour in wall-to-wall words about the importance of living a life worthy of the stewardess image.

"Perhaps you take offense at what you might construe as meddling into your personal lives. But your personal lives will be mirrored in your conduct as a stewardess. It is my wish that each of you always give deep thought before giving yourself . . . how shall I say it . . . giving yourself to other than the man you marry, if marriage shall be your wish. It was stated so nicely years ago by some unknown scholar who said, 'Is an hour of pleasure worth a lifetime of Hell?' "

We sat there trying to look deep in thought at this profound message. Betty Big Boobs broke the silence. "Mah only question is, how do y'all make it last an hour?"

Gruel didn't understand the question at first. Then she did. Class was over and Betty became a stewardess against the better judgment of everyone.

The next to the last night before graduation I couldn't take it any longer and I said, "Rachel, let's go. Let's get out of here and go into town."

"Oh, no," she said. "It's only a couple of days more—let's not get into any big trouble."

"You're not going to let me go alone?"

"Of course not."

We sneaked out the balcony window at the end of the corridor, right next to our room and got down by hanging onto a downspout and some heavy grape vines. Before we left we fixed our beds to look as if they had bodies in them—we knew there was a bedcheck at midnight. Well, it worked fine. We went to the bar where the airline people hung out and we danced and kidded and had a fine time and I met Chuck.

Chuck was a first officer and had already been with the airline for a year. He was very tall with a marvelous smile, a great blond crew cut and crazy blue eyes under huge eyebrows. I'd never seen such blue eyes in a man. He started getting me drinks and paying attention to me and finally I said, "Come on, handsome, we're going to dance."

He said, "You've got to be unreal. You must be from the south."

I said, "You've got it—I'm from Texas and we love everybody."

He was from way up in Minnesota where it's so cold you can practically ice skate in the summer. We talked and kidded as if we'd known each other forever. I hated

COFFEE, TEA OR ME?

to leave, but Rachel's saner head prevailed. We got a lift back to school about midnight. We scampered across the front yard, crouching low to escape the beam of the searchlight and scrambled up our vine and pipe to safety.

The next night, the eve of graduation, there was no holding me. I had to see Chuck again. Rachel and I would be leaving for New York over the weekend. I wanted to find out where he was going to be. He looked too good for me to let him disappear just like that and leave it to chance that we might meet some day on a flight. Or maybe our paths would never again cross. I couldn't bear that thought.

Rachel protested—it was too dangerous to take a chance only hours before graduation. Word had gotten around that any last minute infraction would bring last minute expulsion. Then the whole six weeks would go for nothing. But there was no holding me. So Rachel took super precautions. I don't know how that kid did it, but she had some one smuggle in two department store mannequins. We tucked them into our beds and pulled the covers up to their shiny chins. We swore our roommates to secrecy. Much as we bickered with them from time to time, we knew none of them would turn us in, not even the lofty Cynthia.

We got down our vine and reached the bar and did we have a ball. We had the greatest time of our lives. Chuck and I danced for hours, all those crazy wild dances where you never touch, but even at arm's length you get on the same beam and move with the frantic beat as intimately as if you were twined together. All the fellows from the airline knew Rachel and I were about to be graduated and they insisted on toasting us, so of course we had to toast back. They really shouldn't have let us do all that drinking, but we were flying and no one could stop us.

"He's going to be based in California for the next three months," I told Rachel sadly during a lull in the racket from the juke box. "I won't be able to see him unless I get a California flight."

"My money's on you, kid," Rachel said. "I bet you'll make it in a week."

COFFEE, TEA OR ME?

Then the party closed in on us again, the drinking and the dancing and suddenly it was 3 A.M. and we were bombed. Well, they got us back to the school grounds and we made it to the wall of our dormitory and I looked up and said, "God, how am I ever going to get up there?" I went first and I kept calling to Rachel, "Come on honey, you can do it."

Rachel just stood there at the bottom and said, "I want to die. I want to die." The next thing I knew, she got sick.

I tapped on the window and called Betty and Sally Lu to help us. I slid down again and tried to pass Rachel up to the others. She was completely limp by then. I shoved her up and they almost had her and then she twisted her foot in that blasted vine and there she was back on the ground with an aching ankle.

Now we've had it, I thought. We'll never get her back up and how'll we explain it and we'll be busted in the morning. And this time *I* wanted to die. But I wasn't going to give up without a fight. Somehow the three of us tugged and hauled Rachel up, pulled her clothes off and stood her up in the shower.

"I want to die," she wailed.

"Listen to me," I told her. "You're going to die if you don't listen. You can yell now. Yell all you want. And when the supervisor comes, tell her you slipped in the shower and twisted your ankle. Got it?"

I guess she got it because the supervisor came running and Rachel was bawling and the rest of us were shrieking.

"How did this happen?" she demanded.

"Well, it's graduation day," I explained, "and we just couldn't sleep we were so excited, so Rachel decided to take a shower and I guess she slipped."

Rachel graduated with a cast on her ankle. "I could just kill you," she hissed to me when they pinned her wings on.

Graduation was very solemn and impressive. Our parents came for the occasion and everyone cried a little as we marched down the main stairs in the dorm in uniform singing our class song, a silly set of words put to the melody of *Liza*. The vice president of sales, who we later discovered was having an affair of long standing with Miss Gruel, pinned our wings on us after making a little speech. Miss Gruel told us we were the best class the school had ever had. We knew she told that to all the classes. But we liked hearing it anyway because we all felt the past six weeks had been a turning point in our lives. Even the giddiest of us had gained assurance and self-knowledge. We were ready for the outside world and all the challenges it would bring. We were stewardesses.

There was a parting benediction from Miss Gruel. She sent a memo to the airline brass: "Don't let Trudy and Rachel fly together." I guess it got filed in a wastebasket.

CHAPTER IV

"You're Nothing but a Stew-Bum, George"

Our first flight together, as already chronicled, was less than perfect. But despite its many hazards, we did take away something of tangible worth—George Kelman.

George represented our first experience in accepting dates with passengers. Like every other girl seeking a career as a stewardess, we were fully aware of the reputation the corps had acquired. Our last days at home in Amarillo and Louisville had been filled with stern parental warnings. You had to be promiscuous to want to be a stewardess, was the consensus of family and friends. We would have to spend our days and nights warding off rape attempts of captains, passengers and all those love-'em-and-leave-'em guys. Our folks harped on the dangers so much we almost found them appealing.

But George Kelman, our first passenger date, proved everyone wrong. He was, if there is such a thing, the perfect gentleman.

That night in Cleveland George took us to one of the city's better restaurants. The more we ate and drank, the more George seemed to enjoy himself. We worried, of course, about sitting there drinking when we probably would have to work a trip back to New York in the morning. Stewardesses aren't allowed to drink within twenty-four hours of a flight, and although our return schedule was unknown, it would most likely fall within the next twenty-four. But George was very convincing on this subject.

"Don't worry about that drinking rule, girls," he said as he poured us another glass of Beaujolais. "I've got plenty of Clorets. No one will ever know alcohol has passed your pretty lips. The only thing you have to worry about is a stew-spy. I've looked around the place and I'm sure there isn't one here."

"Stew-spy?" The thought was incredible, too much so to be believed.

"Yes. Stew-spy," he confirmed. "You'll find out all about them when you go to your first union meeting. In the meantime, just take my word for it and watch your step. You can't trust any girl you fly with, unless you really know her. Even then, don't be too sure."

Rachel and I looked at each other with suspicion. Then we laughed and drank more wine.

We checked back at the hotel before leaving the restaurant and there had been no calls. We then proceeded to a nightclub on Cleveland's outskirts, a barn-like place with a rock-and-roll band on a raised platform over the bar and two go-go dancers on the bar itself (much to the discomfort of a few hard-fisted drinkers). It looked like a pick-up joint.

The music was terrible, its din jarring the brain with every rimshot and twang. We ordered drinks from a mousy little girl in a sequined bunny costume, and settled back to watch the action. Stray fellows and girls were everywhere, each trying to outguess the other. One of the girls, a muscular blonde with smeared eye shadow and dirty fingernails leaned against the wall next to our table. Every so often, a young man, with long sideburns and starched dungarees would come over to her, offer to buy a drink and ask, "How's about makin' it outta here with me?"

She always replied, "Git me a Wild Turkey 'n Seven-Up and I'll think 'bout it." He'd trudge off to the bar and she'd wait, nursing the previous drink and scratching her nose.

One hulk of a guy, obviously not heavy in the mental department, came over to her and said, "Hey, sweets, whatta ya say we run 'cross town and do a couple lines a' bowlin'?"

"Bowlin'?" the girl repeated. "Git me a Wild Turkey 'n Seven-Up and I'll see."

"OK, sweets," the hulk replied and went back to the bar to fight the crowd for his order.

"I wonder if she'd go with me if I suggested weight lifting?" George kidded.

"Give her a try," we suggested.

He did.

"Maybe," she answered him with a straight face. Then she realized what he'd said. "You say weight liftin'?"

"Yup."

"Buy me a Wild Turkey 'n Seven-Up and I'll see."

COFFEE, TEA OR ME?

"Let *me* think about *that*," George countered, keeping a straight face as he sat down.

The girl muttered, "Weight liftin'?" again, and called to the hulk who had offered bowling. "Hey Billy, come on over here."

He gave up his spot at the bar and came back growling, "Now I lost my place in line."

"This here guy wants to take me weight liftin'," she told him.

He wasn't sure he understood. But he felt safe in saying, "You some kinda wise guy?" George flinched.

The hulk became bolder. "Come on, fella, you bein' a wise guy to this here girl?"

George looked gravely concerned. He fished a ten dollar bill from his pocket and threw it on the table, and with firm pressure on our elbows made us stand up. He got up with us.

The hulk came close to George, their proximity emphasizing the difference in height and brawn.

"Look, no trouble intended," George said weakly as he tried to slide past his adversary. "Just a little joke, you know. El joke-o, huh?"

"Where was you gonna go weight liftin'?"

"Nowhere, nowhere. Honest. Just a simple jest."

"You don't look like no weight lifter to me."

"And you sure do. Look, I'm sorry. Buy yourselves drinks out of the ten on the table. OK?"

George's generosity stymied the hulk for a moment, enough time for us to take large strides for the door. We heard him muttering, "Weight liftin'?" as we pushed past the bar crowd and onto the exit. A sweaty go-go girl waved goodbye without breaking stride in her jerking and frugging.

The air outside, and the quiet it offered, was welcome. "Someday I'll learn to keep my mouth shut in these joints," George sighed. "I should have known every guy in there was probably a weight lifter. Bad news, these places. Come on, we'll go back to the hotel and have a nightcap. Better yet, we'll find a bar near the hotel."

We found a cocktail lounge near the hotel and went in.

COFFEE, TEA OR ME?

We were barely inside when a table of girls, definitely stewardess types, spotted George and gave him a big Hello.

"Hi, girls," He beamed. We wondered how he knew them but didn't ask. Why shouldn't he know girls? But why stewardesses? Spies? Silly!

We each had a stinger, weak ones, and George insisted he walk us back to our room in the hotel. We expected the inevitable pitch to come in for a drink or, considering there were two of us, an invitation for one of us to go back to his room. But nothing like that happened.

"Girls, I really enjoyed it." He fished in his pocket and came out with a half-used roll of Clorets. "Here, for the morning. Your supervisor will never know you've had a drop. Sleep tight."

"Goodnight."

"See you tomorrow on the flight, girls."

"You're going back with us?"

"Sure. I'm anxious to see how you do with your second flight. Should be interesting."

"But we don't even know what flight we're working."

"They'll probably call you sometime tonight. They always manage to call when you're asleep. They'll call you and I'll know, too. See you then." He turned and walked back to the bank of elevators. We went into our room, very much up in the air about this whole George Kelman thing.

"He knows so much about being a stewardess," Rachel mused as she struggled out of her girdle. Neither of us had been girdle-wearers until becoming stewardesses. The manual said you always had to wear one while working, and slipping into one had become habit.

"Maybe he's some kind of spy," I suggested.

"I don't think so, Trudy, but maybe he's with the airline in another capacity. No, that doesn't seem logical. But he's rich. That's for sure. Imagine flying back with us just to see how we do."

"I think it's a big line."

"Probably, But he's kind of cute, though."

"Uh huh. I wonder what he does for a living."

COFFEE, TEA OR ME?

"Me too. What about those other girls in the bar? They all seemed to know him."

"Well, I suppose he meets a lot of stewardesses with all his travel and everything. He really is cute."

Rachel had her pajama bottoms on and was slipping into her top when she noticed her bare bosom in a full-length mirror on the wall. Rachel was nicely built although on the small side.

"I wonder if he knows Betty Big Boobs," she asked her mirror image.

"Who knows," I answered. "He wouldn't like her anyway. He doesn't look like he has a breast fixation."

We climbed under the covers.

"I like him," Rachel giggled. "I really do."

"I think he likes you, Rachel."

"I don't think so, Trudy. It's you he likes."

"Anyway, I'm glad we went out with him. He's up for grabs. OK? No hard feelings when one of us runs off and marries him."

"You don't need him, you have Chuck."

"Sure—in California. Goodnight."

Everything was silent for a minute.

"Gee, Trudy, I hope he isn't a spy."

"Don't be silly. Goodnight."

"Goodnight." (pause) "Trudy?"

"What, Rachel?"

"You don't think he's queer, do you? I mean, he didn't even try a thing."

"How could he with the two of us?"

"Well, he could have asked one of us down to his room."

"Would you have gone?"

"Of course not."

"Then why do you think he's queer? He knew neither of us would have gone with him."

"I guess you're right, Trudy." (Two minutes of silence this time.) "Have you ever gone to bed with a man?"

"Rachel, what is this? I've told you about Henry."

"I don't mean in a car, silly. I mean in bed. A hotel."

COFFEE, TEA OR ME?

"Of course not!"

"I was just wondering."

"Well stop wondering and shut up. I'm tired."

"Me too. Goodnight."

"Goodnight."

We'd been asleep about a half hour when the telephone woke us both up. Rachel picked it up.

"Howdy. Miss Baker?" a nasal voice asked.

"No, this is Rachel Jones."

"Miss Baker with you?"

"Who is this?"

"This here's Rob at crew scheduling. You two gals are gonna fly tomorra at noon. Reckon all the soup in New York'll be gone by then."

Rachel sighed and laid back on her pillow. "Have you told Mr. Kelman about the flight?"

"Mister . . . who?"

"Forget it. Thanks for the warning on the flight tomorrow. Goodnight."

" 'night . . . Say, what are you gals doin'?"

"We're sleeping. Goodnight."

"You're both brand spankin' new, ain't you?"

"Right. Goodnight."

"You ain't been breakin' any rules, have ya?"

"If it's against the rules to hang up on you, yes. Goodnight." She banged the receiver back in its cradle and rolled over. "Creep."

We slept a solid hour when a door slamming next door brought us both up to a sitting position. A man's voice in the next room said, "Hurry up. I don't have a lot of time." The walls were paper thin.

"Afraid your wife will scold you?" a female voice answered.

"Don't be smart," he said, a little annoyed.

The next noise was a bed creaking. A few giggles, some scuffling, three minutes of silence, and then he said, "Goodnight, hon. Sleep tight. See you next time you're in town." The door closed quietly and his footsteps padded past our door.

"Who's in the next room?" Rachel whispered.

COFFEE, TEA OR ME?

"How should I know?"

"Is it a stewardess?"

"I haven't the foggiest."

"Let's check in the morning."

"OK. Goodnight, Rachel."

"Goodnight, Trudy."

The next sound was the telephone. It was 9:30 the following morning. I answered it. "Hello."

"Hi. George Kelman, here. How about some breakfast?"

"When?"

"Right now. You've got to be at the airport at eleven. Noon flight, right?"

"That's right. We'll be a half hour."

"Fine. Meet me in the dining room and we'll cab it out to the airport. See you at ten."

"OK." I hung up and pushed Rachel out of her bed and onto the floor. I wake up when a pin drops. But Rachel can sleep through a machine gun duel in the next room. "Come on. George is buying us breakfast and picking up the cab tab to the airport." Rachel just curled up on the floor and started to go back to sleep.

"Come on, Rachel, we haven't got much time."

It took a playful kick in the ribs to bring her to her feet. We managed to get ready, pack and out the door by ten, and met George in the dining room. He was sipping orange juice and reading *The Cleveland Plain Dealer*.

"Good morning, Mr. Kelman."

"Hi, girls. I already ordered eggs, bacon, juice and coffee for you. Have a seat."

We raced through breakfast, hardly talking to each other, until Rachel responded to his question about how we slept.

"Great," she told him, "if we hadn't been party to a little scene next door. These walls are like cardboard. Some married man and his girl friend. Kind of interesting."

"Which room on which side of you?" George asked, never looking up from his reading.

65

"The one on the right," I said. "I mean on the left. On the side furthest from the elevators."

He laughed a little. "Lewis' room huh?"

"Who's Lewis?" I asked.

He seemed annoyed at my slowness. "Lewis. Your senior stew on yesterday's flight."

We were shocked. "Miss Lewis?"

He was still annoyed, this time at our naïveté. "Yes. Miss Lewis. So she was swinging a little, huh? Interesting."

Miss Lewis was already on board when we arrived to work our noon flight. Her face was as stern and unyielding as ever. The temptation was great to let something slip to show our knowledge of her extra-curricular activities. Perhaps another few months on the line we would have that kind of boldness. But it was not prudent for two novice stewardesses.

George was quiet throughout the trip. He posed another temptation for us. Should we ask the obvious: how he knew where Miss Lewis was staying? That seemed unwise, too. But the more we thought of George Kelman, the more we became convinced there was something wrong with him. He either had to be officially connected with the airline, a spy for the stewardess union, a bring-'em-back-alive agent for The Amarillo or Louisville Chamber of Commerce, or maybe just a raving idiot who always wanted to be a stewardess.

The flight this time was uneventful. We felt a little more confident about our chores, although we still managed to spill a few drinks and to misplace a passenger's raincoat. (We finally found it on the floor of the coat rack under Rachel's overnight case). George didn't say anything as we left the airplane. But he did wink at Miss Lewis, who stood by the cabin door as he passed. She just looked away and bid farewell to the man behind him.

We went through the sign-out procedures in operations and headed for the taxi line. We were exhausted. The trip, the weather, Miss Lewis and George Kelman had proven too much to handle in such a short span of time.

COFFEE, TEA OR ME?

We should have conserved money and taken the Carey bus back into Manhattan, but a cab was faster, easier and more comfortable. And comfort was highest on the immediate list of priorities.

We collapsed once we hit the apartment. If we didn't have to buy our own uniforms, we wouldn't have even bothered to take them off. Our apartment was furnished with only a couch, two beds, a director's chair and a camel saddle from Arabia. I never got past the couch. Rachel fell instantly asleep on her bed. Then the telephone rang.

"Hi. This is George."

"Please, no," Rachel pleaded. "Call tomorrow, when we've had twenty hours sleep. Not now."

"Sorry to bother you, Rachel, but you've got to eat dinner. Right? It's on me. You name the place."

"George Kelman, whoever you may be, dinner is the last thing on our minds at this moment."

"By midnight you'll be hungry. How about a few pizzas? At your place. Or mine. Or the pizza place. You name it and I'll be there with the mushrooms. That's my favorite kind of pizza. What's yours?"

The fatigue had brought out an unusual testiness in Rachel. "No! No pizza, no eggs, no steak, no oysters, no soup, not even a candy bar. We're tired and we're going to sleep without George Kelman. I mean we're . . . Oh, the hell with it." She hung up with a bang.

We slept until ten the next morning and made it out to JFK for a one o'clock Cleveland trip. Yes, George Kelman was standing there when we arrived, just outside operations. It was beginning to take on a nightmarish quality, this whole George Kelman thing. Or shades of sophomoric romance with the jilted suitor spending seven days and nights following you around.

When we saw him standing there, we started giggling.

"Hi," he said happily.

"Are you going to Cleveland again?" we asked.

"Nope. Not today."

"Why?" Rachel pressed our sudden good luck.

"I'm going to Los Angeles."

"Just what business are you in that takes you to all these places?"

He thought that over for a moment. "Well, none, really. I'm what you could call independently wealthy."

"Sure," I said with sarcasm, "and I'm Doris Duke."

"I knew you didn't look like a stewardess," he quipped.

We looked around for any snooping eyes and ears and put what we felt was the crusher on him. "Look, just what is it with you?"

He was hurt. "Well, I'll be damned. Here I am, a regular guy who's sorry he woke you up last night and comes all the way out to the airport to apologize. Do I have to take a loyalty oath, too?"

"We're sorry, George. Guess we're a little on edge after the first flight and all. How long will you be in LA?"

"Overnight. Be back tomorrow."

"Oh. Well, have a great trip. See you again."

"Gee, I hope so. How about dinner tomorrow night?"

"Can't. Besides, just which one of us are you asking?"

"Both of you. Honest. I'll call you."

"OK. Bye."

"Bye."

We had dinner with George four more times during the following six weeks. He flew with us again to Cleveland, once to Cincinnati and treated us twice in New York. It was all weird; totally weird. In fact, it was downright frustrating that he never asked one of us out. It always was the two of us together. There was never a pass, never a pinch or subtle brush of the hand—nothing. Just a free spending guy with good manners and a happy way about him. We actually came to the point of no longer wondering about George and what he was. To be candid, he had become a great meal ticket, one without the usual strings attached.

We did find out a little more about George a week after our fourth dinner date. We had gone to the theatre the night before, sixth-row center seats, compliments of Mr. Kelman, who couldn't join us because of an out-of-town trip. Rachel, who was flying reserve that month, had pulled a Seattle trip for the following day, and it was on that flight that some of the mystery was solved.

Rachel was surprised when she saw him board the 707 for Seattle. He seemed a little taken back at seeing her, but recovered quickly and gave her a hearty greeting. The other three stewardesses didn't seem to know him, or notice him.

The flight was an hour out of New York when Rachel, doing a head count against the one the senior stew had performed, discovered there was one too many heads. She mentioned it to the senior stew, a chesty little California girl with bangs, and a hustle-bustle way of doing everything.

"I know, I know," she said when Rachel mentioned the problem. "I've got a dummy aboard."

"A what?"

"A dummy. Dummy. A friend. Forget it. Just drop it."

"I don't understand," Rachel persisted out of sheer curiosity. "What's a dummy?"

"Look, sweetie, there's a guy on board I happen to do a few favors for once in awhile. That's all there is to it. It's done all the time. You know when a flight is going to be light so you slip him on board. Just cool it and start serving the food."

Rachel went about her chores, looking into every male passenger's face for a sign, a clue. Which one was the dummy? George Kelman was an obvious choice, with his stewardess connections and all, but that didn't seem to make any sense to Rachel. George was wealthy. Or at least he said he was. Besides, if a stewardess wanted to do him a favor, why risk her job slipping him on the airplane? Why not sleep with him? Then she remembered the possibility of his being fay. Or maybe he was a gigolo, his trips were his payoff. She looked at him again. No. Impossible. Too sweet.

It had to be another man, a boyfriend of the senior stew. And which one that was certainly wasn't any of Rachel's business. She tried to forget about it, content with her new knowledge that it was possible to sneak a friend on board an airplane.

Rachel was the first stewardess off the plane in Seattle. She hurried across the lobby, did her checking out quickly, and stationed herself behind a concrete pillar by the hack stand. "I ought to have my head examined," she muttered to herself as she tried not to look too much like a private eye behind the proverbial potted palm.

What she was waiting for soon materialized. The little senior stew with the bangs came from the terminal with George Kelman. They entered a cab and headed for downtown.

Rachel, devil that she can be at times, thought quickly. She raced for a phone booth and dialed the hotel where the crews stayed.

"Hello. This is Rachel Jones, a stewardess. I just got in on flight 61 with Miss Crowly and Miss Ramkin, and Miss Ramkin and I would like a room adjacant to Miss Crowly's. We have homework to do together."

"Yes, ma'm. I'll put you and Miss Ramkin in room 1131."

"Thank you."

That night, Rachel stayed close to the room. Miss Ramkin had a date, and Rachel sat alone, her ear straining for signs of activity next door.

She dozed off about midnight and was awakened at two by laughter in the hall. It was George's laugh.

Rachel got mad at herself for being such a busy-body, but that didn't deter her from pressing a water glass against the wall. "This is terrible," she scolded herself.

All she'd heard about a water glass being a good conductor of sound was proven wrong that night. Only snatches of the conversation could be heard, a tribute, we suppose, to the hotel's substantial walls.

But she did hear the senior stewardess say, "You can stay if you'd like to, George."

And he answered, "No, thanks. Got to run."

And that's exactly what he did.

Was George Kelman really queer? Or was he simply a

pleasant guy with a fetish for stewardesses? We were baffled.

I was the one who found out about George, quite by accident through a friend of his. I started dating Bill, a New York psychology student, about a month after Rachel's ear-to-the-wall report from Seattle. Bill was an interesting type of young man; bright, moody, subject to long lapses into introverted discussions on matters that concerned him deeply. He went into one of these spells one night in his fourth floor walk-up apartment in Greenwich Village. He lit a cigarette and started talking about sex, how everyone has an individual need for specific sexual satisfaction and about some cases he knew that were unusual.

"I know this guy, George. Really strange. He has an unbelievable fixation on stewardesses. It's so strong, he'll spend every dime he has just to hang around them. It's lucky he's loaded."

I was all attention. I accepted Bill's romantic gesture of lighting another cigarette for me, and asked, "This wouldn't be a George named Kelman, would it? You don't have to answer, if you don't want to. But you'd better."

"Oh, you've joined Kelman Airlines, have you? I didn't know you were one of the flock George can claim victory over."

"No, Bill, honest, he's never even tried to touch me. Or Rachel. But he's always asking us to dinner and even used to fly with us. Frankly, we just wrote him off as a good-natured queer."

Bill laughed and lit another cigarette.

"I don't doubt he never tried to touch you. But, George Kelman is no fag. He's just different. He only makes it with pros. Hustlers. Call-girls. Plenty of money for any girl he wants, any time. But the stewardess thing is another matter entirely. He loves being thought of as a big brother to the girls. Of course, he gives the guys the impression that he's in bed with every one. But he's never even tried. He likes to be the trusted guy with the girls.

He actually considers stewardesses the ultimate in chaste, sweet American womanhood."

"We are."

"You're not."

"They told us we were at stewardess school."

"They must all be sick down there."

"But it all sounds so ridiculous about George. Why?"

"Who knows? Maybe I should, being a psych student and everything. It's just that some guys need this kind of relationship with clean-cut girls. Maybe it's his personal retribution for always sleeping with prostitutes. But one thing is for sure. Every stewardess who's given him a chance to hang around has found him to be a charming and delightful guy. No strain, no fuss. No passes after every date. Just good company. Funny."

I tried to digest it all for a minute and then asked, "Why does he sneak on board airplanes? If he's got so much money, why doesn't he just pay for his trips?"

"He usually does. But getting an occasional free ride is sort of a game. It's like stepping on the grass when the sign says you shouldn't. Some of the girls just do it because they feel a large debt to him for all the dinners, gifts and even loans. You girls are strange. You don't want to *have* to sleep with a guy who spent something on you, but after awhile, you start to feel guilty. He should be getting *something*. Right? So, they give George a free trip."

"I can't wait to tell Rachel. We've been avoiding him lately. Now we'll be more tolerant."

"Marvelous. Another poor soul saved by my expert analysis."

"What would you call George, then. A stew-bum?"

"Good a term as any. Don't push me away." I had been exerting counter pressure on Bill's straying hand.

I got back to the apartment very late and told Rachel the whole story. She was fascinated, disbelieving, but bowed to Bill's academic credentials. I was going over it with her again when the phone rang. Rachel answered.

"Hello? George Kelman. How are you?"

"Great, Rachel. How about some dinner tonight? The two of you."

"George, you have a date, even if you are nothing but a stew-bum."

"Ahhhhh, where did you hear that?"

"It makes no difference. It's just our little term of affection for you. Pick us up at seven."

"Right."

We see George Kelman often. His stable of stewardesses has grown, and he has less time for us old-timers. We've met other stew-bums besides George, but he remains unique among the airport Johnnies or hostess hoppers—other terms used to designate the type. The others, while having a similar fixation on stewardesses, also take normal male actions with the girls they go out with. George remains to this day a paragon of virtue with the stewardess corps. His place in aviation history as big brother-in-residence seems secure.

CHAPTER V

"Can We Fit Eight in This Apartment?"

Take eight girls—one alcoholic, one dieter, one borrower, one compulsive liar, one pet lover, one overall bitch with a nervous curl of her lip, and the two of us, mix them together in a $750 a month penthouse apartment in Manhattan and you have the makings of a chapter in this book. Lacking a nymphomaniac, we make no pretense at trying to outdo *The Group*. We simply present our own.

Pulling New York City as a duty station is easy. With so many flights originating from the city, the need for stewardesses is great. Also, many girls who try New York for the first year of their flying career decide to transfer to other cities. As they say, it's a great place to visit but . . .

We did as most new stewardesses to the city tend to do. We moved into the stew zoo, a large apartment building in the east 60's. But we did try first to find our own apartment, one in which we wouldn't feel back in the atmosphere of the stewardess school. We followed the ads in *The New York Times,* and made every attempt to be the first ones answering any advertisement that looked appealing. We should have saved our energy. New York landlords just don't want stewardesses living in their buildings. We rank only behind racial minority groups in feeling the vise of housing prejudice.

We first applied at a pretty brownstone in the upper eighties where, according to the newspaper ad and the sign outside, there was an apartment available. We rang the downstairs apartment bell, marked super. He came to the door, some mustard from lunch remaining on his triple chin.

"It's taken," he said after looking at us for no more than two seconds. There was mustard on his summer undershirt, too.

"What's taken?" we asked.

"The apartment. It's taken."

"How could it be taken so soon?" Rachel asked, shaking her head back and forth in disbelief.

"Look, goils, take my advice, huh? Go on over on six-

77

COFFEE, TEA OR ME?

ty-fifth where all the other stewardesses live." He started back into his apartment.

"Wait a minute. How do you know we're stewardesses?"

"Ain't you?"

"Yes, we are. But how did you know?"

He shrugged his shoulders modestly. "I don't know. It's a funny thing. All you stews look alike."

Rachel wasn't about to take this lying down. "If the apartment's taken, why haven't you taken down the sign?" she demanded.

The super was impatient now. He rubbed the back of his thick neck and screwed his face up in frustration. "Look, goils. Don't make a fuss. The place is taken. That's it. I leave the sign up because I git lonely and like to have people knockin' on my door. OK? Try the stew zoo."

He slammed the door in our face. We'd never heard of any place called the stew zoo. And his reference to it seemed a deliberate attempt to label us animals. At least that's the way Rachel took his comment. She stood there banging her fist on his door. He responded by turning up a recording of Maria Callas at the Met. Rachel banged louder, screaming as she banged, "Call me an animal, will you? You're the animal. A . . . a pig animal."

I pulled her away. "Come on, Rachel. Forget it."

We tried five other places and were rebuffed in each case. At only one of these places was the landlord open about not wanting to rent to stewardesses.

"Look, girls," he sniveled, "nothing personal. But everytime we let stewardesses in the building, it's trouble. You break the lease and hop on an airplane for god knows where. You have parties all hours of the day and night and it bugs everybody else in the building. You get behind on your rent. Or you load the place with other girls and pretty soon there's ten of you in one bedroom place. Please. Go away. Go over to the stew zoo. It's fun there. Companionship and all that. You know?"

We asked the obvious question. "What is and where is the stew zoo?"

He told us. And we went.

The stewardess population in the stew zoo seldom goes below two hundred. Aside from being a home away from home for so many stewardesses, it's pretty typical of most of the large apartment buildings in New York. We made a lot of good friends there. The halls were never without a uniformed girl of one airline or another. Girls ran in and out of each other's apartments, borrowing stockings and gloves. Evening dresses came and went on loan. It was fun and crazy. There were the stew-bums, George Kelman included, who could be seen coming and going from various apartments, always on a first-name basis with the doorman. The supply of bottles to keep his brown paper bag full usually came from the stew-bums.

We became friendly with Joan Livingston, a stewardess for another airline, who shared the apartment next to us with Jane Baldwin, another stewardess. We got into the habit of dropping into each other's apartment at any hour. Joan and Jane were pleasant enough, although Joan could be snippy and short, her upper lip taking on a strange curl when these moods came to the surface. Her roommate, Jane, we both agreed seemed to drink too much for her own good.

"Jane always looks a little drunk," we kidded with Joan one day as we walked down the hall together.

"I've never noticed," was Joan's cool answer, her lip curling.

We were having coffee one morning, a day off, in Joan and Jane's apartment, when Joan asked, "How would you two like to move out of this place?"

"Do you have anything better?" Rachel asked.

"I sure do," Joan said. "Here's what we're thinking. I've been going with a fellow who's loaded. I mean really loaded. He lives in a penthouse on the west side that cost him $750 a month."

"Marry him," I suggested.

"That comes later," Joan said with a smile. "But listen to this. He's moving out of there for a new apartment on this side of town. And he's offered to sub-let his penthouse to me. There's over a year to go on his lease."

"That's great," I said. "But how are you and Jane going to pay that much rent?"

"By getting other girls to share it with us. You two are the first we've asked."

I did some quick figuring in my head.

"That's over $180 a month. Impossible. We couldn't afford that kind of rent."

"Of course not." She was annoyed at my comment, and her lip started to curl. "That's only four of us. But add four more and it makes eight to share the rent. That comes to $93.75 for each person. That's no problem, is it?"

"Eight people!" Rachel banged her knee into the coffee table as she got up from the couch. "Eight people! Can we fit eight into this apartment? It'll be a dormitory."

"Wait'll you see it," was Joan's reply.

We saw it that night. Her boyfriend, a fortyish bachelor, let us in with an over-zealous welcome. He gave Joan a long kiss, and then proceeded to show us the penthouse. It was splendid. And the problem of fitting eight girls vanished after we looked at each of the four huge bedrooms.

"What have you been doing up here all by yourself?" Rachel asked Richard, as he poured us all a drink.

"I just love room," was his reply. "I can't stand to be cooped up like you usually are in New York. I hate to leave this place but I've found something even better. I can't pass it up."

We sat there and took in the living room as we sipped our Scotch and water. Jane drained her glass with one long, continuous swallow. It was refilled by Richard. The room was magnificent. Every inch of the floor was covered with deep, rich red carpeting, accented in front of the grand piano, the fireplace and the ceiling-high bookcases by white animal skins. The furniture was sort of early Chinese, primarily black, with various dragon designs and rising suns in appropriate places. Jane was on her third drink when I asked, "How can we ever furnish this place?"

Richard laughed, a rich man's laugh when asked a silly question about money. He looked at Joan and said, "I love this girl friend of yours and I'm giving her all the furniture. Besides, I need a change. I'm buying all new for my next apartment. Everything you see here is staying."

"But what's the landlord going to say about eight girls moving in here?" Rachel was always the practical one.

Richard smiled another rich man's smile. "He can't say a thing. I've loaned him money at various times, and you might even say I own part of this building. I own part of him, too. You just move in and enjoy it."

Jane walked a little unsteadily as we left. Joan stayed behind with Richard.

"Jane, I don't understand something," I said as we walked out of the building. "If this guy loves Joan so much, why doesn't he just hand over the apartment to her? Why does she have to share it with seven other girls?"

Jane shrugged for a long time in preparation for her answer. She laughed a couple of times, too, at something only she was thinking. She never did answer the question.

Rachel and I had reservations about moving into the penthouse. The thought of living together with that many others was pretty scary. But the stew zoo paled in comparison to the elegance of that penthouse. And the experience of living in such splendor even for a short period of time would be worthwhile. We decided to go ahead with the move.

Joan naturally assumed a position of power. After all, it was her boyfriend who made the move possible. It was now *her* elegant furniture that we would be enjoying. It was her deal, and she knew it. Her lip took on a grand twist now, and she tended to speak with disdain. But we really didn't care.

Joan brought the other four girls into the picture. There were Sally, Marie, Helen and Sarah. We accomplished the assault on the penthouse in one day, and soon settled into a routine that seemed to work very nicely. That is until we got to know each other.

COFFEE, TEA OR ME?

Jane seldom left her room. We'd never met a girl who said less and drank more. It was kind of funny to see her weave into the kitchen or across the living room. How she managed to keep sober when flying the line was something we discussed frequently, but the fact that she continued to fly was proof enough of her success.

We seldom saw the other girls. Everyone seemed to be on a different shift, a fact of stewardess life that makes living together more easily accomplished. For the first month we were never all in the penthouse together. But on the first day of the second month, we did happen to find ourselves together. And Joan acted on the occasion.

She beckoned all of us to the living room and announced she had something to talk about. We straggled in, each in her own particular costume of relaxation. I was in my usual Levi's and sweat shirt. That's the only way I can relax, in Texas pants and a shapeless, baggy top. Not glamourous, but the most comfortable clothes in the world. Rachel, on the other hand, relaxes in regular street clothes. She always has on a nice dress and stockings. She looks so ladylike I sometimes can't stand it. Joan was wearing a sleek Japanese kimono, a real one she had picked up in Tokyo. Jane was in an ancient muumuu. Sally had on tight orange stretch pants with a poison green turtle neck pullover. We all suspected that Sally was color-blind; nothing she wore ever matched. The poncho outfit and boots belonged to Sarah. The granny dress with high collar and long sleeves was Helen's idea of what to idle around the house in.

Marie sported her usual Bermuda length shorts and buttondown oxford shirt. An outsider would have thought we were quite a sight. We hardly looked at each other as we flopped around on the floor waiting for Joan to start the meeting.

"Well, here we are. I hope you're enjoying what Richard did for us."

"Who's Richard?" asked Helen.

"He's the one who made all this possible," Joan answered with a haughty rise to her voice. "Anyway, I think with all of us living so close together, we should have some sort of rules. I think we need them."

"She sounds just like Big Momma," I whispered to Rachel who had taken off her shoes and was polishing her toenails.

"Shhh," Rachel cautioned.

Joan went on.

"I've written up a list of rules, simple rules, and had them run off on a duplicating machine. I'll pass them out now and you can read them."

Jane excused herself and disappeared into her room. She came out a few minutes later looking more relaxed.

Joan passed out the white paper with the purple printing on it. We each took one and began to read.

TO: Residents of the penthouse
FROM: the rules committee
SUBJECT: General operating rules
1. Each pair of girls will clean up their own bedrooms.
2. Bedrooms are privileged areas. Do not enter anyone's bedroom without prior permission.
3. Label all food stored in the refrigerator or kitchen closets.
4. Men may be entertained in any general area of the apartment or in your own bedroom. Work out any conflicts with your roommate. Try to encourage men to use their own dwellings for certain intimate activity.
5. Arguments will be settled by the rules committee.
6. No loud noise at any time.
7. 2% late charge will be levied for late rent payments for the first three days. 5% after that.
8. Each set of roommates will have their own telephone installed in their bedroom and will use only that phone.

"Who's the rules committee?" Helen asked.

"Jane and I," was Joan's answer.

"Why you two?" was Helen's next question. It seemed a logical one, except to Joan.

"That was decided when Richard allowed me to ask you girls in to the penthouse."

COFFEE, TEA OR ME?

"Who's Richard?" Helen didn't give up easily.

Joan simply ignored the question. Jane went back to her room for another moment's worth of relaxation.

"Are the rules clear?" Joan asked in a loud voice.

No one answered.

"Good. That's all for this meeting."

We all went back to our rooms.

"I think the power is going to her head, don't you?" I asked Rachel when we were safely alone.

"She is a little overbearing," she agreed.

"The others are a good bunch."

"Yeh. They seem great. Gee, I wish there were some way to help Jane out. All that drinking, I mean."

"She sure puts it away. I like her, though. And underneath all Joan's veneer, she does seem to stick by Jane. That's pretty nice."

Another month went by in the penthouse without serious incident. We were spared any more meetings, too. And we began to know our roommates in this housing venture.

Sally, a pretty but shy little brunette, was as sweet as could be. The delightful thing about her was her habit of telling little white lies. She couldn't help embellishing the stories she told, usually with the story improved by her embroidery.

Helen, tending to overweight, was on a perpetual diet. She'd been on one for six years in a never-ending battle to satisfy the airline's rigid weight checks that came often and unannounced. Yogurt was her staple food, her portion of the refrigerator a virtual supermarket display of the world's yogurt varieties.

Marie was a darling, in her own way. She loved animals. Any animals. In her room, which she shared with Sally, were six birds of varying origins and species, a live mink in a cage and a baby alligator in a large fish tank. His name was Nelson. He was frightening even in his infancy.

Helen roomed with Sarah. Sarah loved to borrow things. Sometimes she returned them. Most of the time she didn't.

COFFEE, TEA OR ME?

That was our group. The diversity of interests and problems seldom posed any serious threat to the penthouse's tranquility. Not until the fourth month of residence when all the individual quirks meshed together to create a night from *The Twilight Zone*.

That night Rachel and I watched Johnny Carson until we'd fallen asleep. We'd been asleep for maybe an hour when the sound of our bedroom door being thrown open brought us both up to a sitting position.

Standing in the open doorway was Jane. She was drunk. Stoned. Her head was going from side to side as if getting up steam to say something. She finally did.

"Where is it?" she muttered, her voice with that slurred quality whiskey in abundance will bring about.

"What in the name of . . ." I was cut off.

"Where is it, I said?" She stepped into the room now, almost falling over the threshold.

"Where is what?" Rachel yelled.

Jane flipped on the overhead light.

"My bottle. My bottle. Where is it? You stole it."

Rachel laid back on her pillow. "Will you please go to bed, Jane," she requested softly.

Jane let out an ear-piercing scream. Then, she leaped on Rachel's bed and pulled the blanket off. "Gimme my bottle," she yelled, trying to punch Rachel as she said it. Rachel rolled out of bed quickly and ran around in back.

Jane's scream had awakened the entire apartment. Joan was the first to arrive, closely followed by Helen.

"What's going on in here?" Joan snapped.

Jane was leaping up and down on Rachel's bed.

"She stole my bottle," she said.

"Who stole your bottle?" was Joan's reaction.

"She did," Jane yelled, pointing to the both of us.

"We didn't steal anything," I protested.

"Yes, you did," Jane continued. "Sally said you did."

"Sally?" we said in unison.

Marie now came rushing into the scene.

"Shhhhhhhhh," she said with exaggerated facial and

COFFEE, TEA OR ME?

hand gestures, "you've woken up the animals. The birds are all chirping and Nelson is restless."

Once the visions of Marie's menagerie in flight passed, thoughts came back to the original problem: Who took Jane's bottle? Did someone take Jane's bottle? Did Sally say we took her bottle?

"Where's Sally?"

"Sleeping."

"How can she sleep when an alligator can't sleep?"

"She's always been a sound sleeper."

Jane had tolerated this aimless chit-chat for as long as she could. She went to Rachel's dresser and began digging through lingerie for the elusive bottle.

Marie left the room and reappeared with a sleepy Sally.

"What's the matter?" she mumbled, rubbing her eyes and stretching.

"They woke up Nelson," Marie told her.

"Oh." (Yawn)

"Nelson is not the problem," Joan said sternly.

"The birds, too?" Sally asked. (Yawn)

"Everybody, except you, Sally."

"Oh." (Yawn)

"Did you tell Jane that Rachel and Trudy stole her bottle. Did you, Sally?" Joan could be a hard quizmaster.

Sally performed two quick yawns and scratched her stomach.

"No, I didn't say that."

That set Jane off. "You did, you did, you did," she yelled at Sally.

"No I didn't. I just said maybe they did. Jane said her bottle was missing and I said maybe Rachel and Trudy took it." (Yawn)

Rachel and I smiled smugly. "See?" we said. "It's simply a case of mistaken identity."

"Do you know anything about this, Sarah?" Joan asked her. Sarah was sitting on the floor in the corner. She jumped up when Joan spoke.

"Not me. Not me. No, sir. Not me."

"Well, *somebody* took my bottle, that's for sure," Jane lamented.

"Sarah?" I said with a strong upward inflection. Sarah avoided our eyes. She did one of those little toe-in-the-sand movements and cleared her throat.

"Sarah?"

"Why would I take someone's Scotch?"

I stood there feeling like Sherlock Holmes in the last reel of *The Late Show*.

"Ah hah," I said pouncing. "No one ever said it was Scotch that was stolen."

"Oh," was Sarah's reply.

"Is that all you can say, Sarah? *Oh?* After we've caught you with a slip of the tongue that proves you took Jane's bottle? You're always borrowing things. You must have borrowed Jane's bottle." I was pressing my discovery to the hilt.

Sarah stifled a yawn and said calmly, "Well, Jane always drinks Scotch. That's how I knew."

Jane tottered unsteadily in the corner while all the cross-examining was going on. "That's not at all true," she said with a strange annoyed tone to her voice. "I'm especially fond of bourbon."

"What did you do with the bottle?" Joan asked Sarah.

Sarah stood firm. "I didn't take any bottle."

Everyone seemed to accept Sarah's finality. They turned to us again.

I started to giggle. Rachel joined me. Joan got mad.

"This is a very serious matter," she intoned with all the piety of a layreader on Christmas. Joan could do this quite nicely. She seemed forever preaching about something, her actions seldom matching her words.

"We know it is." But we couldn't stop laughing.

The night ended with nothing solved and everyone mad at everyone else. Rachel and I chuckled ourselves to sleep.

We were about to leave the penthouse the next morning for our flight when Marie came flying out of her bedroom, tears running down her cheeks. In her hand was the lifeless form of Nelson, the alligator. It's hard to tell when an alligator is dead, especially from a distance. But Marie confirmed it.

"He's dead," she shouted.

"How?"

"I don't know." She was heartbroken. The little reptile didn't move in her hands.

We went into Marie's room. Sally sat sleepily on her bed. The birds were all chirping happily, a thing birds probably always do when an alligator dies.

We went over to the fish tank where Nelson drew his last breath and looked into the water. The water was never especially clean, but that morning it had a definite bronze tone to it.

"What's in the water?" Rachel asked Marie, now calmed down just a little.

"I don't know. Is anything in the water?"

"Sure." Rachel dipped her finger into the tank and sniffed it.

"Smells like Scotch."

"Scotch?" Marie said with horror.

"Yeh, Scotch. Take a sniff."

Marie did.

Then she dipped her own finger into the tank and licked the water on its tip. "It *is* Scotch," she moaned.

"Maybe he died of cirrhosis," Sally said from the bed.

"Who did this?" Marie shrieked at the top of her voice.

That scream did it. Everyone came running into the room.

Everyone chattered away at once.

"A little respect for the deceased, please." Rachel suggested.

The chattering was still going on when we left for our flight. We returned that night to a grim penthouse. Jane was drunk, bless her heart.

"Well, who did Nelson in?" I asked Joan, who sat quietly reading a book.

"Sally said maybe you two did."

"Here we go again."

"Did you?"

"No."

"I didn't think so. Jane and I have solved the problem, though." (The rules committee, remember?)

"How did you do that?"

"Marie will be leaving in the morning."

"Marie? Did she poison Nelson, her own alligator?"

"No, of course not. But those animals all over the place were just too much for anyone to bear. She's leaving with her zoo." Joan went back to reading.

Marie did leave the penthouse. The mystery of the missing bottle and the dead alligator were never solved, although Rachel and I came up with a solution we felt was plausible. We figured Sarah borrowed the bottle and Sally knew it. She accused us to protect Sarah. Then, Sarah got scared and dumped the bottle in Nelson's tank to get rid of the evidence. We gave up trying to figure out what she did with the actual bottle. You can't solve everything.

So Marie moved out and Libby moved in. Libby was a friend of Helen's, their particular closeness bonded by a mutual need to diet constantly. Libby was a discothèque dancer in Greenwich Village. Sally moved in with Sarah, and Helen roomed with Libby. Together, they cornered the market on yogurt. They also turned the penthouse into a gymnasium for their numerous exercises for figure improvement. Things went along for a month until Libby, or Helen, we're not sure which, accused somebody of eating her yogurt.

Sarah admitted borrowing "a little teeny bit," but Sally said she thought Sarah had borrowed a lot. The only one in the clear was Jane who often said yogurt and whiskey just didn't mix.

And so it went. Our chic, glamorous penthouse soon fell into a long shadow of bickering, a human inevitability where girls are concerned, especially eight of them. Rachel and I departed for an apartment in Greenwich Village where we stayed-in relative bliss.

It's true that our experience in New York is probably not at all typical of most stewardesses. Those who remain seem to find some sort of fun out of living there. Certainly the penthouse hadn't contributed a great fondness for fun city. But it's also true that New York is a tough place to live for any stewardess.

For instance: The telephone company, that great symbol of everything bad about a monopoly, is very reluctant to give a telephone to a stewardess. We understand they're reluctant to give a telephone to anyone, but the fact that a stewardess works for an airline and, by virtue of that simple employment circumstances has easy access to airplanes, thrusts a dagger of deep mistrust into the hearts of the telephone company's employees.

It's the same with department stores. These money-making giants of commerce seem certain we'll spend a day in their store with our new charge card, buy at least $50,000 worth of goods, and immediately wing off to Saudi Arabia to avoid payment of the bill. What amazes you is when you receive one of those form letters stating you are a preferred customer and a credit card is waiting for you at the Preferred Customer, Gold Plated, A-1 First Class, Chosen-By-God credit desk. Just try and get it.

We've since found these problems to be common to other cities besides New York. But it just doesn't seem as bad. Everything is magnified in New York.

If you, stymied in becoming the world's greatest Wall Street broker, concert pianist or most famous actor on Broadway, should decide to pursue the career of a stewbum, knowing where we live in the cities of this nation will be helpful. The following listing is published for your use.

New York
    The East 60's and 70's of Manhattan
    Forest Hills
    Jackson Heights
    Kew Gardens

Chicago
    Aurora
    Near North Side
    Apartments near airport

COFFEE, TEA OR ME?

Miami
- Coral Gables
- Villa Springs
- Miami Springs
- Coconut Grove

San Francisco
- San Mateo
- Belmont
- Redwood City
- Sausalito
- Downtown

Los Angeles
- Westchester
- Inglewood
- Gardena
- Long Beach
- Manhattan Beach
- Van Nuys

Denver
- Aurora
- Downtown

Houston
- Downtown

Dallas
- Apartments near airport
- Downtown

Atlanta
- N.E. side of town
- Chamblee
- East Point
- Buckhead
- South side of town

Boston
   Back Bay
   Beacon Hill
   Brookline

Washington, D.C.
   Georgetown
   Arlington (Virginia)

Also, there are definite places where we have fun. As a stewardess working a flight, we aren't able to serve more than two drinks per person. But that doesn't mean we can't have more than two drinks when off-duty and in any one of our favorite bars. If you ever feel in the mood to have more than two drinks with a stewardess, give these places a try, each a known hang-out for sisters of the skies.

St. Louis
   Any bar up and down Gaslight square

New York
   Sullivan's
   Friday's
   P. J. Clarke's (or any P.J. joint)
   Wagon Wheel
   The Baron Steak House
   Sammy's
   York
   Clos Normand
   La Popotte
   Le Marmiton
   Rattazzi's
   Hawaii Kai Club
   Dawson's Pub

San Diego
   Mickey Finn's
   Coronado Island

COFFEE, TEA OR ME?

Atlanta
- Mr. Brother's Place
- Sans Souci
- Kitten's Korner
- Ruby Red's
- Al's Corral
- The Red Barn
- The Lion's Head
- Top of the Peachtree
- Fan & Bill's
- Yohannan's
- The Malibu Room
- The Round Table
- The Falcon Lounge

New Orleans
- Al Hirt's Place
- Pat O'Brien's
- Pete Fountain's
- Whis-A-Go-Go

Miami
- Tie One On
- The Eden Rock
- 600 Lounge
- The Villas
- The Dream Bar

Washington, D.C.
- Beef Treat
- Blackie's
- Junkanoo
- Palladian Room
- O'Donnell's

Mobile
- Quarter Note

Hawaii
- Duke Kahanamoku
- Don-Ho's

COFFEE, TEA OR ME?

Las Vegas
- Stardust
- Silver Slipper

San Francisco
- The Crown Room
- Chuck's Place
- The Two Turtles
- Basin Street South
- hungry i
- Big Al's
- Playboy Club
- Gay Nineties
- Alioto's
- Whis-A-Go Go
- Doros
- Red Garter

Los Angeles
- Manhattan Beach
- The Chatter Box
- Shakey's Pizza Parlor
- Disneyland Bar

Toronto
- Skyline Motel Bar

Chicago
- The bars of Old Town
- The bars of Rush Street

CHAPTER VI

"This Is Your Captain Speaking"

You can always recognize a captain from the calluses on his finger from pushing the call button for coffee. Sometimes we think that's all the captain does up there —summon us for coffee. Most captains are great guys. They have a sense of humor, they know how to treat a girl, they take care of their girls. Good captains are extremely protective of their stewardesses. They don't permit any funny business, by anyone, where their girls are concerned.

I'll always bless the captain of one of my early flights. The two senior stews were stiff, unfriendly girls and I was decidedly ill at ease. Just before dinner a passenger toward the rear of the plane signaled. I went back. A man sat there. His pants were unzipped and he was fully exposed. He grinned up at me with a nasty expression that froze my blood. I panicked and ran to tell the senior stew. She coldly suggested that I inform the passenger of his condition in case it was an accident. I approached him gingerly and said, "Sir, I'm sorry, but would you please zip your zipper."

He leered at me and said, "Why don't you let me put a tiger in your tank, young lady?"

I was completely flustered. The other stews were clearly not going to be any help. I went forward and told the captain. Without a word the captain turned the controls over to the first officer, put his hand on my shoulder an instant to reassure me and strode to the rear to deal with the situation. He got the man closed up all right. Two policemen met the passenger at the next stop and hauled him away. The captain rang for me immediately after the incident. "You all right, honey? You OK?" He sensed how distressed I was.

"I'm shook, but I'll make it."

"That's a good girl. Don't let the goons get you. Wait for me in Toledo. I'll take you to dinner."

That captain was a born big brother. At dinner he kept me laughing steadily with stories of his boyhood in North Dakota. He showed me pictures of his seven-year-old twins and his Great Dane puppies. His easy chatter crowded all thoughts of the distasteful encounter from my

COFFEE, TEA OR ME?

mind. At my hotel door, he tilted my head back, kissed me on the forehead and said, "You're a good girl, Trudy. You'll be OK now. Sleep well." Now that's my idea of a captain. I only hope his wife is good enough for him.

On the other hand there are some captains, not many of them, who think the whole point of taking a plane from one city to another is to make a lunge for a stewardess two minutes after landing. Sister stews have told us some pretty horrendous tales about captains. You could begin to think that some of the most over-sexed males in the country are right up front in the cockpit of your super-powered, fan-jet, dyna-lift, whisper-quiet airplane. Waiting for only one thing—to paw their way into your chaste chamber at the hotel.

What never ceases to amaze us is the stamina and staying power of these pilots, most of whom are over fifty years old. They're not old for the same reasons old men are selected at the stewardess school. It's taken a pilot a long time to gain the necessary hours and experience to command a multi-million-dollar jet aircraft. There's been a lot of talk recently about the upsetting effect jet travel has on the bodily functions of crew members. Maybe there is a physiological reason for captains' retaining their sexual drive, even after the age when most men find it necessary to develop another hobby. Maybe the key to potency is more jet travel. (We now lay claim to any airline advertising campaign based on this assumption.)

Of course, a few months on the line and you soon develop your own code of conduct with the cockpit crew. Either you Do or you Don't. And you try not to tell your roommate or your hairdresser. You make up your own mind whether your captain really does have the right to all your services. Captains realize that the longer a girl flies the line, the harder she'll be to conquer. Stewardesses who've been around will generally have latched onto one particular captain or have acquired other interests. So those on the make stalk the new girls, fresh from school where Big Momma made virtue sound dull and walls were for climbing.

It was on Rachel's third flight that she was introduced

to the "manual flush" routine so popular with cockpit crews where a new girl is concerned. It was a light flight and dinner had been served when the little light flashed in the galley indicating that service was needed in the cockpit. It's an unwritten rule that the junior girl handles the cockpit chores, unless a senior girl has something going up front. This day, Rachel was the one. The other girls had evidently sworn off crew members for the week and simply pointed to Rachel.

She nervously pranced up the aisle, fluffing her dark hair and straightening her skirt. The flight engineer patted her fanny as she slid by him, a gesture Rachel assumed was normal cockpit procedure. Besides, she wasn't about to be labeled a square so early in the game. She stood silently, in back of the captain's right ear, his head just reaching her chest.

"Rachel," the captain said with a smile as he turned to show his wrinkled profile, a must for all captains, "we seem to be having trouble with the flushing apparatus in the lavs."

What could she say.

"Yes, sir."

"It looks as though we'll have to go to manual flushing techniques this trip," he continued, frowning to indicate the gravity of the situation.

Rachel quickly flipped back through her mental file of procedures and could remember nothing of a manual flushing problem. But that didn't prove a thing. Would a captain lie about something like this?

"We're very busy up forward here, as you can well imagine, Rachel. I'm placing you in complete charge of the manual flushing procedure. That little button in front of me, the one farthest away, activates the manual flushing operation. Every twenty minutes, I want you to come forward to the cockpit and flip that button. You'll flip it and hold it for forty-five seconds. Got it?"

"Yes, sir."

"Better give it a try now, Rachel."

The only way Rachel could reach the button was to lean over the top of the captain's head. She strained to

COFFEE, TEA OR ME?

get her finger to the switch, her breasts melting comfortably around the captain's ears. Finally, after much squirming, she managed to reach the button and flip it.

"Hold it steady for forty-five seconds," the captain commanded, his head rigid back against her bosom.

Rachel started to sweat as she kept her finger on the switch. She kept shifting her weight from foot to foot, each movement rearranging her breasts on the captain's head and neck.

"Manual flushing completed," snapped the co-pilot in crisp military tones.

"Roger," the captain confirmed.

"Whew," Rachel sighed.

"See you in twenty minutes, Rachel."

Most new stewardesses are put through the manual flushing routine. Some come back to the galley cursing the captain. Some, embarrassed, say nothing. Some can't wait for the twenty minutes to pass. Good all Rachel's attitude was that it could have been worse.

Another favorite trick is to hoist a new stewardess up into the overhead coat rack before passengers have begun to come aboard. The crew then sits and watches the girl try valiantly to get down, tight skirt and all.

We give it back at times to the cockpit crew. A co-pilot (commonly called a first officer on most airlines) or flight engineer making his first flight as a crew member with the airline can look forward to having his sleeves sewn shut, his cap insignia turned upside down and his coffee served in one of those dime-store dribble cups.

Captain Smyth was a fine pilot, one of the airline's best. He was also a religious fanatic. When he wasn't pushing a 707 around at thirty thousand feet, he was guiding his own congregation of six hundred people in a church he founded about ten years ago. It had no affiliation with any recognized religious order.

Captain Smyth was a nice guy to fly with. He was always polite to his stewardesses and would tolerate no dirty talk in his cockpit. Many cockpit crew members refused to fly with him. They took offense at his pious approach to flying. But there were always a few first officers and flight engineers who held similarly strong religious beliefs, and when they'd get together on a particular flight, we'd term the cockpit, "Boeing's Basilica."

If you flew often enough with Smyth, you soon found yourself turning to him for fatherly advice. In effect, he'd set up his own flying confessional. And it's amazing how many girls took advantage of his religious leanings.

One night in the crew motel in New Orleans, a pretty brunette took her tale of woe to Captain Smyth's room. It seems she'd become deeply involved with a married passenger and his marriage was threatened as a result. She told our self-ordained captain the entire story, and waited for his words of wisdom.

"I want you to take off your clothing and lie on the floor," were his initial words of advice. "You must lie there awake all night and pray to the spiritual bodies of the universe that they may wipe you clean of this sin."

"You're joking?"

"Joking? Hardly. Do as I say and I'll remain at your side for the entire night, if need be. You can gain through my strength."

Naturally, the story got around. And that ended any evangelism as far as Captain Smyth and his girls were concerned. He's still a fine pilot, but the stewardesses working his flights now confine their problem-telling to a psychiatrist boy-friend or roommate.

At times captains can be trouble for a stewardess, even though their intentions are honorable.

Marge Bascom was a striking blonde girl who had been with the airline for over two years. She had a particular friendship with a veteran captain that, she claimed, never went beyond the platonic stage. She was a pretty open gal, and there was no reason to disbelieve her.

Her trouble with this captain came after a delayed flight into Kennedy from El Paso. They finally arrived in New York at 1:30 A.M., and the captain offered to see Marge home to her apartment in Manhattan. His wife was away and he thought he'd stay in town rather than trek home to Westchester.

They took a cab into the city and went up to Marge's apartment. Her roommates were out of town on layovers. When she offered to make him a drink, he accepted, and settled down on the couch as she prepared martinis in the kitchen.

"Mind if I change into civies?" he yelled through the archway.

"Be my guest," she answered.

"Give me a minute out here before you pop out," he warned. (It *was* platonic.)

"Take your time."

This captain, with the honorable intentions, was down to his shorts and T-shirt when a key turned in the front door and a tall, young man stepped into the foyer.

"What the hell?" he gasped.

"Who are you?" the captain asked, a little dismayed by his state of undress.

"Marge," the young man shouted, storming past the captain into the kitchen.

Zap, smack, whop, came from the kitchen and the young man tore out of the room.

"You bastard," he hissed at the captain who was racing to get dressed. "You dirty bastard." With that, the young man made his exit with a flair of slammed doors and profanity.

Marge emerged from the kitchen holding her mouth. A thin line of blood trickled from its corner and her eye was beginning to puff.

"What is this?" the captain asked as he went to help her.

"That *was* my fiancé," she said. They never did make up, and Marge is still flying the line looking for another intended.

There was a time when a crew could stay together as a working unit. The airline allowed the captain, first officer, flight engineer, navigator and stewardesses to bid as a unit for various trips, and it wasn't uncommon to find a congenial group flying together for a year or more.

But those days are over. And ironically, the change

COFFEE, TEA OR ME?

was brought about by ex-stewardesses who married captains as the result of this cozy situation.

Every airline has an organization of ex-stewardesses who band together to rehash old stories and aid their former airline in matters of policy and publicity. In reality, the girls primarily use the organization to maintain the illusion of still being glamorous stewardesses. It's an organization Rachel and I have pledged to each other to avoid at all costs when our flying days are over.

But they're an influential group of women, and when they decide to put the pressure on a given airline, their collective voices are listened to. That's what happened to the permanent crew situation. Many, or perhaps most, of these ex-stewardesses married crew members whom they got to know quite well when they were flying as a team. Many of them managed to steal captains from spouses of long standing.

Once they won their Flash Gordon from the other gal, they were put in her shoes. And they didn't like it. So, using the power they had, they convinced their airline that crews should not be allowed to fly together for any extended period of time. They won. Their victory spread to other airlines and pretty soon you couldn't fly with that great crew any longer. The silly thing is that this maneuver didn't really accomplish a thing. If a husband is going to stray, he'll do it no matter how new his crew is to him. But the girls feel more certain in their own hearts that they've insured a long and happy marriage. Maybe we'll react the same way when we're married, grounded and scared of losing our hero. We hope not.

Of course, even with the break-up of permanent crews, it's still possible to fly with a particular favorite pilot. Every crew member works on a bid system when it comes to receiving monthly assignments. The stewardess bid results come out before the cockpit crew results. If a captain has something going with you, he can usually, if he has the needed years of seniority, bid for those trips you've been awarded. But this situation can lead to great sadness.

COFFEE, TEA OR ME?

A stewardess with another airline was madly in love with a handsome captain. They'd carried on an affair for six months, and he'd always bid for and receive most of her trips.

The sadness came one day in flight operations. She hurried up to him with the glad news, "I got San Francisco again, Harry. You'll have no trouble getting it, too."

"Gee, I'm sorry, Lucia, but I got stuck with Buffalo and Toronto. What a rotten break."

"Buffalo and Toronto? You've got enough seniority to get any trip you want. I can't believe you'd lose out and end up with those dog runs."

"I tried, Lucia, I really tried. I'm sorry." With those words of apology, Harry walked away to the hellish fate of a Buffalo non-stop.

But Lucia wasn't about to take this turn of events without a little checking. She slithered down to the departure gate and watched Harry climb onboard with a new stewardess, who was sort of a cross between Sophia Loren and Gidget. It was obvious that Harry decided to fly the milk runs because they were the only ones the new gal could bid and win. Lucia learned there and then that a sure tip-off of a dying romance between senior captain and stew is when he suddenly becomes junior again, both in seniority and outlook.

Most crews will get together after a flight for a dip in the motel pool. It makes no difference what the hour is, and 2 or 3 A.M. swims are common. We all splashed into the pool this particular night in Miami with the exception of our captain, who begged off without any specific reason. We were having a wonderful time in the cool water when he finally did appear and ran up on the edge of the high board. He perched there, minus blue serge uniform and wings, and sprang up and down in readiness for a swan dive. Oh, yes—he was also minus his swim trunks.

There he was, our leader, posed proudly like an out-of-shape statue in all his natural glory. Occasional spot lights around the pool perimeter reflected off the water to illuminate his splendor. Then, with a healthy Tarzan scream, he leaped into the water to join us.

We all paddled around for an hour. Our captain wasn't drunk from all we could ascertain. It was a simple matter of flying fatigue.

"Roll me in the clover and do it again," he sang as he lazily paddled back and forth across the pool. His singing brought a few complaints from sleeping guests at the motel, and the manager, as understanding as he was with airline crews, came out and asked us to leave the pool. We did, forming a circle around our nude captain.

We asked him about it the next morning at breakfast and he mumbled something about the threat of the H-Bomb and starving children and other vague references. We didn't press the issue, and his subsequent dips in the many pools we frequent were always with trunks.

There are so many stories about captains. Some are true, some are almost true. Many are simply too grotesque and sordid to write about. In their professional role of commander of a giant commercial aircraft, they're fine, expert professionals performing a very responsible job. Passengers seldom have to worry about their captain. Stewardesses are the ones who sometimes worry.

Rachel has a favorite captain story. One wintry night there were about ten stews sitting on the floor in our apartment drinking red wine, listening to Oscar Peterson records and swapping girl talk. We went through quite a bit of wine that night and the competitive spirit became keen. Each girl tried to top the others. The stories became more and more personal and I suspect now as I look back less and less truthful. After a while there was a kind of lull. I turned to Rachel, "You've been very quiet over there. Haven't you been raped lately or anything?"

"Well, now that you mention it . . ."

All Rachel needs is one prod and there's no guessing what'll come next.

"C'mon, tell us. What happened?" the girls begged.

"I never told you about Louis Lamb, did I?" Rachel settled herself against a pile of cushions. "You know, the big deal captain who thinks he's God's gift? I wasn't going to tell anybody, I mean, it's kind of sick. Pour me another glass." I did.

"Well, I was working some trips with him couple of months ago and we laid over in Detroit. I kind of liked him. He's a good-looking guy, you have to admit that. So he took me out and we drank a lot and pretty soon he had me talked into staying with him. We went back to his room and after a while he went into the john and I got undressed and waited under the sheets. It took him forever to do whatever he was doing. And then . . . Oh, pour me another wine, huh?"

"C'mon, get to the point," I said.

"Yeah, let's hear it," the others chorused.

"OK. So I'm in bed and all of a sudden the john door opens and out he comes, not a stitch on, and he's got his arms out at his side, like wings on an airplane. And he starts running around the room and dipping from side to side and making motor sounds, like, *Rrrrrrrrrrrr*. I swear he was nuts, really nuts. All over that damn room and I sat up and boy, I was scared. Then all of a sudden he zoomed at the bed, *Rrrrrrrrrrrr* and he said, 'OK, baby! Maybe you've had it from the best. But you've never been screwed by a 707.' I'm not kidding, girls. That's what he said. Boy, did I get out of there fast. I hate to look like a kid, but I'd just as soon have it like I've always had it. I guess I'm just a country girl at heart."

We all laughed for at least twenty minutes. There were girls sprawled all over the floor, laughing like crazy. The next morning I said to Rachel, "Come clean. That Louis Lamb story. Did it really happen?"

Rachel looked at me, her brown eyes round as searchlights. "Why, Trudy, would I lie to you? Ever?"

"I don't think you'd lie to me. But you could have been putting those girls on last night. Did it happen?"

"Like I said." She put her arms out and went, *"Rrrrrrrrrr."*

I started laughing all over again. There's no telling with Rachel. But this I do know: captains can be a strange breed.

CHAPTER VII

"You Must See So Many Interesting Places, My Dear"

My visits back to Amarillo always take a particularly pleasant turn when I stop to see my Aunt Laconia, a fascinating person, and the only family member pleased with my stewardess career. Aunt Laconia is a librarian and naturally reads a lot, mostly about places she's never been. Aunt Laconia should have been a stewardess. She was a beautiful girl in her youth.

When I visit her, we usually pass the first ten minutes with general chit-chat about Amarillo, the family and local gossip. Then, when it's time for tales of my travels, Aunt Laconia begins with, "You must see so many interesting places, my dear."

Before I begin my travelogues for Aunt Laconia I have to give her a careful rundown of a day in the life of a stewardess. Otherwise, she'd think we're fresh as a daisy and raring to go the minute we hit a new town. We like to go all right. Stewardesses are young and swingers and we'll have plenty of time to catch up on our sleep when we're older and grounded. But even with all the enthusiasm in the world on our side, there are times when we're simply too bushed to do the hot spots.

You, the carefree passenger, may snooze your way from New York to San Francisco or dip into a light novel or watch a shoot-'em-up movie. Meanwhile, here are a couple of things that we're doing:

Our flight leaves at two in the afternoon. We check in at operations at one, and hustle down to the airplane. We go through all the setting up and you, our paying customers, come on board. There are one hundred thirty of you.

Flight time is about five hours. And here's how we spend it.

. . . We prepare and serve two hundred sixty diverse drinks, all from the liquor cart that was designed to fit in the aisle, not to function as an effective bar-on-wheels. One of you becomes irate because we don't serve mint juleps. It's not our fault. Nor is it when the pre-mixed martini isn't dry enough. And we're sorry we hit that turbulence that caused us to spill ginger ale on your only suit.

. . . Now come one hundred thirty hot towels. We ex-

COFFEE, TEA OR ME?

plain to eighty passengers what to do with them. And our hands become TV-rough and red from handling them.

... Collect the towels. Set up one hundred thirty trays. No, we don't have special trays for children. No, we don't have peanut butter and jelly on board. No, you don't have to eat. Yes, if you're going to eat, you have to do it now. No, you can't have another drink. No, we do not have *Playboy* on board (men always ask that and wait for our reaction. It's our least favorite line and we wish they'd stop).

... Serve one hundred thirty meals. You ordered a kosher meal? Gee, the caterer didn't put one on board. (Should we tell the next passenger who ordered a special meal that the airline never delivers on those orders? Should we simply make up our own kosher meal for the next passenger. We've done both.) We're sorry the steak isn't rare enough. It's a shame you don't like bacon crumbs on the salad. We're sorry, we're sorry, we're sorry. Our legs are beginning to feel it now, the running up and down, the bending, the apologizing, the rat-race.

... Coming up are one hundred thirty desserts. Don't yell at us because the ice cream is too frozen to push your spoon through. I'll bet your mother did make better apple pie.

... After-dinner drinks now. We're still pouring wine from dinner. Some are getting drunk now. And some of those are getting obnoxious.

... You're too cold? We'll make you warmer. Too warm, now? We'll make you cooler. Sorry, but we don't carry *Downbeat*. No, I won't go to bed with you. Yes, I will go to bed with you. We're really tired now. We've run up and down getting you water, matches, cigarettes, magazines, Kleenex, pillows, blankets, writing paper, telegram blanks, post cards, the typewriter, the razor and anything else you might want—within reason. No, even outside of reason.

... There's San Francisco below us. And we know what you're all thinking as you file off the airplane past us. Who, what, why, when, where are we going to swing tonight? Yes, sir, here we are, those swingers of the sky,

COFFEE, TEA OR ME?

about to tear up hilly old San Fran and have an orgy on a houseboat in Sausalito and drink ourselves silly and still show up tomorrow morning with our smiles, hair and uniforms in place, sans wrinkles and ready to serve you in the best tradition of our airline.

Well, you know, you're not altogether wrong.

We check out of the airport about five, reach downtown San Francisco at six, take a shower, put our hair up, think, boy, this is one night I'm going to do nothing but sleep. It's shut-eye from now until I'm called for the 8:30 A.M. flight back tomorrow. Nothing will get me out of bed. Nothing.

The only trouble is that in about ten minutes the phone rings. It's Susie or Grace or Mark or Phil—one of our pals from this flight or other flights. "Hi, Trudy, hi Rachel! C'mon, there's a party in room 1026 and then we're going down to the wharf." I say I'm too tired. Rachel says she's too tired. We're both too tired. But while we're protesting, we're already pulling the rollers out of our hair and reaching for our shoes. "Come on, Rachel," I say, "let's go!" And we're off to a big night in San Francisco.

Most of our layovers now are only eighteen to twenty-four hours. In the past when planes were slower we often stayed in a place for forty-eight hours or more. Then we have more time to sight-see and get to know a city. But even with lots of time, stewardesses aren't much for visiting museums and trotting around to historic sights. The museum stuff that I tell Aunt Laconia I usually get from travel booklets. She likes to much to hear me talk about culture. I always play down the nightspots; she isn't very big in that department. But stewardesses are.

Here, then, is a stew's eye-view of some of the livelier towns in the U.S.A.

San Francisco: Just the simple act of taking a walk can be an enjoyable experience in San Francisco, with its hills and white buildings and cool-wet bay breeze. The night life is the best, although all the topless craze of late seems to have caused some confusion in the minds of San Fran's

COFFEE, TEA OR ME?

eligible dates. We love dating there. We love a drink at the Top of the Mark. We love listening to jazz at the Matador or Jazz Workshop. But we *don't* love going to watch some Iowa farm girl flop her silicone breasts around on the top of the bar. As they say at county fair girlie shows, "Ladies free 'cause there's nothin' inside you ain't seen before." But, topless or not, San Francisco will always reign supreme.

Boston: Boston is a nice city. And it has so many nice, eligible college men. It does help your cause if you're at all conversant with urban renewal and local politics, two apparent running manias with Bostonians. We always manage to find time for a ride on the swan boats on the Common, beer, beans and sandwiches in Harvard Square and maybe even a little sailing on the Charles. Most stewardesses try for at least a year's duty in Boston. All those educated, potential lifelong mates are a pretty potent motivation.

Miami: Never a dull moment in Miami, unless you're looking for lazy, dull moments under the sun. The beach is Miami is relaxing, and you can squander away your time watching the beach boys flex or the bar girls outflex the beach boys. All that crystal blue water and towering white cloud formations can make you wish you didn't have to leave. You might even bump into Jackie Gleason on the golf course, which can be a massive experience.

Dallas: We'll include Houston, too. That's because this Texas haven for humidity holds a special spot in my heart. We were flying a Miami-New York trip when I started feeling stomach pains. They got worse, and pretty soon I was doubled over in the aisle, passengers and fellow-stew hovering around me. It was my appendix—burst. We detoured quickly to Houston where an ambulance whisked me away to the hospital. Once the pain was gone, I began to wonder how mad all those passengers were about having to go to New York via Houston. But then the get-well cards started to pour in from over half the passengers and I stopped worrying. The traveling public does have a heart.

COFFEE, TEA OR ME?

In Dallas, the stewardess sport is to cruise the streets in search of young oil tycoons. Once you've exhausted that possibility, you go after old oil tycoons. Failing all chance at an oil windfall, you can daydream over the Chinese junks or "his 'n' her" bathtubs at Neiman-Marcus and wish there was an oil tycoon to . . . Well, you know.

Chicago: The local gals seem unusually jealous of all the laying-over stewardesses in their windy city, and manage to keep prize males out of sight and reach. This is a shame because Chicago is such a ball to visit with all the pub crawling, especially in the winter when it's too cold to do much else but pub crawl. Maybe our union can negotiate a truce with Chicago's female population. On second thought, our union doesn't seem to have any negotiator that hard-fisted to pull off that trick. We'll just have to keep pub crawling in search of some escaped males. Luck to us.

St. Louis: For some natural reason, winters are colder and summers hotter in St. Louis than anywhere else. But in the spring and fall, St. Louis offers a great deal to do and see. In your plaintive moments, you can sit and wait for some hot-shot pilot to fly a 707 under the newly completed Gateway to the West arch.

Atlanta: Once you've found the inner circle, you can find a swinging time in Atlanta. For some reason, Atlanta likes stewardesses. A lots of bars cater to us, and one little favorite spot, Kitten's Korner, is fast to put it on the house for us. It's definitely *our* favorite house in Atlanta.

Cleveland: For all that smoke and water pollution, Cleveland has its charms. Besides, with a good crew, we can have fun anywhere, even in a steel mill.

Detroit: They make cars in Detroit, and men make cars. Detroit has an ample male population who know where the action is and who are willing to spend money to make it happen. We like Detroit.

Los Angeles: Los Angeles is a thing all to itself. It's great and it's horrible. Some of the greatest times we've had occurred in Los Angeles. When those memorable times weren't happening, we hated LA. It's just one of those places, we guess.

COFFEE, TEA OR ME?

Memphis and Nashville: If you like Dixieland Jazz, and we do, you like these two southern cities.

Montreal: We date mounties in Montreal and have parties in cabins on the river. Sometimes our dates take us for rides in their canoes which is fun and, due to the structural design of a canoe, provides relative protection from too vigorous advances. It's also a drag if you're looking for vigorous advances. Or wet.

Although we work for a domestic airline, we have plenty of chances to see the world. Through exchanges with other airlines, we can spend a weekend in London for $39. We can to to Paris for less than $50. Everywhere we get 75% off at hotels and we pick up all kinds of free passes. I spent four days in Paris that I'll never forget. I adore Hawaii. The stews there spend a lot of time in Don Ho's famous night club. I once flew from Miami to Lima, Peru, for a weekend and still had change from a $20 bill when I returned.

Aunt Laconia doesn't believe me when I tell her that I once took off from Atlanta, went to Chicago and on to Los Angeles to have a drink with some friends. I came back the same way, took a quick shower and was off on a working flight to New York. A couple of days later a friend called and said, "I was trying to get you Tuesday night. Where were you?"

"Tuesday . . . Tuesday," I said, "let me think a moment. Was that the night I went to the movies? Oh, no. Tuesday I was having a drink in LA."

CHAPTER VIII

"You Must Meet So Many Interesting Men, My Dear"

My same Aunt Laconia will occasionally interrupt my tales of travel to say, "You must meet so many interesting men, my dear." This is her shy, sly way of prying into the sex in my life. I do not try to let her down when it comes to my romantic interests. But naturally, I don't mention *all* the men in my life. I don't think Aunt Laconia really wants to hear the gory details. Then again, maybe she does. Still I never take a chance with the whole truth. Even when I confine my tales to storybook young college men who share ice cream sodas with me through two straws, she asks with a sweet and hopeful smile on her face, "Is he the one?"

"I don't think so, Aunt Laconia, maybe next year."

I've debated often whether to tell Aunt Laconia about Chuck. She's a pretty shrewd old gal and if I started talking I'm sure she'd sense that this one is more serious than all the others. She's bound then, one way or another, to tell my parents. And after that on every visit home they'd all be staring at the fourth finger on my left hand and making not-so-gentle hints. I've decided to leave that part of my life a closed book as far as my family is concerned.

I didn't see Chuck for about four months after I got to New York. I thought about him a lot. A million different nights I said to Rachel, "What do you think? Will I hear from him?"

She had unshakable confidence that Chuck would reappear on the scene in a big way. "Give him time," she assured me. "He'll turn up."

Several times I spotted his name on crew lists, so I knew he'd been in and out of New York. It was a crisp early fall day and I was alone in the apartment when the phone rang. "Are you wearing your jeans?" a man's voice asked.

"Sure. Who is this?" I asked.

"Good. I'll pick you up in half an hour. On my motorbike. We'll go for a ride."

"Who is it?"

"Why, Trudy, I'm surprised. I thought you Texans were friendlier. It's Chuck." And he hung up.

He must have called from around the corner because

COFFEE, TEA OR ME?

he was at the door in a couple of minutes. He was wearing boots, dungarees, an old orange flight jacket and a crash helmet. He swept me into an enormous kiss that lasted nearly forever, but wasn't half long enough, and then he dropped down on to the sofa. "Where've you been?" he demanded. "Pin a pair of wings on a girl like you and you disappear. Did you miss me?"

You must know by now that I'm not often at a loss for words, but I was tongue-tied. "Yes, I mean I was here . . . in New York. Where . . ."

"Forget it," he said. "Let's go."

His motorbike was parked just outside our building. He handed me his helmet and showed me how to strap it on. "We'll have to get you one of these things," he said. "This time you'll have to wear mine. You sit there." He pointed to the small rear saddle. "And hold on here." He arranged my hands around his waist. "Hold tight. We're blasting off." It wasn't a very big scooter, but it made a take-off sound like a 707.

"Where're we going?" I shouted into his ear as the wind rushed by. The automobiles on both sides of us were much too close for comfort. We missed pedestrians by mere inches. But I could sense his sure command of the vehicle and a great feeling of exhilaration began to take hold of me. We sped up to Radio City, wove in and out of the shopping crowds on Fifth Avenue, zoomed over to the East River Drive, hurtled along the river to an ancient, decaying wooden wharf, way downtown among the skyscrapers where old men were fishing in the afternoon sun. We parked the bike, sat on a splintery log and talked. That is to say Chuck talked. I was still too dazzled to find my tongue and every time I looked into those blue eyes of his I fell apart all over again.

He talked about his special assignment in California. He'd been on loan from the airline to a plane designer working on experimental new planes. That had been exciting but his real love was flying and he was happy now to be back on the line. He wanted to know everything that had happened to me since my first day as stewardess. I told him about that crazy first flight and the lady stuck

COFFEE, TEA OR ME?

in the john. I told him about other flights and about people I'd met, about Rachel and Betty and the others in our class. Once I got started talking, I could hardly stop. The words just poured out. We jabbered away on that dock until the wind rose and it turned cold.

"C'mon, I'll take you home," he said. "You can change your clothes and we'll do the town tonight."

Rachel was in the apartment when we got there. "Hi," she said to Chuck, as casually as if she'd seen him the day before. "What'll you drink?" She fed him bourbon while I went to dress. When I came out of the shower, Chuck was gone and Rachel was packing her overnight bag. "What's up?" I asked.

"Chuck's gone to change. He's staying with a friend a couple of blocks away. He'll be right back."

"What are you doing with that bag?"

"Didn't I tell you?" Rachel asked, all innocence. "I'm going to Great Neck for a couple of days to visit the Morales'." Rachel had an admirer who was a metallurgist from Colombia, South America. Through him she'd met a whole crowd of wealthy Latin Americans. She hadn't said a word about going to see the Morales'. I was sure she didn't really have a date with them.

Well, I didn't tell Aunt Laconia about the next two days. Not that she wouldn't have liked to hear. But there are some things a girl can't tell—even to her best friend. I didn't tell Rachel much either. Not when it's so real and important, you don't go yakking away.

"Is it the real thing?" Rachel asked two days later when Chuck had collected the last of his socks and shirts and Rachel had unpacked her overnight bag.

"Well, yes and no."

"What does that mean?"

"It's big with us all right, but . . ."

"But what?"

"But we're not going to do anything about it. Not now, anyway."

"What do you mean? You meet Mr. Right. Then you kiss him goodbye. Why? He isn't married or anything, is he?"

COFFEE, TEA OR ME?

"No, but he's been married and that's the problem."

It was kind of hard to explain because it wasn't altogether clear in my mind. But one thing was sure. Chuck believed in marriage more fully and intensely than any man I'd ever met. He had a kind of holy feeling about marriage. It had to be right and it had to be forever. He'd married several years earlier a girl from his home town who couldn't take the life of a flyer's wife. Marian couldn't stand the separations and the worry. After six months she'd given him an ultimatum. He'd have to give up flying or she'd leave. He couldn't stop flying. It was all the world to him. Marian got a divorce.

Chuck wasn't going to let that happen to him again, ever. For a couple of years, ever since his divorce, he'd avoided entanglements, refused to get serious with any girl. He was still avoiding entanglements. "Trudy," he'd said, "I have a feeling it may be us someday, you and me. But if it is, it has to last as long as we do. I won't settle for anything less. You're just beginning. You've got a million places to go and a zillion guys to meet before you're ready to settle down. You may not be ready for years. I'm not going to hurry you. Take your time. Get all your living done. I'll be around. You'll be hearing from me." He ruffled my hair once more. Kissed me again, picked up his bag and a few minutes later I heard the zoom of his bike.

So I didn't tell Aunt Laconia about Chuck.

Instead I told her about handcuffed prisoners we've had on board, political big-wigs, Don Juans, men who say funny things. There was the Catholic priest and the Seventh Day Adventist minister sitting together on one flight. The priest ordered a Scotch and water. The minister said, "I'd rather commit adultery than drink."

The priest looked up at me and said, "I didn't know I had a choice today." That was a fun trip.

With some hesitation I told about the stewardess who dated a photographer and began posing in the nude for him. On one of her flights the captain buzzed for her. He pointed to the centerfold photograph in a cheap men's magazine where she saw herself displayed in all her natural skin. "Anyone you know?" the captain asked jovially. The poor girl gave the photographer the gate.

I gave Aunt Laconia an edited version of my encounter with Mr. Relick. I met him during my one and only flight to Mexico City. I was on reserve, and pulled this flight when one of the regular girls became ill. I was pleased with the prospect; I hadn't the needed seniority to bid successfully for the Mexico City run, and Rachel's envy enhanced the windfall.

It was a wonderful trip down. The airline created a Mexican fiesta mood for the passengers, and everyone seemed exceptionally cheerful. We spent the night in Mexico City. The thrill of being in a foreign country buoyed me after the long flight. The crew, regulars on the Mexico run, took me everywhere, showed me everything and I fell into bed at three in the morning with a head full of *magnifico, bueno, si-si* and *buenas noches*. The first officer made a mild overture about spending the night, but took my polite negative response calmly.

The next morning we departed Mexico City with a full load, mostly wealthy businessmen, a few with their families. One of the men, a Mr. Relick, was particularly charming. He was courteous to the girls, never asked for anything without prefacing it with Please. Besides, he was handsome, about forty, with that attractive graying at the temples. We found time to talk a bit toward the end of the trip, and he asked me to join him for coffee in New York. I accepted. I was pleased to be asked, and frankly hoped it would prove interesting.

We had our coffee at the terminal, and I found out a few things about Mr. Relick. He was divorced, maintained a home in Mexico City, apartments in Paris and New York, and was successfully engaged in international import and export. I proved a good listener and he asked me for a date.

I bubbled all about him to Rachel as I showered and prepared for the evening. I evidently went overboard because she asked, "Isn't there anything wrong with him?"

"I don't think so, hon. Come to think of it, there is one flaw. With all his charm and sophistication, he has a little rough edge to the way he talks. I like that though. Know what I mean?"

"No."

"Oh, you do so know, stupid. Like Anthony Quinn or Jack Palance or Harry Guardino. A little bit of dem and dose. But manly, like he's lived."

"That ruins the whole thing. He sounds awful."

"Oh shut up. You're just jealous because I came up with a winner."

"Where are you going to dinner?"

"I don't know, but I bet it'll be nice."

"I hope so."

"Should I wear a girdle?"

"Definitely not. Bill Harris says girdles are the curse of American women. He says unless you really need one, you shouldn't wear it. And you don't need it, Trudy." Bill Harris was a flight engineer Rachel was seeing.

"But Big Momma said we all need it."

"Big Momma's a thing of the past. No girdle. Go loose tonight."

"What do you think he'd like me to wear?"

"Well, Trudy, if he really talks like you say he does, he'd probably like to see you in sequined slacks and gold high heels. No girdle. Guys never like girdles."

I wasn't wearing a girdle when Mr. Relick picked me up. We took a cab to an elegant Italian restaurant with "21" prices. Mr. Relick's charm became even more pronounced as the evening wore on. The most interesting thing was that his tendency to fall into a Brooklyn speech pattern also increased. He knew all the right things to say, but had trouble maintaining what was obviously a forced urbanity. Strange but delightful.

We continued the evening at Basin Street East where we enjoyed Duke Ellington and his band, a favorite of Mr. Relick's. The Ellington magic swept me up as it did the rest of the crowd, especially when the band played a medley of Ellington evergreens.

"All the guys in the band—Carney, Hodges, Brown, Anderson, Gonzales—they all hate to play the medley, Trudy. They've played those tunes at least eighteen thousand times, and it gets old. But that's what has to be played. He plays a lot of new stuff, but the crowd always wants to hear "Indigo" and "A-Train" and those things. Great band, isn't it?"

"Wonderful," I responded. "I love it." I did notice the bored expression on some of the musician's faces, now understandable in light of my escort's explanation.

"What a marvelous evening," I said as we climbed into a cab.

"I bet you can't wait to get home and out of your girdle, huh?" It wasn't a particularly charming thing to say, but humorous in light of my earlier conversation with Rachel.

"I'm not wearing one," I answered, realizing the answer wasn't any more charming than the question.

"I wasn't prying," he said quickly.

"I know."

"Well, since you don't have a girdle to get out of, how about making it to another place? I know a great coffee house in The Village. I'll buy you an espresso."

"Great. I'm off tomorrow. The night is young, Mr. Relick."

I can't remember the name of the coffee house, but it was what I supposed such a place should be. All around were dirty-looking young men and women, each trying very hard to conform to the non-conformist image. Mr. Relick and I sipped our espresso and he reached across the table and took my hand.

"Trudy, being out with you is great. Really great. I'm truly enjoying myself and I've got something to repay you with."

What a switch. He wasn't asking me to repay him, the usual feeling on the part of the fellow who's paid for dinner and expensive entertainment.

"Oh, Jim," I said with complete sincerity, "I don't deserve a thing. The fun has been all mine."

"No, no, Trudy. I insist."

He was drunker than I had realized, and his speech was now quite slurred and heavy, a great deal of the charm gone from it.

COFFEE, TEA OR ME?

He lowered his voice, glanced around, and looked me straight in the eye. With the secrecy came a hardness, a businesslike look, but more ruthless than that. He suddenly looked like Bruce Gordon, the actor who always played Frank Nitti, the enforcer on *The Untouchables*. He sounded like him, too.

"How would you like a grand a month, Trudy? Tax free."

"A grand? That's a thousand dollars, isn't it?"

He chuckled. "That's right. A thousand bucks. How would you like that?"

"Do I have to blow up an airplane?"

"No, no. Nothin' like that. Very easy loot. You're not against money, are you?"

"This sounds too easy, the way you tell it."

"Well, you interested?"

I sat there pondering his question very carefully. The evening had been fun, and I had a sinking feeling whatever was going to come next would in some way ruin that fun. But maybe I was wrong. I had to appear interested.

"Sure I'm interested in money. Everyone is."

"OK, Trudy. Here's the deal. And I'm trusting you a hell of a lot to even offer it to you. You know I'm in the import business. Well, one of the things I import is marijuana."

There wasn't another soul in the world at that moment. Everything ceased—all sound, movement, color. I felt a sickness creep up into my stomach, and my hand started shaking on the table.

"I don't feel very well," I said and started to rise. "I'm sorry. Please excuse me."

"Wait a minute," he said shaking his head back and forth and grabbing my arm. "Sit down."

I sat, but said, "Please, Mr. Relick, I want to leave. I don't like any of this." I wanted to hit him, or scream for the police, but he was frightening, sitting across from me. I just wanted to forget there was ever a Mr. Relick, a Duke Ellington or a Mexico City. I wanted this whole day and night to disappear.

COFFEE, TEA OR ME?

"Don't get shook, Trudy. I'm not askin' you to *use* dope or anything like that. Hell, I don't use the stuff. I just want you to help me out when you come up from Mexico now and then. Not all the time. Just sometimes. There's no trouble. You girls come in and out without anybody botherin' with you. Just carry some stuff once in a while. That's all."

The coffee house was full, and I was afraid someone would hear us. I leaned across the table and whispered to him, "Look, let's just forget about this. OK? I never heard what you said and that's it. Please. I can't do anything like that."

"Don't be stupid. Do you think you'll be the only stewardess who's smuggled stuff across lines. Trudy, some of the international girls make a fortune doin' it. And there's no risk. If anybody did find some stuff on you, you just say some crook must have put it there. Some crook like me. No sweat. Besides, I've already got a girl, one of your buddies probably, working with me. It's easy out of Mexico. How about it?"

"No. Please don't ask me again. I enjoyed tonight and want to forget it ended this way. Please!"

I grabbed a cab by myself and went back to the apartment, looking behind at every corner to see if he was following me. Once inside I bolted the door, and leaned heavily against it. My sobs came in heaves, their intensity bringing Rachel from the bedroom on the run.

"Trudy, baby, what's the matter?" she asked as she put her arms around me. "So he likes girls who wear girdles, So what?"

We stayed up the rest of the night as I told her of my evening. I finally stopped shaking long after the sun had risen, and Rachel persuaded me to lie down and sleep. I woke up a little after noon and there was Rachel, my good friend Rachel, sitting reading in a chair.

"Feel better?" she asked.

"I guess so."

"Want to call the police?"

"I'm afraid, Rachel, to do anything like that. I just want it to never have happened."

"I know how you feel. But you should call them, I guess."

I didn't. As wrong as that may be, I didn't do anything. I wanted only to obliterate the entire affair from my life.

Six months later I picked up a copy of the *Daily News* and read that Mr. Relick had been picked up along with other mobsters in a raid. They had been meeting someplace when the police interrupted their assembly. His picture was there, that same handsome face I first encountered on my Mexico City flight. I've never heard of him again.

Getting involved with the gangster element as a stewardess isn't too difficult. Rachel and I know a girl who dated a mobster in Detroit. He was a nice-looking young man, maybe a little too slick, but attractive. He told her he was a trouble-shooter for a finance company.

They dated every time she had a layover in Detroit, and her first inkling of his true occupation came one night at his apartment. They had been to bed, gone out for dinner, and were back in bed when he asked, "Do you love me?"

"I don't know," she answered in all fairness. "Maybe I do. I don't know yet."

"I was just wondering. I was just wondering if you liked me enough to do me a favor."

The stewardess sat up and sipped from a brandy snifter at the bedside. "Well sure I'll do you a favor. I don't have to love you to do that."

"Maybe not. But it would help. I might as well level with you. There's this guy coming in town soon and he means a hell of a lot to me financially. What I wanted to ask you to do was . . . well, sleep with him for a couple of nights."

"Wait a minute," she snapped in natural indignation at his request. "If you think I'm going to be a . . . a whore for a buddy of yours, you're crazy."

The Detroit hood got up from the bed and slipped into his shorts. "Look, I just asked. It's not like I want you to do it for nothing. You'll get paid . . . by my company.

You'll be doing me a favor and makin' fifty bucks besides."

She was furious. "Pay me?" she yelled. "It's bad enough being asked to do it as a favor. But pay me?"

He was almost dressed now. "That's right, baby. And there'd be lots more where that came from."

She quickly got out of bed and dressed. She was on her way to the door when he grabbed her by the arm and swung her around.

"You broads make me sick. You screw anybody who buys you a decent dinner and holds your hand, but taking hard cash for it makes you vomit. I told you I was in the finance business. Sure I am. But a different kind. I make finance out of broads like you. Only they ain't all like you, and that's a big break for me. I'll level with you. I run a string of call-girls. Hustlers. And you could make a bundle just workin' a little on the side when you're in town. Big bread, baby. And all you gotta do is lay on your back like you've been doin' with me and enjoy it."

She swung at him but he was faster. He slapped her back against the wall and threw the door open. "Get outta here."

We heard the story fourth-hand, but had it confirmed later by the girl herself. You can be sure this is a story I didn't tell Aunt Laconia.

Pimps and dope pushers aside, Rachel and I both agree that Lucius Dumbarton was the craziest man we've met in our flying career.

Lucius was a happening director.

"What's that?" Rachel asked as she brought him his second drink. It was a quiet night flight in a nearly empty plane.

"I direct happenings." Lucius formed his fingers into a rectangular hole through which he peered out the plane's window.

"What are you doing?" was her second question.

"It's like a movie, baby, a movie. You know? Andy Warhol does wild things like this. Really beautiful. Like, try it. Make a lens with your fingers."

COFFEE, TEA OR ME?

Rachel tried. The rectangle kept becoming a circle, and when she looked all she saw was fingers.

"You still didn't tell me what a happening director is," she tried again.

"You know, happenings. You've never seen a happening?"

"Afraid not, Mr. Dumbarton."

"I'll take you to one of mine. You'll dig it."

"I see." She didn't.

"I'll bet you didn't dig what I was doing a minute ago, when I was looking out the window."

"You're very right. I didn't."

"See. I knew it."

"You're very perceptive, Mr. Dumbarton."

"Call me Lucius."

"Fine, Lucius."

"I'll tell you what I was doing before, Rachel. That was your name, wasn't it? Rachel?"

"You're right again."

"I knew it."

"I'm impressed."

"Good. You'll be more impressed when you dig my happenings. Oh, yeh. Before. What I was doing was being a camera. A motion picture camera. You just set up the frame with your fingers and let it roll. Like Andy, only he uses a real camera. He just lets the camera roll on one thing. Like The Empire State Building. Or a banana. Or a ping pong ball. And things happen. Like, no one plays ping pong while Andy is filming. Oh, no. That ball, or that big building just sits there. Maybe for a half hour or more. Just that thing doing nothing. Beautiful. Power, baby. Insight. Inner conflict between the man and the machine. War and peace and the womb and plaid stamps. Beautiful. So beautiful. I do it myself all the time. With my fingers. Nothing moves, like. I set up on the sky, maybe. Just that plain, blue sky. Better gray. More power. And you know what? One time a bird, a big damn bird, flew right into my picture and that isn't all. He actually came back again, from the other side, and came

128

right through again. Oh, if I only had film in my fingers that time. Tooooooo much."

Rachel was quick to display her ignorance of such beauty. "That's all these movies ever do? Nothing moves? Nothing?"

"Of course nothing moves." He was scornful. "If the building moved it would blow the whole thing. It's like you take a guy and sit him on a chair and let the camera roll. No movement. Just maybe a twitch in his eye. And he can blink. Or maybe you do it with a cat who's asleep. That's been done already. A whole hour of this sleeping cat. Wow!"

"Did a bird fly across his face?" Rachel was kidding, but maybe she wasn't.

"You're putting me on, right? How could a bird fly across his face? I mean, like, he's asleep in his bed. Dig? A bird . . . his face. Oh, man, am I gonna have to hip you."

"I'm afraid so, Lucius. It'll take a lot of hipping, too."

"Beautiful. Tell you what. I'm running two happenings next week. Classics. You'll understand better when you see them. One is called *Miscegenation*. It's like one guy and a watermelon. There'll be a lot of social significance with this happening. Wait and see. The other happening is called *Meat Meet*. You'll absolutely die with this one."

Rachel accepted his offer, despite his advance billing of the events, and met him at a small Spanish restaurant in The Village the night of the happenings. He was wearing exactly the same unwashed clothing, his hair was one week longer, and no soap company could boast of increased profits on his account.

He remained silent and morose throughout the meal, so much so that Rachel asked, "Are you having a happening now?"

Lucius just shook his head back and forth and never took his eyes from the table top. "No, baby, no. But dig this tablecloth."

Rachel looked down. It was a red and white check, and contained large, permanent grease stains.

"Are you going to make a movie of the tablecloth, Lucius?"

"Oh stop talking, baby, stop talking. Like, things were happening on that cloth. Did you see that fly? I mean, you didn't even see the fly, did you?" Lucius flailed his arms around in the air. "Oh man, that fly was making it right into the scene. Right into it."

Rachel was sorry she'd interrupted such a monumental event. "Maybe the grease on the tablecloth attracted him. Maybe he'll come back."

"Ah, screw the fly," Lucius said with great authority. He motioned for the check.

They walked many blocks until Lucius turned off into the dark doorway of a loft building. Rachel scurried in after him and followed him up pitch black stairs until they reached a large, metal door that admitted a shaft of light underneath from inside. Lucius pushed it open and she followed him in.

Rachel described the happening scene two days later. It went this way:

"Trudy, you wouldn't believe it . . . never in a million years . . . It looked like a big warehouse and there were all these weird people sprawled out on the floor . . . One guy was actually making love in the corner with a girl . . . and there were guys holding hands with guys and . . . oh, my . . . Well, the only light was from some purple bulbs hanging from the ceiling . . . They were like floodlights . . . Lucius told me they were ultra-violet lights and they're important to a happening . . . (I evidently shook my head at this point) . . . You don't know why either, huh? . . . Anyway, in the middle of the floor was a big blanket . . . He told somebody to change the direction of the lights . . . He told the couple in the corner to stop it . . . They did stop . . . Pretty soon music started playing . . . It was southern music . . . Like *Dixie* and *Stars Fell on Alabama* . . . Out came this skinny fella with a loin cloth around him . . . It really didn't cover him at all, especially when he sat down on the blanket like an Indian . . . You could see everything . . . This same boy was painted black all the way down one side and white all the way down the other side . . . Split right in half . . . A girl in a mink coat and nude underneath carried out a whole half a watermelon and patted the skinny guy with the loin cloth on the head and laid the watermelon down in front of him . . . He picked it up and started chomping away . . . He chomped and he chomped and that couple started making love in the corner again and Lucius was making little groaning sounds and everyone watched this nut eating watermelon with the juice and seeds all over him . . . Trudy, he ate that damn watermelon for forty-five minutes . . . I kid you not . . . forty-five minutes . . . The couple in the corner just kept going at it . . . Everyone else seemed to be getting their kicks from the watermelon man . . . Finally, he got up, rubbed the juice and seeds all over himself, hugged himself tight, rubbed some black make-up on the white side and white make-up on the black side and then do you know what he did? . . . He cried . . . He bawled and ran out of there . . . Everyone was cheering and applauding . . . It was awful . . . awful . . ."

Rachel was too tired to go into detail about the second happening, *Meat Meet*. It consisted of five men and five women, each wearing only a loin cloth, getting on the blanket and rolling all over each other. It was a great big tangle of arms and legs and other things. Lucius was one of them. Pretty soon the spectators started getting up from the floor, dipping paint brushes in cans of paint, and dabbing the colors on everyone on the blanket.

The bodies on the blanket were in a constant state of motion while Muddy Waters' records played in the background. Soon, everyone was covered with the multi-colors of the paint. Then, out came the nude girl in the mink coat carrying a big bucket full of ketchup. She dumped it on the mass of bodies. They spent a half hour rubbing it into each other. Finally, the happening was over.

The bodies then disappeared into corners where they wiped each other off with burlap bags. Lucius came back to where Rachel was sitting on the floor and plopped down beside her. He was still covered with paint and ketchup. All around were couples—men with women, men with men, women with women.

"Oh, you were really in luck tonight, Rachel baby," Lucius informed her proudly. "Things really happened, didn't they?"

"It was . . . wonderful, Lucius. Just great." She felt horribly uncomfortable in her woolen dress and heels.

With those words of encouragement, Lucius grabbed Rachel, pushed her onto her back and climbed on top of her. He kissed her and ran his hand up her leg.

Rachel is no lightweight, and she pushed him off. "Stop that, Lucius. Don't touch me again." She looked down at herself and gasped when she saw the paint and ketchup smeared on her dress.

"Look what you've done to my clothes," she shrieked. "Just look, you . . . you . . . you happening director."

"Shhhhh, baby. No scene. Don't sweat the color. And don't ruin the total happening. Oh, don't do that. I mean, the happening's happened, and now's the time for the big impact. We've got to fulfil the magnetic cosmos of two forms, two human elements, two sweaty, salty bodies. You and me. Now!"

"You're nuts," Rachel yelled. Everyone was watching.

"Beautiful," one tall, slender Negro purred from underneath his white companion. "Beautiful happening."

A girl whistled her approval. "Oh yes, girl-girl. That's the way it is. Tell it that way. Make it happen."

Rachel fled the room to a thunderous ovation.

"It was the best happening they'd ever seen," she told me as she finished her tale.

"I'll bet Betty Big Boobs would have been a better happening," I teased.

"I was going to say she was there but didn't think you'd believe me."

"Or Cynthia," I further suggested.

"You know, Trudy, that's what that damned stewardess school needs. A happening. A Lucius Dumbarton happening. Let's put it in the suggestion box."

We didn't of course. But visions of Big Momma, the meat man, Cynthia, Betty and the faggy hair stylist being

COFFEE, TEA OR ME?

painted as they rolled together on a blanket provided a whole day of inner grins.

Yes, we've had them all on board—wealthy men, poor men, imaginative men, dull men, men who offer jobs, men who give lavish gifts just for the fun of it and men who give little gifts with many strings attached. Yes, we meet interesting men. And good or bad, meeting men is the name of the stewardess game.

CHAPTER IX

"The Radar Is Built In"

As we've mentioned, captains rate highest on the list of stewardess dangers. Second on that list are married male passengers.

We have, out of necessity, developed an inner radar system that is part of the game we play among ourselves. To keep long flights from becoming boring, we use the radar to guess the marital status of each male passenger, his nationality and profession, on the basis of the kind of approach he makes to us. The nationality and profession portions of the game are described in Chapter XIX. This chapter deals only with the "Is he married?" sequence.

As the men come aboard, we make snap judgments as to their state of freedom. Then, as the flight progresses, we have the opportunity to verify our initial opinions. The most obvious tip-off is that common and widely used banner of matrimony: the wedding band. Not that we accept credit for correctly identifying a married man who's wearing one. Men who wear a wedding band are automatically disqualified from competition.

We're referring to the man who removes his wedding band just prior to boarding the airplane. He's kissed his wife goodbye in the departure lounge and, as he walks up the loading ramp, he slips his ring off and places it in his pocket. He boards the airplane secure that he's removed all traces of his spouse and the restrictions she places on him.

But he underestimates the ingenuity of his stewardess. We've trained our eyes to detect the slightest trace of pale flesh on his ring finger. And in ninety-nine per cent of cases, that ring in his pocket has left just such a pale mark. Of course, the more he's out in the sun, the more pronounced the mark is likely to be. But even men who only see the sun on their walk to the train will fall victim to this give-away.

I suppose he doffs the ring when his mind begins to reflect back on all those stewardess stories he's heard. He remembers hearing from Joe, a guy in his office, how he made a stewardess in the back seat of the airplane on his last business trip. He recalls the office boy telling how he is pulled into strange stewardesses' apartments and raped

COFFEE, TEA OR ME?

nightly. He pictures the stewardesses who will be working his flight as busy, lusty, quivering mounds of flesh just waiting for him to come aboard so the bacchanal can begin. He figures he'll have a better chance if these sex pots of the sky don't know about his wife and seven kids. So, off comes the ring, exposing maybe a year of lily-white skin. He might as well wear a sign.

When he comes on with a big wave of the hand, we automatically check him off as married, on the make, and devious to boot. But let's give him credit for being imaginative. Let's assume he's gone so far as to carry a small tube of flesh-colored make-up. Or maybe he wears gloves all the way. Or never takes his hands out of his pockets.

That brings into action our second method of determination. We ask a simple question when he's off guard.

"Do you live right in Manhattan, sir?"

"No, I live in Smithtown. Out on the island."

That's it right there. A bachelor will generally live in the city. Only a married man with grass-loving kids would live so far out and put up with the rigors of commuting. Sure there are exceptions. And many times this married man from Smithtown, realizing he's come up with the wrong answer to our question, will try to make himself on of those exceptions.

"Yes, I decided to leave the city and all its dirt and noise. I love nature and the outdoors, the horses I keep, the dogs, the tranquility. I love the country."

But we don't buy that rationalization. He's had it as far as we're concerned, unless we're looking for a married man to date.

Now let's assume we've still not being able to make a positive classification of this unidentified flying object—the male passenger with the leer in his eye.

Go to stage number three. How does he make his approach? Is he aggressive or cool? Does he force the issue or make it casual?

Married men don't have a great deal of time to wine and dine a girl they're after. They can't afford to pursue her casually over a long period of time. They want her *now*. And their approach reflects this pressure of time.

COFFEE, TEA OR ME?

But a single guy will take his time. He'll make it sound interesting, fun, and exert little or no pressure. There's an amazing difference between these two species of men, and the differences are quite pronounced.

Now, we've ascertained their marital state. Or maybe they've freely admitted they're married, and even owned up to a couple of children. At this point they begin their talk campaign, hoping to win us over to their side. Some of their conversation goes as follows.

—"My wife just doesn't understand me." (This ancient line is only used by very out-of-touch men.)

—"My wife loves me too much. It's stifling. I'm smothered by her love. I need to be with a woman who doesn't love me, like you, someone who can face me objectively." (This is fairly enlightened and can be so refreshing in its absurdity that you might fall into the logic.)

—"Once the children came, my wife forgot I was even around." (Another old line, but valid in too many cases.)

—"We bought a dog and ever since my wife has forgotten I exist." (Come on, fella.)

—"It's the bomb. Tomorrow may never come." (That's a good reason to get a good night's sleep, as far as we're concerned.)

—"I went to Sweden once." (Is he trying to tell us he'd had an operation?)

—"It's good for a man to have different sexual experiences. Why, Doctor Joyce Brothers says . . ." (Why don't you call Dr. Brothers?)

—"This is the Twentieth Century." (He's fairly bright, at least.)

—"It's good for a man to stray once in a while. He appreciates his wife more." (Flattering to us, huh?)

—"My wife is so immature. I need a mature woman, someone with insight, understanding, someone to confer with on an intellectual level." (Who, me?)

—"My wife and I have an agreement. She knows I run around a little." (It's a sure bet he's scared silly of his wife and the last thing he wants to happen is for her to find out.)

—"If you do go out with me, promise to be very quiet

about it. My wife would kill me." (At least he's honest.)

—"We're getting a divorce soon." (Call me from Mexico.)

—"My wife is frigid. That's not easy for me, you know." (Her either, Charlie.)

—"I'm writing the great novel of our times and I need to live, to experience all of life." (Have you ever been to a happening?)

"I'm seventy and still need love." (Have you written your will yet?)

And so on.

No matter how we feel about dating married men, each of us ends up with at least one in our careers. The only time I've become really involved was when I truly didn't know he was married. My radar completely broken down and I believed everything he said, including the fact that he could only date me on Wednesday because he went to school every other night of the week, including Saturday and Sunday. I hate to tell you how I found out about his wife. It was one of the darkest experiences of my life. Thank god she was the calm, reasonable woman she was.

I was at home reading a book a captain had given me, a gripping novel about the peacetime Army, *Stockade*, when the telephone rang. I picked it up, still engrossed in the book.

"Hello."

"Hello, I'd like to speak with Trudy Baker please."

"This is Trudy Baker."

"And this is Mrs. Pearl." I was elated. The book I was reading was written by Jack Pearl, and for a moment, this woman seemed connected with him. But that fantasy lasted only a fraction of a second. Then I realized I knew another man named Pearl. His name was Bob Pearl, a draftsman, the man I'd been dating every Wednesday night for the past six months.

"Bob Pearl's mother?" I asked timidly.

"No, his wife."

What do you say in such a situation? I said nothing and let her continue.

"Miss Baker, I've known all about you and Bob. Don't ask me how. It's really irrevelant. But what I do want to say is I'd like to stay married to Bob. But I won't if he'd prefer to continue seeing you. I've offered him a divorce but he's declined."

"Mrs. Pearl," I said slowly, "I'm sorry. I did not know Bob was married. He said he wasn't and I believed him. I'm sorry."

"Didn't you find it unusual that he could only take you out on Wednesday?"

"Yes. At first. But I stopped thinking about it. I was happy with Wednesday."

"Well, at any rate, I do demand that either you stop seeing him or I'll start divorce proceedings. Bob says he doesn't want that and I now leave it in your hands."

"Mrs. Pearl, I want nothing to do with your husband. Believe me, nothing."

"Thank you. I'm sorry he lied to you."

Quite a woman. That was the end of that.

Actually, there's one kind of passenger any girl will date, or at least go to dinner with, whether or not he's married. That's the man who sits there quietly, behaves himself like a gentleman, but you know that he's aware of you. You're sure that he wants to ask you for a date but doesn't know how. As he's leaving, he'll often say something like this: "That was a very nice flight. I enjoyed it and you're a nice stewardess. I'd like to have you on my flight again. The next time I'm on your flight, maybe I can buy you dinner."

That's fine. Even if he's married, most of us will go out with a guy like that, have dinner, enjoy his company and that's it. No wild time. No big sex thing. But we're both in a strange city, away from home and we want to spend a pleasant evening. There's no harm in that. Of course, it can happen that from such a casual beginning there can develop a very deep and complicated attachment. That's a risk we take.

Yes, the radar is built in. What we do with its findings is another matter.

CHAPTER X

"They Looked So Normal"

There isn't a great deal you can say about homosexual men and women you meet on a flight, except maybe to comment that there are more of them than you might think. Just as we're able to size up a man's marital status, profession and nationality, we've become quasi-expert in labeling the gay guys who fly with us. It really isn't difficult when you think about it.

Some make it easy for us through their outward mannerisms. It's a fairly safe bet to say, "Here comes a fay one," when the subject of your comment floats up the loading ramp, his feet six inches off the ground, twinkle-toes past you and lightly settles in his seat, one leg daintily crossed over the other in best feminine fashion.

Much tougher to recognize are those with big biceps bulging under their coats, rugged faces, and harsh, manly ways of speaking. They're dangerous, if only because you can fall in love with one before you know he isn't capable of returning the affection.

Certainly, there are times and conditions when a homosexual is preferable. Many girls working foreign lines testify that a good portion of the male stewards working their flights aren't as masculine as you might expect, and this very lack of drive for the opposite sex insures these girls a relatively safe trip, especially in the close confines of the galley.

Then too, a fay fellow can be valuable simply as an escort, when escorting is the sum and substance of what you expect on a given evening. There are many girls who maintain a warm friendship with a homosexual man, and enjoy his company on those occasions when all she wants is a pleasant fellow to take her to dinner, the theater, and to bring her home without pawing and panting. But as a steady diet, none of us wants that man around.

We've found that most effeminate men on our flights are extremely passive. They generally possess a high degree of intelligence, are witty, too polite, and offer no trouble to a stewardess. But despite these apparent advantages, their very presence is unnerving and disconcerting.

The biggest problems with a homosexual on a flight

COFFEE, TEA OR ME?

come when he's an overt one, a practicing queer with little discretion for the time and the place. We've all been involved in these cases, and they can leave you shook for days.

I remember one young man, neatly dressed and from all appearances a gentleman, on a flight from Dayton to Houston. He sat in seat 6B.

We were airborne and just leveling off at cruising altitude when a passenger signal light flashed in the galley. It was for seat 6A, occupied by an elderly businessman who had settled down to paper work the moment he came aboard. I walked down the aisle to answer his signal and as he saw me coming, he got up and met me in the aisle.

"May I have a word with you?" he asked, his expression one of disgust.

"Of course, sir," I answered, and led him back to the galley.

"Look, miss, I don't want to be a complainer or prude. But I wonder if there isn't something can be done about the young man sitting next to me." He was referring to the neatly dressed young man in 6B.

"What's the problem, sir?" I expected him to say he had excessive body odor, or was playing a wooden flute or maybe he was even reading *Playboy*. Perhaps the sight of the center fold-out was bothersome to this businessman trying to work.

"I don't even want to get into a description of it with you, Miss. I think the best thing would be for you to go down the aisle and look at what he's reading. You'll understand then."

It seemed a reasonable request, and I did as he suggested. I wish I hadn't. There was the young man in his seat, his eyes focused on a magazine he had in his lap. It did have a center-fold like *Playboy,* but this one had nothing to do with girls. Folded out was a full-length photograph of a nude man posed against a tree. He was the pin-up of the month. It wasn't the first time I'd seen a man in the nude, but the setting and timing left me in a slight state of shock.

COFFEE, TEA OR ME?

I came back to the galley where the businessman stood patiently.

"That's awful," I said.

"Yes, it is. The thing I want to know is what we can we do about it. I'd ask to change my seat but it's obvious there isn't a vacant seat in this airplane. But I won't spend my whole trip looking at his . . . his pin-ups."

"I think the captain should be advised about this."

"That probably would be a good idea, Miss."

I went to the cockpit and explained what the problem was.

"Pictures of naked men?" the captain asked with disbelief. "Come on, Trudy. You're kidding."

"I'm serious. A fold-out, no less. And his seat partner, a distinguished type, isn't happy, boss. I suggest you come on back and straighten things out."

The captain, a tall Texan with droopy eyes, came back and approached the young man with the magazine. The magazine was still on his lap but turned to a different page. This page featured a large advertisement for a community shower gadget that would attach readily to any shower enclosure. The illustration showed six men standing nude in a circle as water flowed from the overhead rig. One was washing another's back.

"I'm gonna have to ask you to put that magazine away, young fella," the captain drawled. "It's . . . well, it's indecent, if you follow what I mean."

The faggy fellow raised up in his seat and surveyed the captain with great scorn and resentment, as a woman might do when confronted with someone of financial position at an Episcopal tea.

"Indecent?" the faggy fellow echoed in an annoyed whine. "You're indecent, Captain Marvel." He broke into a high-pitched giggle and blinked his eyes at the bewildered captain.

The captain pondered the man's reaction to his request and decided to take immediate action. He reached down and gave the magazine a pull. "Gimme that thing," he demanded.

COFFEE, TEA OR ME?

The homosexual hung on tightly. "Don't you dare touch this," he screamed, "Or I'll have you demoted . . . and whipped!"

"The hell you say," the captain retaliated. He gave an extra pull and came away with most of the magazine. The homosexual was left holding the corners of a few pages.

The queer young man turned red with anger. His lips quivered, he breathed hard, and he turned around to everyone within hearing distance, which took in most of the passengers.

"This man is a sadist. He's violating my rights as an individual and a citizen. He should be whipped. That's right. Somebody help me."

No one moved. They returned to their magazines or to looking out the windows. The captain just stood there, his prize, the bulk of the magazine, tightly clenched in his fist. He turned on his heels and stalked back to the cockpit. I went in with him and asked what I should do.

"Not a damn thing, Trudy, unless he makes any more trouble. He'll probably settle down now. Let me know if you need me again."

Before I left the cockpit, I took a moment to look at the magazine. It was some sort of official publication for homosexuals. It was the sickest magazine I've ever seen.

The fellow in 6B kept quiet for the rest of the flight. The businessman returned to his seat with great reluctance and no further trouble came from that section of the airplane.

It was on arrival that the homosexual decided to raise a little hell with the captain's confiscation of his magazine. He waited in the lobby until the captain came off the airplane, and boldly walked up to him.

"You big bugger," he snarled in the captain's face, his hands waving about like Bette Davis. "I hope you get some horrible disease from the next girl you're with."

He wiggled away, his tight pants accentuating his girlish derrière.

"I'll be a son-of-a-bitch," the captain muttered as he walked over to us. "These damn fags'll take over the whole damn world."

148

We still kid the captain about the incident. He says he's kept the magazine as a reminder of the experience. I don't need anything to remember it.

Occasionally, we receive a complaint from a male passenger who claims another man is making propositions to him. In these cases, we try to switch his seat. When that isn't possible, we ask him to grin and bear it, a difficult request to make of any virile man. It's bad enough for a girl to be stuck next to a guy who makes unwelcome advances, but it must awful for a man to be annoyed by a member of his own sex.

We can see only one solution. We advocate the offering of half-fare tickets to all homosexuals. Why not? They give reduced fares to everyone else. By doing it for homosexuals, we could at least pinpoint them and assign seats accordingly. Of course, this would bring up the problem of whether to seat them together and put up with a non-stop flight of male hanky-panky, or intermingle them with normal passengers and suffer the consequences. Either way, we know there'd be trouble. But you have to admit a half-fare for perverts is an interest concept, no matter what its pitfalls.

"Please take your hands off me . . . I said *stop it!* I'll punch you . . . I really will . . . Don't do that . . . *Watch it"!*

Was this Rachel in the back seat with a boyfriend? Me in the back seat with my Braille-reading buddy?

No.

It's what you might have heard had you eavesdropped on the two occasions when Rachel and I were confronted with Lesbians.

Sure, we've had those women who come aboard, their hair done up in a butch haircut, wearing no make-up, and dressed like any normal, virile man. But they're no problem. You know who they are and therein lies the safety factor. The same goes for the asexual type. They are, according to what we've read and observed, above sex of any kind. Obviously, they pose no problem to anyone.

It's the seemingly feminine, pretty, sexy girl who really throws you when she pinches your leg or makes a habit

COFFEE, TEA OR ME?

of pressing too close when there's room to avoid contact.

My particular confrontation was with an Olympic swimmer. I met her at a party while living in the stew zoo. It was a good party in that it attracted many people from outside the airline business. We get tired of talking airplanes all the time.

Gretchen was a lovely girl. She'd competed in the Olympics, was currently a swimming instructor, and was constantly surrounded by men at the party. All that swimming had given her a lean but muscular body, her shoulders larger than most girls. She had a radiant smile and short but carefully styled blonde hair. You couldn't help like her, man or woman.

She seemed to be enjoying and inviting all the male attention that was directed at her. There she stood, a drink in her hand, smiling broadly, as each guy tried harder than the other to impress her. Toward the end of the party I was in the kitchen with a few people when Gretchen came in for a drink refill. The others left the kitchen soon after she arrived.

"It must have been fun traveling to the Olympics," I said as she prepared her drink. "I'd love to hear more about it."

"Yes, it was fun," she said without looking up. "It was a marvelous experience. Do you live in this building?"

"Sure do. I call the stew zoo home."

"When do you fly again?"

"Tomorrow. A noon flight. I'm going out tonight after the party to stay with some friends in Rego Park. It's close to the airport. Besides, I always enjoy getting out of the stew zoo for a night."

She looked at me and flashed a broad smile. "It doesn't seem so bad here. Lots of friends with common interests and all that. Say, I live in Huntington. That's on the Island. I have my car in town. I'll be happy to drive you out after the party and drop you off in Rego Park. I take the Expressway anyway."

"You'd still have to go out of your way."

"So what? I'd love to drive you. Count on it, OK?"

"Gee, that's fine. Thanks. Anytime you want to go."
"We'll stay another hour if that's all right with you."
"Perfect."

We left the party together and climbed into her Mustang. We were at the Midtown Tunnel in no time and once through it, Gretchen pushed the car to about sixty-five. Long John Nebel was on the radio, and we laughed at the debate he was having with someone over whether Catholic priests should be allowed to marry.

"I don't think anyone should be allowed to marry," was Gretchen's remark, a throaty chuckle punctuating the comment.

"Why not?" I asked, laughing with her.

"It all seems so silly, really, I guess I'm just a little drunk."

She pulled off the Expressway at the Rego Park exit and followed my directions. It was a gloomy night, and a few drops of rain began to pock the windshield.

We were proceeding down a dark street when she pulled to the curb, cut the engine and the car's lights.

"What's the matter?" I asked. I assumed something wrong with the car had prompted her action.

"Nothing, Trudy," she answered. She sat passively behind the wheel and watched the rain drops as they ran together into tiny rivulets on the glass.

"Don't you feel well?" I asked. I didn't sense anything to be afraid of, and was expressing normal concern.

"No, I guess I don't feel well." With that, she reached over and took my hand from my lap. "Would you understand?"

"Understand what?" I still didn't get what was happening.

"Understand someone who looks at things differently from you. I am different, Trudy." She slid across the seat, neatly sliding over the console. Then she kissed me on my cheek, letting go of my hand as she did and letting it drop back into my lap. Her free hand clamped on my breast.

Now I knew what was going on. I always feel a little

COFFEE, TEA OR ME?

silly in retrospect admitting my slowness in the situation. But once I knew, I acted quickly. I jumped out of the car and stood there in the rain.

"I'm sorry, Trudy. I'm sorry," Gretchen pleaded out the open door. "I'm sorry. Please get in. I'll drive you to your friend's house."

"You seemed so, so normal—" I stuttered at her.

I walked away from the car. Fortunately, Gretchen pursued me long enough to hand me my overnight case through the window.

The last thing she said was, "I'm sorry, Trudy. Really sorry. Please don't tell anyone."

I didn't answer. Long John's voice could be heard through the open window saying. "I don't care what a man is. If he's got needs, he's got 'em, collar or no collar." With those apropos words, she drove off. I've never seen her again.

Rachel's run-in with a Lesbian was more bizarre than mine. Rachel always does things on a big scale. She infiltrated a whole den of them quite innocently.

She'd become friendly with a department store buyer on a flight from New York to Salt Lake City. The buyer, a stunning woman, invited Rachel to visit her in New York. A few weeks later Rachel received an invitation to a dinner party.

At the party were five others, including the hostess. There were two men, or as Rachel put it, 'sort of men.' The other two guests were both women, 'sort of women,' in Rachel's words.

After dinner, during which all of New York's artists, writers and politicians were analyzed in terms of their phallic symbolism—a train of conversation Rachel simply accepted as sophisticated—everyone retired to the living room.

An hour later, the hostess asked for silence, opened a desk drawer and brought out a large, gray envelope. She took from it what appeared to be photographs, and without a word handed the pictures to Rachel.

There were seven, eight-by-ten pictures, each showing

the hostess and the other girls in the dinner party in various poses of lovemaking. Everyone giggled as Rachel perused the file. Anyone else, as shocked as Rachel was, would have quit with the first one. But that's Rachel. Her philosophy dictates that once something bad has begun, you might as well take it all in before you react. She studied each picture, aware of the eyes intently studying her face for signs of a favorable reaction. After looking at all seven she put the photographs down and turned to the hostess.

"I have to leave, now," she announced flatly, "I have a lover who gets very mad when I'm late. She really gets violent."

Rachel took her coat from the closet and walked out of the apartment. Once outside she pressed her ear to the door. Inside, someone was saying, "She *is* one of us. Let's invite her again."

The hostess could be heard replying, "Don't be an ass. She made fun of us. I hate her."

"I hope she gets pregnant," one of the gay fellows threw in. They all giggled and Rachel walked away.

Passengers come in all styles and types. But as long as they buckle their seat belts, observe the No Smoking sign and don't pinch us as we pass, we couldn't care less.

CHAPTER XI

"You Ought To Be in Pictures, Sweetie"

No matter how long a stewardess works at her job, she never becomes too jaded to feel a little twinge of excitement when a celebrity comes aboard. Meeting celebrities was something we all expected would happen when we decided to fly for a living. And we've met them, all in the confines of an airplane where there's no make-up, script writer or out-of-focus photography to cover the blemishes, both physical and personal.

Taken as a group, celebrities are usually more difficult to handle than normal, everyday passengers. Their lives are lived in expectation of attention. Why not? They usually receive the attention they look for.

Naturally, we have favorite celebrities with whom we fly. These are some of them.

Arthur Godfrey—A charming man, and one who knows as much about flying as the captain up front.

Henry Fonda—As easy to get along with as pie. Married to a former stewardess, which might provide additional understanding.

Al Hirt—Loads of fun and will even take out his horn and play a few notes if you've served him a few times before. He once ran that whole jam session for us on a flight.

Bob Hope—Funny, considerate and easily pleased. "Why aren't you in pictures?" he asks the stew every time she goes by.

Van Cliburn—a very quiet gentleman.

Lee Marvin—One of the most regular-guy celebrities we've served.

Eddy Arnold—Never fails to thank us and tell us how nicely we did our job. Drinks the airline dry on every flight, but never anything stronger than milk.

Robert Kennedy—Nothing political in our praise. Good sense of humor and will ask for a direct line to the White House.

Jack Jones—Very nice, and a good card player.

Ford & Hines—Nutty but nice. Gave a friend of ours a trip into New York City from JFK in their black limo.

Joan Rivers—Her routines about flying are favorites of

COFFEE, TEA OR ME?

the stewardess corps. We tried not to steal anything from her for this book. She can steal anything she'd like.

Duke Ellington—"We love you madly," Your Highness. We go to see and hear him play in cities all over the country. We always give him first-class service.

Phil Harris—Just makes us feel good.

Jack Sterling—A most amazing man when you think of his getting up that early for so many years and still being pleasant.

Skitch Henderson—A good pilot himself. His giggle can perk up many a dull trip.

Chet Huntley—Doesn't frown as much on an airplane as he does on TV. Delightful man. No matter how busy he is always takes time to tell the stewardess it was a great flight.

Mike Douglas—Never really feels secure when flying but covers it up pretty well. We've never met a star who's more sincere and easy going.

George Hamilton—Sits quietly in his seat and says Thank You for everything. Always a pleasure to have on board.

Jonathan Winters—So funny . . . he's in character for every mile of the flight. Once did for us his episode about the oldest airline stew in the world. He hobbles down the aisle, talking about the days of the Wright Brothers when he was first a stew and complains that the jet age has knocked him out. It's hard for him to compete with the beautiful 20-year-old stews on the new jets. We break up every time we hear him.

Johnny Carson—You can't get tired on a trip with him. He tells us to come up and be on his show. I bet if we showed up he'd put us on the air.

Jack Benny—You know he really is thirty-nine.

Phyllis Diller—I thought I'd see something out of a crow patch when I heard she was coming aboard. Actually, she's one of the most charming, attractive women you could meet. Love her sense of humor.

Merv Griffin—You can't top him. He talks to us the way we like to be talked to, understands what a tough job we have.

COFFEE, TEA OR ME?

Miss America 1965—If she hadn't been crowned Miss America I think she would have wanted to become a stewardess.

Lucille Ball—One of the most delightful people I've ever waited on. She's just precious and I love her flaming red hair. She's got talent she's never even shown to the world.

Elizabeth Taylor and Richard Burton—I panicked when I heard they were to be on the flight. How would I look? How would I act? Would I please them. Please, God, don't let me ask for their autographs. Don't let me spill a drink on them. Well, I found them just wonderful. Elizabeth Taylor is probably the most beautiful woman I've ever seen in my life. You have to see her close up to realize how beautiful she is. Both of them sat there quietly, a perfect couple, never asked for anything special. I guess she sensed I wanted their autographs but didn't dare ask them. They both wrote their names on a piece of paper and handed it to me and I nearly fainted when I saw it said, "To one of the nicest stews we've ever traveled with." I treasure that paper with my life.

Other good-guy celebrity travelers are:

Steve Allen	Joe Garagiola
Bob Newhart	Charles Percy
Bob Considine	Van Heflin
Hubert Humphrey	Hoagy Carmichael
Jimmy Durante	Jimmy Breslin
Peggy Lee	Jackie Robinson
Ella Fitzgerald	William B. Williams
Brad Crandall	Tony Bennett
George C. Scott	Tony Martin
Ed McMahon	Tony Randall
Red Sutherland	Richard Nixon
Julie Harris	Gregory Peck
Truman Capote	George Burns
Charlton Heston	Herb Caen
Sonny Tufts	Louis Nye
Frank Fontaine	Peter, Paul & Mary
Jimmy Cannon	Alfred Hitchcock

Veronica Lake / Janis Paige
Louis Sobol / Bud Collyer
John Peckham / James Mason
Lionel Hampton / Jack Lemmon
Fred Robbins / Jack O'Brien
Edie Adams / Frederick A. Klein

The following celebrities have also flown with us:
Jack Paar / Broderick Crawford
Joan Crawford / Joey Adams
Robert Goulet / Judy Garland
Art Linkletter / Johnny Mathis
Celeste Holm / Jerry Lester
Susan Hayward / Julie London
The N.Y. Yankees / Sidney Poitier
Ed "Kookie" Byrnes / Hedy Lamarr
Jack Carter / Zsa Zsa Gabor
Gary Morton / Allen Funt
Jerry Lewis / Mort Sahl
George Jessel / Danny Kaye
Anthony Franciosa

CHAPTER XII

"Wow! We're Going To Work a Press Trip!"

*MEMO FROM: Supv. Carlson
TO: T. Baker
ACTION: Special assignment.
Report Mr. Craig PR Dept.,
Main Office, 0930 8 May.*

"I got a memo, too," Rachel told me when I showed her mine. "Wow! Sounds like we're going to work a special party or something with Huntley and Brinkley and Walter Cronkite and all those people."

"Let's call Dan and see what he knows about this. He must know who Mr. Craig is."

I dialed the number of Dan Lindgren, our airline's public relations representative at Kennedy Airport. We'd met Dan one day when he was frantically trying to find two stewardesses to pose for a publicity picture. He'd dragged us out of the snack bar, only after Rachel made him show his airline ID card, and herded us over to the fountains in front of the International Arrivals Building. We took off our shoes and stockings and were wading around in the pool portion while a news photographer snapped us from every angle. It was supposed to be a cooling picture in the midst of New York's record heat wave.

Things went nicely until a Port Authority police car drove up and arrested Dan for trespassing in the pools. Dan managed to talk the cop out of confiscating the film, but was taken away from the scene to explain things at headquarters. Despite all the police nonsense, the picture made the papers, and we proudly sent many copies back home to parents and friends.

We'd run into Dan occasionally after that in the terminal. He was usually with a big, handsome fellow named Sonny Valano, the airline's official photographer. It was Sonny who answered the phone when we called.

"Sonny?" Rachel asked.

"Yeh."

"This is Rachel."

"Who?"

"Rachel Jones. Remember the pool . . . And the cops?"

COFFEE, TEA OR ME?

"Oh, yeh. How've you been?"

"Fine."

"Good. Wait a minute."

There was a moment of silence. Then we could hear Sonny screaming profanities at a messenger who had obviously arrived late. Sonny muttered as he came back on the line. "OK, Sally," he said, "What can I do for you?"

"This isn't Sally. This is Rachel. Rachel Jones."

"Oh, yeh. How are you, Rachel?"

"Fine."

"Good."

More silence. I broke it this time.

"Sonny, this is Trudy and . . ."

"Who?"

"Trudy. Trudy Baker. I was in the pool, too."

"Oh, yeh. How are you?"

"Fine."

"Good."

"Sonny, we've gotten special assignments for some press flight. We're supposed to report to a Mister Craig Tuesday morning. Do you know what it's all about?"

"Sure. I requested Rachel and Trudy."

"How could you request us if you can't remember our names?"

"I keep a file."

"Oh."

Sonny excused himself again to take some prints off the dryer that were about to go through for the second time.

"Sorry, Trudy, but . . ."

"This is Rachel."

"Right."

"I was saying, Sonny, about this press trip and wondering who Mister Craig was."

"Jeez, I left a roll of negatives in the soup. I gotta run. Here's Dan."

Dan Lindgren got on the phone and we all went through the identification process again.

"Dan, we were asking about Mister Craig. Who is he?"

"Yuuk."

COFFEE, TEA OR ME?

"Oh."

"But don't tell him I said that. We work for him."

"OK."

Dan explained about the trip. "It's to introduce our new 727 service to Atlanta. We fly a whole plane-load of press types down there and wine 'em and dine 'em and bring them back the same night. Big drag but Sonny thought you'd like to work the trip."

"We'd love to go. Just the two of us?"

"No. Sonny got a third girl. I think her name is Betty O'Riley or something similar. Know her?"

"Yuuk."

"Oh."

"But don't tell her I said that."

"OK."

"How've you been, Dan?"

"Terrible, Sonny and I were out here until two this morning working with a gang of faggy photographers and lesbo models. They were doing a brassière ad. You know, broad in bra on wingtip under moonlight? And I've got to be here tonight to VIP a columnist's dog. It's a poodle, I think. And we've got a newscaster up in the club getting boozed up. He's flipping because his flight was delayed an hour. And Sonny has to shoot a retirement dinner for some captain. And, let's see. Oh, yeh. John Craig, the guy you have to see, our boss, is coming out tonight to meet his wife. They're going to LA for the weekend. And boy, do I dread seeing him. He'll smile at me and pat me on the back and ask how my family is. I'll tell him everyone is great. He figures that's all he has to do for me for the next six months. He read at Dale Carnegie or someplace that you always ask your employee how his family is. Then you can knife him for another six months. He's really bad news. But he's the fair-haired boy of the new V.P. and he's swimming in power. Oh, I almost forgot. An African starlet is arriving at eleven and we have to do a picture and a release. And, some circus lions and tigers are being shipped to Memphis on air freight. More pictures, if they can get the model to put her head in the cat's mouth. See? That's how I am."

COFFEE, TEA OR ME?

"It's a shame I asked."

"Anytime. Have fun with Craig. He's really not very bright, and you can put him on easily. See you on the trip."

We saw John Craig on the appointed morning. He was kind of seedy looking in a corporate way, a refugee from the low-paying city rooms of newspapers to the higher-paying conference rooms of public relations. He liked girls and he told us so. It was disconcerting to talk with him; he seemed to go into deep thought before every sentence, even a simple one like "Hello."

"Hello," we said back.

"I saw your picture in the paper and thought you'd be perfect for this press flight. I always appreciate a good-looking couple of stewardesses."

"But Sonny said he was the one who . . ."

Craig cut Rachel short. "Yes, good old Sonny. Good boy. OK, here's what we have planned. We'll have a meeting with Mr. Looms in about ten minutes. He's our vice president for public relations. Brilliant man. I think he'll like you. It's his first press trip and he's a little on edge about it. He's never been in the aviation industry before. Lots of PR experience, though. He's been with eight different companies in the past seven years. All of them as V.P. That's quite a record."

It obviously was, but we didn't know how to take it. It sounded bad to us. Anyway, we were still thrilled with the thought of serving all those big names of the press. And, management was certain to notice us. What worth such notice would bring was dubious, but it seemed important nonetheless.

The meeting was held in Mr. Looms' spacious office. The carpeting was thick, and we enjoyed sinking into it with each step as we took chairs across from the massive desk. Behind it sat a head, a huge, balloon-like head with red, wavy hair. Below the hair was a large, forced smile. He looked like a clerk who issues marriage licenses.

Other people started coming in, including Dan Lindgren, Sonny Valano, John Craig and an assortment of men and women of the PR department. Looms swiveled around so his back was to the people. When everyone became very quiet, Looms spun about in his chair and slammed his fist on the desk.

"Let's get one thing straight," he began, his tone extremely angry. It seemed a strange way to start a meeting. "I want a perfect press trip next Sunday. A perfect one. I won't tolerate any mistakes. Understand that?"

Heads went up and down.

"We're really going to sell this airplane. Atlanta is just the beginning. Pretty soon, we'll be offering it to passengers coast to coast."

A big man interrupted. He was obviously his own person as he blew his nose in a red railroad handkerchief. "Stewart," the man said, "this airplane will never fly coast to coast. It can't. It doesn't have the range. It was never meant for coast-to-coast travel."

Looms obviously didn't like this kind of factual backtalk from a subordinate. He slammed his fist on the desk again and yelled, "Scotty, stop trying to destroy this project."

"But Stewart," the big man went on, "it's silly to talk about coast to coast for a 727."

"Goddamn it," Looms screamed, "you know what I mean. I need straighter thinking than that."

The big man, Scotty, sat back with a sigh, a look on his face indicating thoughts of other and better places to be at the moment.

"As I was saying," Looms drove forward, "I won't tolerate any mistakes on this trip. I want this whole project to have magic, drive, sparkle. Got that?"

Everyone wrinkled his brows in thought except Scotty, who just blew his nose in nasal defiance. Then, Mr. Craig raised his hand, a silly smile on his face.

"Mr. Looms, I've been giving this whole project a great deal of thought. Even on the weekends, when I'm with my family, I want it to go off right. I think the key to its success is to try our hardest to put some magic, some drive, you might even say sparkle into it."

Looms' face lighted up and he became excited. "That's the kind of thinking I mean," he proclaimed to everyone.

"That's exactly what I mean. You do see what I mean, don't you, John?"

John Craig assumed a semi-humble pose and said through his smile, "Yes, I do, Stewart. Yes, I do."

"See," Looms said to the group. "That's the kind of thinking I'd like to feel I'm surrounded with. You're all paid enough to think that straight."

Scotty belched and said he had something to do. Looms' eyes followed his imposing form out of the room. Dan Lindgren leaned over to me and whispered, "There goes the smartest guy in this whole damn airline. Looms hates him for that."

Looms stood up for the first time. "I know what you're all thinking. You're all thinking I'm a bastard and a tough guy. Well, I am. But I know how to get the most out of my people. Always have, everyplace I've been. And we'll have a perfect press trip." His scalp was beaded at the edges of his red hair.

Craig stood up in a gesture to end the meeting. "I think I speak for everyone in this room when I say how fortunate we are to have your kind of leadership, Stewart. We'll give 'em hell on Sunday." Craig wasn't sure if it was Christian to give 'em hell on Sunday. But Looms was obviously pleased by his comment about leadership. And Craig was pleased Looms was pleased. They beamed at each other as we all left the office.

The flight was to depart Kennedy at noon the following Sunday. We arrived at ten, and after checking in with crew scheduling, went down to the lounge area. There was a crowd of people drinking from the make-shift bar set up in the corner. Sonny lounged against a wall, a Yashica-Mat camera around his neck.

"Gee, the press gets here early, don't they," Rachel said.

"What press?" he responded. "It's all PR people. The press won't arrive for another hour."

We noticed a tall, gaunt man standing talking with Mr. Looms and some other men. It looked like our airline's president, Mr. Lincoln, at least as we remembered him

COFFEE, TEA OR ME?

from his picture. Sonny confirmed that it was. Looms spotted us, broke away from his group and bounced up to us.

"Hi there," he said. "I'm Stewart Looms, vice president of public relations. I didn't get a chance to say hello at the meeting last week. I hope you're pleased I selected you for this trip. I saw your pictures in the paper and decided right then and there you would be perfect." We looked for Sonny but he had quickly walked away.

"We're delighted," we said.

"Good. You just stay near me and everything will be all right. And don't let that tough talk of mine at the meeting scare you off. You've got to be that way with your staff. I've been very successful with it. Eight vice presidencies in the last seven years. That's really going some, wouldn't you say?"

"Oh yes, Mr. Looms."

The press arrived and headed immediately for the bar. Looms was everywhere back-slapping and chat-chatting, always with an eye on Mr. Lincoln. We strained to recognize any of the press people in the lounge. There wasn't one who even looked vaguely familiar. We asked Dan Lindgren about it.

"Why should you know any of them?" he asked in return. "You don't really think Craig is capable of lining up any names, do you? This whole thing is a game. Craig ends up inviting guys from *Turtle Breeders' Quarterly,* assistant editors from make-up magazines, secretaries from NBC, CBS and ABC so they're represented on the sign-in sheet, and maybe a guy or two from a daily paper who live off free PR food and booze. The best bet he came up with today is the managing editor of a New Jersey weekly, a personal friend. Like I said, it's all a game. Craig fills the place with bodies and Looms, silly Looms, thinks he's done a fantastic job."

"That's awful," Rachel said.

"Sure. And Mr. Lincoln thinks Looms has done a great job because of all the people. When nothing appears in print or on TV, they all chalk it up to bad breaks. It's all pretty silly, when you think about it."

COFFEE, TEA OR ME?

"How much do they spend to be silly this way?" I asked.

"Fifty, maybe sixty-thousand. But don't worry about it. Enjoy it now. Pretty soon everybody will be drunk and you'll be fighting for your life."

"What a sick way to make a living," Rachel commented as the absurdity of the thing began to sink in.

"Not really," Dan said. "It's just this bad when you have a psycho like Looms running the show. It used to be better. Lots of great people in this department. But they'll all pick up and leave soon."

"You too, Dan?"

"I've already got lines out all over town."

The lounge was bulging at the seams now. People were everywhere, drinks in their hands and a great deal to say to each other. Each received his periodic pat on the back from Mr. Looms, and there was never a PR man too far away with an instant drink.

All the chatter was brought to a halt when Looms leaped up on the table and held his hands up to the people. "Quiet, please. Quiet, please," he said, looking to Mr. Lincoln for approval of his approach. The president just scowled.

"Hey, ye gonna need coats in Atlanta?" a drunk yelled from the rear of the room.

This question seemed to fluster Looms. He asked a staff member at the side of the table about the coats and the staff member said everyone should bring coats.

"Yes, indeed," Looms answered the drunk, "coats in Atlanta."

"Hooray," another drunk yelled from the bar.

Looms continued. "Well, ladies and gentlemen, it's time to get on down to the big bird." He chuckled at his terminology—terribly inside. He looked at Mr. Lincoln who seemed pained. "Well, as I said, we can go down to the 727 now and get in our seats for the trip to Atlanta. Everybody ready?"

No one answered Looms, which upset him. He jumped down from the table and patted Mr. Lincoln on the back.

COFFEE, TEA OR ME?

"Well, Mr. Lincoln, guess we're ready to go. Sure got a fine group of people here, didn't we?"

Mr. Lincoln took a final sip of his drink. "Who are they all, Looms?"

Looms was quick on his feet. "Oh, you know, top echelon folks from the nets, wires, dailies . . . that caliber. We're right in there with the best today." Lincoln snorted and walked away from his PR man.

Looms spotted Craig as he was walking out with the group and grabbed his arm. "John, we've got top people here today, haven't we?"

Craig was fast on his feet, too. "You bet, Stewart. What we've done is to really dig and find the people who can produce . . . really produce for us. No sense having the managing editor of *The Times* or *Newsweek*. They can't do anything for us. We've got the do-it guys. The guys with some magic and sparkle."

"Good boy, John." They walked out together proudly. Behind them came the last member of the magical press corps, the cartoon editor of *Welfare Weekly*.

We helped the drunks into their seats, fumbled with their seat belts, gave the special PA announcement for the occasion, and sat back as the plane streaked down Runway 31-Left at Kennedy. The wheels had barely left the ground when everyone seemed to get up at once. They clustered in the aisle, first in a large group in the rear, and then moving up to the front.

Someone spotted something out the left side of the airplane and they all piled over to see, the plane taking a shuddering change in flight characteristics. It was that way the whole trip; back and forth and up and down until the pilot must have simply given up trying to maintain any sort of straight and level flight.

Dan Lindgren was right. The entire flight was a valiant fight to keep the booze flowing and the drunks in line. Looms kept running into the galley with nasty mixed drink orders like whiskey sours and daiquiris for one guy or another, and Craig would always come in right after him to check on whether we were following orders.

COFFEE, TEA OR ME?

The only one who seemed to be enjoying the whole affair was Betty O'Riley. She almost missed the flight, racing in at the last minute with a story about how this fantastic male model just wouldn't let her out of bed. Once we were airborne, she was right in the midst of all the elbows and hands with a tray of Scotch or bourbon and a big smile.

Sonny took lots of pictures, his strobe unit flashing all over the cabin. It wasn't until we were seated at dinner in Atlanta that he confided to Rachel and me that he had forgotten to bring any film, and was doing all his picture taking for effect only. Betty was attracted to his camera like a snake to water. She managed to be in every scene photographed, including some with Mr. Lincoln. It would be a sad day when she found out there was no film.

We landed at Atlanta and taxied up to a waiting line of black limousines. The drunks were poured into cars and off we went to a downtown hotel. At dinner the press type on Rachel's right passed out just as the main course was served. He fell headfirst into the mashed potatoes, much to the chagrin of Mr. Lincoln. Others fell by the tableside as the dinner wore on. The only saving touches were the caustic comments interjected by Sonny and Dan.

After dinner, we were all hustled to a nightclub that featured an exotic dancer, an off-key singer and a comic who, after being encouraged by the fifty dollars Mr. Craig gave him, told some jokes about the airline and New York. More drunks fell asleep at their tables, a woman from a cosmetics magazine got sick, and Looms made a scene about bad service.

All of these misadventures didn't prevent Rachel and me from having a good time. At dinner and at the night club we were treated like guests, not employees. We danced with Sonny and a couple of the press fellows who could still get around. We spent a lot of time turning down drinks. It seemed a shame to say No to all that free-flowing booze. But under the friendly but stern eye of the airline's president we didn't think we should take the slightest chance. Several times I could see Rachel glancing over at Mr. Lincoln.

COFFEE, TEA OR ME?

"What are you thinking?" I asked.

"I was wondering if he'd like to dance."

"Why don't you ask him?" I suggested.

Rachel shook her head. "I wasn't wondering that hard." For once she didn't respond to my needling. "Why don't *you* ask him?" She flung the challenge back at me.

"I think I will," I said, pushing my chair back.

Rachel was startled. "You wouldn't really, would you, Trudy?"

"Just watch me." By the time I'd walked over and tapped Mr. Lincoln on the shoulder, *everyone* was watching. I hadn't counted on such a big audience.

"Excuse me," I began, but realized my voice was too diffident. I'd have to come on much stronger if I didn't want to end up with egg on my face. I put on my heartiest Texas tone. "C'mon, President, baby, let's dance."

There was an instant of frozen silence. Then Mr. Lincoln stood up tall and serious and said, "I'd love to, Miss Baker." Now there's a man who's really a sport. We had a lovely dance—luckily it was a slow number. I don't think Mr. Lincoln would have been up to the dog or a fast twist.

Sonny patted me on the back afterward. "That was the best thing that happened this whole trip." What truly astonished me was Mr. Lincoln knew my name. I've never gotten over that.

The limos drove everyone back to the airport for an eleven o'clock departure for Kennedy. Once we were inside the airplane Dan Lindgren took a head count and came up one short. Finally, after much questioning, it was learned that the eighteen-year-old daughter of a woman on board was missing. The mother, an administrative assistant at a local New York television station, was riproaring drunk. She really didn't seem to care about her missing daughter.

The PR staff, those still standing, fanned out in all directions to find the missing girl. Someone vaguely remembered she was in one of the cars coming from town, so she certainly must have been at the airport. They

COFFEE, TEA OR ME?

searched under parked cars, up trees, in empty airplanes and in the stalls of the bathrooms. Nothing.

Then, a half hour later, Sonny came down the corridor with a limp girl slung over his arm and shoulder. He had found her curled up behind the closed bar of the terminal, her head resting on a bottle of rye.

Everybody accounted for, we flew back to New York. This leg of the trip was peaceful because everyone was asleep, except Mr. Looms and a few of the PR people. Betty leaned all over Looms and he loved it. Rachel and I talked to Sonny. Dan was asleep in a seat next to the lost-and-found girl, who kept thrashing her arms around and yelling, "I hate you, Mother, you bitch." No one else seemed to hear or care.

More black limousines were waiting at Kennedy for our triumphant return. They left carrying their precious cargo of press people to various destinations. We were walking out to try and catch a cab back to the city when Mr. Looms came running up behind us. We assumed Betty had scored with him, but she was seen leaving the terminal with the captain of the flight.

"Girls," Looms said with a tired gleam in his little eyes, "I'll take you home. We can have a nightcap at your place and I can tell you about the whole concept of these trips." He was actually standing on his toes as he spoke, like an over-the-hill ballet dancer.

"No thanks," we said. "We're beat."

"Don't be silly. I'll get John Craig and we'll meet you someplace if you'd like. You know, I can see that you get a lot more of these special assignments. As the vice president, I can do that." Craig came running up to us with great relief—he'd found his leader.

"Goodnight," we said and turned away from them to go outside.

"I'll see you again, girls," Looms said with a nasty turn to his voice. We could hear him, just as the door closed behind us, say to Craig, "I told 'em I was too tired."

CHAPTER XIII

"Please, Not Another Press Trip"

MEMO FROM: Supv. Carlson
TO: T. Baker
ACTION: Special assignment.
Report Mr. Fowler, Sales Dept.
Main Office, 0930 11 June.

As with the notification of our press trip, Rachel received her second memo the same day mine arrived. We went to see Miss Carlson together.

"Congratulations, girls," Miss Carlson beamed as we walked through her office door. "You must be popular."

"The question is, with whom?"

Miss Carlson checked a file she had in front of her. "According to Sonny Valano, that press trip you two worked was the biggest success they've ever had. He suggested you for this next assignment."

"It's not another press trip, is it?"

"No, it isn't. Look, if you two don't want these assignments any more, I'll be happy to take your names off the list. I get asked every day by at least a dozen girls how they can get to do special assignments. If you can't use the extra ten-dollar daily fee, forget it."

"Don't be hasty, Miss Carlson," I responded quickly. "We love doing these things. Anything at all."

"Not anything," Rachel said, a smile lighting her face.

"OK." Miss Carlson had had enough of this banter. "Go see Mr. Fowler in the New York sales department. We're becoming involved in a big promotion and part of it calls for stewardesses being interviewed on radio and television. Sonny says you two are pretty glib."

"Sounds like fun," I offered. "Just the two of us?"

"No. Sonny also said you two and Betty O'Riley worked beautifully together on that press trip. She'll be with you."

We didn't reply.

"What's the matter? Betty's ego getting to you? She's really a good gal down deep. She grows on you."

Rachel was about to add, "like fungus," but thought better of it. "I'm sure down deep Betty O'Riley is a lovely person," Rachel managed coolly.

We reported to Mr. Fowler at the specified time and

COFFEE, TEA OR ME?

place. He was a very pleasant man and seemed eager to see us enjoy the assignment.

"The first thing you girls are going to have to do is be interviewed on a local radio show. You've probably heard of it. The Big Wilson show?"

"Sure," we responded. "He wakes us up every time we have an early flight. Funny fellow."

"Wonderful guy, too," Mr. Fowler assured us. "The interview is set for Friday morning. They're doing the show as a remote from the skating rink at Rockefeller Plaza. You'll be on sometime between nine and ten."

"We thought Betty O'Riley was in on this also."

"She is. She couldn't make it this morning but I've arranged a briefing this evening for her. You know her?"

"Sort of."

Mr. Fowler told us all about the promotion and the interview, and impressed on us the fact that we had nothing to worry about. "Biggie is a very easy going guy, girls. He'll lead you right along in the interview. Just be yourselves."

We could only foresee disaster for the airline if Betty O'Riley acted as she normally did. But that was Big Wilson's problem, we decided. We even resolved not to follow Rachel's suggestion that we pass a note to Big Wilson on which we told him Betty's nickname.

"We can't do that," I protested. "What if he slipped on the air and said it?"

"Don't be silly, Trudy," Rachel said in defense of her idea. "Professionals don't slip when they're on the radio."

"I don't care. As much as I don't like Betty, we have no right to do this to her. Besides, one look at her and anyone around will come up with that nickname himself."

I won out.

We arrived on time at the skating rink, and were greeted by Frank Deveau, the show's director. Betty was already with Mr. Deveau, in the midst of a long, involved story about her most recent beau, when we barged in.

"Where's Big Wilson?" we asked after Mr. Deveau arranged for coffee for all of us.

COFFEE, TEA OR ME?

"The news is on and he went for a walk. You've never seen him?"

"No. We were talking about him on the way over. We've decided he's under five feet tall and weighs about one hundred pounds."

The director smiled. "How did you know?"

We were pleased we'd envisioned Big Wilson so accurately, with only a voice to go on. "Well," I said modestly, "we figured the nickname Big was a joke. You know, one of those show-business jokes."

Frank Deveau laughed. "Good thinking. He'll be back in a minute. He gets up at 3:30 every morning to make the show at five, and I think he walks to keep awake."

Frank introduced us to the show's engineer, another very pleasant fellow named Jerry Schneyer. Betty took an immediate liking to him. She must have thought she was back in the cockpit of a 727, because she immediately blinked her eyes and asked, "What are all those li'l dials and lights and things? My, how much y'all must have to know.

Jerry Schneyer looked up from what he was doing and leaned over to Betty. "No, it's all done inside. They just put me out here for show. You know, keeps the people interested." With that, he turned back to what he was doing.

Betty turned and flashed her eyes at Frank Deveau. "My, Mr. Deveau, ah do declare ah didn't know that. Isn't that just the cutest thing?"

"Yes. The whole thing is a fraud," he concurred.

The remote broadcast was being handled within a portable three-sided room, the walls hinged together to form a back and sides of the set. A large crowd was gathered in front.

"Hi, Biggie," we heard someone in the crowd yell. Then someone else said the same thing. We looked hard into the crowd for the little fellow to come through. Instead, a very large man stepped up onto the slightly raised platform on which a small piano, desk, engineer's equipment, director's desk, clock, microphones and other broadcasting paraphernalia stood ready for use.

COFFEE, TEA OR ME?

"Anybody see Big Wilson?" he asked us.

"We're waiting for him," we replied.

"Me too," he said.

All of a sudden, Frank Deveau pointed to the big man we'd just spoken with, who immediately sat down at the little piano's little bench and started to play ragtime. After a few bars, he stopped and said into the microphone suspended above him, "Good morning, good morning. This is ol' Biggie and it's good to see ya all here this morning."

"That's Big Wilson?" I whispered to Frank Deveau.

"No," he answered. "It's Ocar Levant in disguise."

Betty giggled. "Ah jus' love show business."

Deveau ignored her.

Biggie played a few more bars on his piano, did a commercial for wine, urged listeners to listen to Mimi Benzell at noontime, and gave the time and temperature. Jerry played a recorded commercial, after which Biggie came back with, "We're about to lose our beloved director, Frank Deveau. He's over there applying for a job as a stewardess. All in favor of Frank being a stewardess? Hands. Hands down. You've got good taste, Frank. Keep it up."

Betty assumed his remark about good taste was directed at her. She wiggled in her chair and smiled broadly at the audience gathered in front of the set.

"When are we going to be interviewed?" we asked Frank.

"Few more minutes. After he interviews some of the people standing out front."

Wilson did those interviews after playing a Les Brown record. "OK, OK," he mumbled into the mike as he got up from the piano bench. He certainly had earned his nickname. He had to be six foot five at least, and we guessed his weight to be three hundred. We were told he didn't weigh that much but we held to our belief. "Let's chat with a few of the folks out here this morning. Merry Jerry Schneyer has the traveling microphone and let's see . . . You, sir . . . what's your name?"

The audience interviews lasted maybe three or four

COFFEE, TEA OR ME?

minutes. No one said anything startling and Biggie was on his way back to the platform when a little old man grabbed him by the sleeve. He turned around and the little old-timer threw him a salute.

Wilson chuckled. "Well, hello there. What's your name?"

He held out the microphone in front of the man's face. The man took the microphone from Wilson's hand, much to Biggie's surprise, looked at it quizzically and held it to his ear.

"What say?" he asked Wilson, now secure with his new-found hearing aid.

Everyone broke up. It was a marvelous scene. Wilson came back to the platform, his large frame shaking with laughter. Frank Deveau was doubled over in his chair, and how Jerry Schneyer managed to keep from pushing all the wrong buttons in his hysterics was a tribute to his experience. The little old man saluted again and walked away.

"We'll be right back after the 9:30 news."

Big Wilson called us up to the microphone at about 9:40.

"All right, all right. We've managed to steal these three lovely young ladies away from Frank Deveau who is currently sitting in the corner sulking . . . or are you sleeping, Frank? . . . Anyway, I may begin to fly again . . . You are three beautiful hostesses . . . or do they call you stewardesses?"

Betty jumped in with an answer. "Well, Mr. Wilson, honey, some airlines call us some things an' some airlines call us other things. Actually, we're hostesses in the true sense of the word. We're taught that every li'l pasenger should be treated with pipe and slipper courtesy an' . . ." Betty was about to recite the entire training manual.

"I'm sorry I asked," Wilson proclaimed.

Betty laughed hard, and jiggled herself for the audience.

"Well now, what are your names? I know your names but no one else does. On second thought, don't tell your names."

COFFEE, TEA OR ME?

We were totally confused.

"Go ahead. Tell us your names."

We did.

The rest of the interview went smoothly. It was true what Mr. Fowler had said: Big Wilson was a wonderful interviewer. We managed to get in the name of our airline a few times, a fact we were sure would please the management.

"Well, girls, it was marvelous," Biggie concluded the interview. "I may even take up flying again."

We smiled. And Betty asked, "Oh, Mr. Wilson . . . May ah call you Biggie? (giggle) . . . Ah didn't know you were a pilot!"

"I'm not. But my friend, Vern Ostermeyer is. Do you ever fly with Vern?"

"Ah don't know any Captain Ostermeyer," Betty said after searching her memory.

"That's a shame. Shame. Thanks again, girls. It was real fun talking to you. And you tell your boss, whoever that is, you deserve a raise. Or I'll tell him. Or somebody'll tell him. OK?"

We asked Frank Deveau after the interview who Captain Ostermeyer was. He replied, "Famous Cleveland pilot. A lot of people flew high with Vern. Very high. You're too young, I guess. Ask your boss."

We asked Sonny later about Vern Ostermeyer. "That's the name Big Wilson has given to V.O. whiskey. V.O. Vern Ostermeyer. Got it?" We were very sorry we'd asked.

Betty wanted to stay and talk with Big Wilson some more, but reluctantly agreed to take a tour of the NBC studios. It was set up by Jim Grau, head of promotion for the WNBC radio and television stations in New York. The tour was fascinating. When it was over, Betty asked Bill Schwarz, Program Director for WNBC, "Ah'd love to be in television. Ah just love show business. It's in mah blood."

"I'd see a doctor," was Mr. Schwarz's reply.

She wasn't to be denied. "He really is big, isn't he?"

"Who?"

"Big Wilson."

"Not really. It's done with mirrors." With that, Jim Grau wished us well and returned to his office.

"Ah jus' love to make jokes with all those show-biz folk," Betty said as we walked back to the sales office. "Ah understand them."

"I think they understand you too, Betty," Rachel resonded with a wide grin. Betty hummed *There's No Business Like Show-Business* all the way to the office.

Since our unparalleled success with Big Wilson, we've worked numerous other special assignments for the airline. Of all of them, our experience at a big political convention in Atlantic City must rate as the highlight. Or low point. It depends on how you view it.

We must first explain our initial reaction to Atlantic City itself. Never having set foot on the fabled boardwalk of that resort city, we naturally assumed it was a city of rich old men and ladies who strolled the boardwalk summer after summer, retired at nine in the evening, and performed exactly six touch-your-toes each morning upon arising.

See how wrong you can be?

Atlantic City is the swingingest city we've ever seen. Certainly, as the site of such an important convention, the city had geared up its natural resources for the occasion. But all they did was amplify what is always there: An all-night, whoop-do-do, give-'em-hell honky-tonk town with wall-to-wall prostitutes and mosquitoes.

There are, of course, as you would expect in a convention city, some lovely beach-front hotels. We didn't stay at them. We were quartered at one of those pink stucco places outside of town where the number of summer insects was rivaled only by the number of hookers running in and out of most of the rooms.

Our job, along with four other girls, was to greet visitors, mostly press, at the airline's hospitality suite. It was set up in one of the public rooms at a boardwalk hotel, and the traffic was even heavier than you might expect. At first, we were told to ask for press credentials when people came to the door. But that system simply didn't work out, and we abandoned it in favor of an open-door policy. Once the word got around town that the party was for one and all, the major problem was keeping up with the demand on the liquor supply. We must commend our public relations people for their efforts in this regard.

We spent a total of two weeks in Atlantic City. By the end of the first week, we were certain neither of us would be able to make it through the second. By the end of the second week, we were equally certain neither of us would ever feel as young as we did two weeks before. It was that grueling.

Our routine at Atlantic City was simple. We arrived at the hospitality suite at 10 A.M. We helped serve donuts and coffee until 11 A.M. at which time the airline's bartender arrived on the scene. At 11 A.M. sharp, the donuts were put away for another day, and only liquor was served.

We were allowed an hour for lunch, and then acted as hostesses until 6 P.M. We were given an hour for dinner. We then went back to our positions at the door until 11 P.M. After that, our time was our own.

We tried to enjoy Atlantic City's nightlife the first few nights. But it didn't work.

First of all, the nightlife is hardly what anyone from any major U.S. city would enjoy. It's low-brow, dirty and amateur. It's major clubs feature talent that is long on stamina and short on ability. The clubs all close from 5 A.M. to 6 A.M., a city ordinance requiring this respite for cleaning purposes.

Also, any girl in one of the clubs who doesn't have an escort on her arm is immediately labeled a hooker. She has to be, and we can understand any man thinking she would be. Even the most hardened of men who were working at the convention for the airline agreed they'd never seen so many "professional girls" in their lives.

On the few nights we did venture into town after our stint at the hospitality suite, the scene usually went like this.

Setting: Bar stools. Many people. Bad singer on stage.

COFFEE, TEA OR ME?

Blue and red lights whirling around and reflecting off silver spangles.
HE: Hi, baby. Drink?
ME: (SAY NOTHING. IGNORE HIM)
HE: I said hi, baby.
ME: (STILL IGNORE)
HE: Drink, baby?
ME: No!
HE: That's good. No sense wastin' the time.
ME: (IGNORE. DON'T UNDERSTAND FIRST TIME)
HE: Let's go.
ME: Where?
HE: My place. Yours? Up to you.
ME: Go away.
HE: How much?
ME: Go away.
HE: I got twenty.
ME: Listen you creep. Get Lost, I'm   I'm different
HE: Whatta ya do that's different? Maybe I'll pay more.

Or,

HE: Hello there.
ME: (ASSUME HE'S NICE YOUNG MAN) Hi.
HE: Let's go.
ME: I don't even know you.
HE: (MUMBLES TO HIMSELF) What is this routine?
ME: I don't just walk off with strangers.
HE: Name's Mark. Hey, you are a hooker, right?
ME: I'm a stewardess.
HE: (GIGGLES) Great gimmick. Let's go. How much?
ME: For what?
HE: Well, how 'bout French.
ME: Irish.
HE: Irish? Never had that. That's somethin' new.
ME: Huh?
HE: Ok. Irish it is. How much?
ME: Three hundred dollars.

HE: Three hundred? For how long?
ME: Five hours. Two drinks, dinner and a junior pilot ring. First run movie, too.
HE: Sorry I bothered you.
ME: Me too. Bye!

There was obviously money to be made in Atlantic City during that convention. Unfortunately, we just aren't the kind to take advantage of such a situation. A few stewardesses are.

Other special assignments have found us handing out travel folders at department store promotions, checking coats at an appliance dealer's convention, and posing for pictures to be used in publicity releases. Rachel was once interviewed by a newspaper from her home town; local-girl-makes-good kind of thing. They photographed her serving a meal to Sonny Valano, window shopping at Bloomingdale's, reading a book in our apartment and walking away from a BAC-111 with a captain. It appeared as promised, and they ended the piece by saying, "This vivacious local girl, now a glamorous member of the elite corps of jet-setting airline hostesses, stated her biggest problem was keeping track of her hectic social life in New York. Obviously, she's captured the hearts of New York's bachelor set, sad news for the Louisville beaus left behind."

Rachel's mother was on the telephone the night the article appeared.

"What are you doing up there?" she demanded. "Sounds like you're just flittin' away your time runnin' around with too many boys."

"Momma," Rachel said pleadingly, "I haven't had a date in three weeks. The newspaper guy was a jerk."

"Well," her mother sighed with a resigned finality, "newspapers don't lie. That's all I can say."

"Don't worry, Momma. I'll be home soon. Bye."

"Bye, Rachel. And don't you let any of them fast-talkin' boys up there get you in trouble."

"I won't, Momma. Bye."

"Bye."

COFFEE, TEA OR ME?

The fringe benefit we liked best was working charter flights of businessmen. A big company will charter a plane to fly its sales executives to Kansas City or its brass to LA. These are men who're used to flying so they don't give you any trouble. They work hard and they like to relax hard. The liquor is poured in cascades on these flights. The usual two-drink limit is off and stewardesses can drink, too. We can also accept tips.

On one charter from New York to Houston we had all cattlemen aboard. We broke out the bourbon the minute we were off the ground and we had all those meatmen bombed before we were past Washington. When we landed in Houston I got hold of the PA and instead of making the usual announcement, I shouted, "Head 'em up and move 'em out!" Those tall Texans got off roaring. I'm not exaggerating when I say I got 12 Texas hats, a pair of souvenir boots, and $150 in tips.

That was what we call a hot flight.

CHAPTER XIV

"There's Another Drunk in 3A"

Government regulations say that we can only serve a passenger two drinks in tourist and three in first class. We don't go along altogether with that ruling. Most passengers don't want more than their limit. But if we have a man aboard who is drinking and having a good time and holding his liquor well, we don't see a reason in the world why he shouldn't have another. He can handle it. He'll feel better for it. He'll thank you for it and remember your airline. So it's really good business. We especially enjoy seeing a passenger who climbs on the plane with a grouch at the whole human race get off at his destination purring like a kitten. Only liquor can do that.

We must confess that there've been times when we've taken the rules into our own hands. We've given extra drinks to a man we've sized up as a good drinker. We've slipped doubles to passengers when the circumstances seemed right. If you recall, on our very first flight we poured doubles into that ill-fated woman who got stuck on the john. We made her life bearable that day. I suppose that if there were many stewardesses who were alcoholics like our ex-roommate Joan, they'd be busy converting the whole flying public to unlimited liquor consumption. But we don't think that's a very big risk for the airlines.

Since most passengers don't use their full quota, there's no great problem about getting an extra little bottle for that hard-fisted sales manager in 5A. But even when the whole plane is drinking to the hilt, we have ways of accounting for the extra servings. One of my favorites is to spill a few drops of Scotch or whatever on the carpet. You smear it around with water to make a big wet spot, but not enough to remove the scent. Then you report that you were walking down the aisle with two trays of six drinks when the plane lurched. Naturally you had to open twelve more bottles.

A good drinker on a plane is one thing. A drunk is altogether different. Nobody likes a drunk. This goes double and triple for stewardesses.

When a drunk comes on board, we shut the aircraft door, climb to thirty thousand feet and there we are, a

COFFEE, TEA OR ME?

captive audience for the fellow with the bulbous red nose and ninety-proof breath.

All the drunks holding an airline ticket don't actually succeed in getting aboard. The airline and its personnel have the right to deny passage to anyone deemed too intoxicated to fly. They can exercise the same sort of restrictions on people with excessive body odor, filthy clothing and, most recently, men wearing earrings. The problems arise when the man with earrings or smelling like a Bowery bum is president of one of the ten top Blue Chips.

You can see the problem. Tell the president of a large company that he's not wanted on your airline, and you can talk thousands of dollars of revenue out the window. The airline becomes very upset when this happens, and few ticket or ramp agents will risk incurring that kind of wrath.

When we spot a drunk staggering up the ramp toward the aircraft, we don't hesitate to go out to the passenger service person in charge of that flight and ask that he be removed. The captain can always demand that a person be taken from the plane. He's in charge of that flight, and what he says goes. But while the plane is sitting there on the ground, the captain will generally leave decisions to the ground personnel. As we said, airline employees think long and hard before denying passage to paying customers.

Sometimes people think we're just being nasty when we complain about a passenger who has had too much to drink. That isn't the case. We simply don't want to have to clean up his seat and the passenger himself after his stomach has rebelled against the whiskey he's poured down. We really don't want to spend our flight listening to his jokes, usually all bad, but hysterically funny to him. We don't want that overweight businessman, perhaps a sweet person when sober but switched into an Errol Flynn by martinis, to pinch and maul us all the way.

In short, taking care of one hundred thirty passengers

COFFEE, TEA OR ME?

is hard enough. One drunk is worth at least ten people. We can do without him or her.

You can't always recognize the drunks on your flight at boarding time. They all don't enter the plane stoned. Some can't hold their liquor, and the two drinks they're served during the flight send them into a drunken whirl. Some are on a very strict diet, or taking medication, and very little whiskey loops them. Some have been drinking for two hours at the airport bar. They seem to hold their liquor beautifully, but they're really on the verge of intoxication. The first drink on board is the one that does it. The second transforms them into a flying nightmare for us.

Then there are the people who never get drunk. They want to be drunk, but don't like to drink enough to reach that state. So, they act drunk. They think being drunk will be interpreted by us as a sign of a swinger, a devil-may-care jet-setter. Usually, these make-believe drunks are frightened about flying and use the drunk routine to explain away the shaking hands and trembling lips.

We've had some memorable drunks aboard our flights. I remember particularly Mr. Lunts, who commuted regularly between New York and Chicago. Now any regular traveler with an airline is a prized possession. He's given special membership in the airline's private club, is greeted and escorted by the airline's passenger service people, and receives general VIP treatment. Usually, when he comes aboard, we're told of his status and are asked to handle him with extra special care.

The first time I had Mr. Lunts as a passenger, I requested he be removed from the flight.

"Don't be silly," I was told by the ramp agent working the departure. "That's C. X. Lunts. He's with us every week. Take good care of him."

"He's drunk," I protested.

"So what?" was the reply.

"So what?" I came back with. "What about the other passengers?"

The ramp agent was very firm. "Mr. C. X. Lunts is al-

COFFEE, TEA OR ME?

ways drunk when he flies. But even when he's drunk, he pays for his ticket and sends all his employees on our airline. Now if you stop and think for a minute, his money helps pay your salary. And mine too. And it helps feed my children and helps keep my wife off my back about all the new things she wants. In short, Mr. C. X. Lunts goes with us, no matter how gooned he is. That's the word."

I stood there shaking my head up and down to indicate understanding. "Message received and understood. What does the X stand for in his name?"

"I haven't the slightest idea. Why don't you ask him. But wait till after he's had his two drinks. It might be an embarrassing thing with him."

There had been no doubt in my mind that Mr. Lunts was drunk when he came aboard. He weaved happily up the loading ramp, never quite sure which way he would lean next. He was a tall, skeletal man, his angular height giving the impression he was a pole bending in a strong breeze.

"He looks like the Leaning Tower of Pizza," Rachel commented after he passed us at the door.

"More like The Leaning Tower of La Guardia," I mumbled. Rachel liked the description. She laughed.

We were waiting in line for take-off clearance when Mr. Lunts first made his presence on the airplane known to everyone. He stood at his seat, turned to the other passengers and announced, "This is the most wonderful airline in the whole wide world. And these are the most wonderful young ladies in every corner of this valued and im . . . im . . . impassioned land of ours and yours and mine." He sat down with authority, pleased he had set the record straight.

The next time Mr. Lunts decided to exert his individuality came when he opened his attaché case. We were airborne only a few minutes, and hadn't begun serving drinks or dinner yet.

His case was filled with miniature bottles of booze, the same kind we serve on flights. He began passing them out

COFFEE, TEA OR ME?

proudly to everyone within reaching distance. They all seemed quite pleased with their gifts.

I went up to him and said, "I'm sorry, Mr. Lunts. But airline regulations allow only two drinks per passenger. I'll have to ask you to put those away until we've landed."

He looked hurt. Really hurt. He stood up, faced the cabin again, and said with great sincerity, "Ladies and gentlemen, I am truly sorry. Truly sorry. In my haste to be . . . to be . . . to be gangrenous . . . Uh, gangre . . . to give each and every one you gathered here today in this wonderful, sleek modern facility a voice . . . uh, a gift, I violated the sacrilege. . . . a sacred by-laws of this wonderful airline, and these wonderful girls here present. So, if you will be so kind and present, please put all those li'l bottles away and don't drink not even a tiny weeny drop 'til we come to our departure . . . ah, destination." He sat down to the clapping of a few hands.

He declined dinner, saying, "I never eat when I'm driving, and I hope our fair admiral up in the starboard cockport of this sleek, modern airplane feels the same way that I do now about these and other matters of ramification."

After dinner, Mr. Lunts led a few of his fellow-passengers in a rousing community sing, the chief song "The Star Spangled Banner," with a few bars of "If I Had a Hammer" thrown in for emphasis.

Upon landing, Mr. Lunts assured us he was planning to inform management about us and our superior attitude and performance toward our job. As he put it, "You are the exemplifying advantage of aviation history today, young ladies, and furthermore, your skillful laying down . . . ah, laying down . . . ah, laying down of the regulations and personal habits of every admiral will be forever in my heart . . . and hand. Good day."

We see Mr. Lunts a great deal whenever we pull New York-Chicago as a route. He's always drunk, never very unpleasant, and always promises to praise us to management. He gave us each ten dollars for Christmas, and has

COFFEE, TEA OR ME?

never argued when we've reminded him of certain rules. Even with his happy way of getting drunk, he poses a problem. But all drunks should be like Mr. C. X. Lunts, if there have to be drunks on airplanes at all. By the way, the X in his name means nothing. A former business partner was also named C. Lunts, and the X was slipped in to help differentiate various aspects of their dealings. He might come up with another story when he's sober, but finding him in that state will probably never come to pass.

Unfortunately, Mr. Lunts is the exceptional drunk. In contrast, we offer Mr. Lippingdone.

We met Mr. Lippingdone only once. It was on a flight from New York to San Antonio. It was horrible. Mr. Lippingdone is at least three hundred pounds. He boarded the airplane on that particular day in our lives, and proceeded to bump into Rachel as she stood in the open doorway greeting passengers. He completely lost his balance, and his bulk flattened her against the wall with a devastating thud.

He immediately turned on her and snarled, "Why don't you stand somewhere else? You're blocking the whole door." With that warning, he stumbled into the cabin, falling left and right as he made his way up the aisle.

"Either that son-of-a-bitch flies or I do, but not both," Rachel cursed as she felt for broken bones. She stormed off the plane and grabbed the ramp agent by the arm.

"Listen," she said, "there's a two-ton drunk on the plane and I'm not flying with him."

The agent laughed. "Oh, Lippingdone? Big pain in the rear end. But he's close with the board of directors, and the word is VIP him to death. Big stockholder, too. Sorry, sweetie, but he's yours. Maybe he'll fall asleep."

"You bet he will," Rachel warned with determination in her voice. "I'll make damn sure of that if I have to slit his throat to make it come about."

Lippingdone was trouble from the minute we took off. We received numerous complaints from passengers about his foul language, foul actions and general foul self. He spilled his dinner all over himself and screamed at me, "I

COFFEE, TEA OR ME?

want to see the captain, god damn it. You set the tray to tip over on me. I know that for a fact (belch). I know all the people you work for on this (belch) airline, and I intend to see that you (belch) and your friend get your asses fired (belch)."

We tried to steer clear of him and succeeded until the light flashed on in the galley indicating someone wanted service in the forward bathroom. We looked at each other in despair. Lippingdone had gone in there moments before. Neither of us wanted to be in that small bathroom with him. We pointed at each other. Rachel with a sigh made the supreme sacrifice.

She knocked on the door and Lippingdone threw it open.

"There's no soap in here," he bellowed. "No soap!"

"It's right there, Mr. Lippingdone," Rachel said with all possible kindness, pointing to a pile of small bars of soap resting on top of the vanity.

"You call that soap?" he menaced, banging his hamlike fist on the counter. "That's not soap."

It was then that Rachel noticed the small, round window in the bathroom. She couldn't believe it at first. And when she finally did come around to accepting what she saw, she had to bite her tongue from laughing. Even this painful technique didn't keep some audible snickers from coming out. Lippingdone went into a rage.

"Laugh at me, will you? Laugh, huh? I'll have your ass fired." He thought she was laughing at the soap problem. Then he followed her eyes and realized she was laughing at the window. It was carefully covered with toilet paper, the edges of the paper held to the wall by Scotch tape.

Lippingdone turned a deep red. His whole body trembled with rage, his lips twitched and his jowls shook. Rachel couldn't contain herself any longer. She broke into gales of laughter which made Mr. Lippingdone's condition even worse.

"This is marvelous," she said between outbursts. "The other passengers will love to hear about this." She turned to leave the lavatory but Lippingdone grabbed her by the arm.

"Don't you dare. I happen to be a modest man, something you wouldn't understand."

"Oh yes, I do understand, Mr. Lippingdone."

"Damn it," he muttered to himself, furious he'd forgotten to remove the paper in his furor over the soap. "Damn it," he repeated, only louder.

Rachel pulled herself together. "Look, Mr. Lippingdone, you've been nothing but trouble for us all day. I won't say a word about the window if you promise to shut up and sit in your seat. Not a word all the way to San Antonio."

He shook again with vehemence. Rachel thought he was going to strike out and hit her. But he didn't. He said, "Oh, all right." He sulked out of the lavatory as Rachel removed the paper from the window and flushed it down the john.

It worked. Our fat Mr. Lippingdone sat silently for the rest of the flight. Rachel told me about what had happened, and we had a marvelous laugh behind the closed curtains of the galley.

We stood at the door at San Antonio as the passengers left the plane. Mr. Lippingdone was last to leave. As he came by us, head down, hands stuffed deep in his pockets, I handed him a little thing we'd made up in the galley from a napkin. It was a perfect circle, just the size of the lavatory's porthole. Written in lipstick was, *For Your Next Flight!*

Of course there are certain drunks you excuse. We've had drunken soldiers flying out of San Francisco after spending their tour of duty in Vietnam. Who can blame them? We've had people with large problems that led them to drink too much before boarding the plane. Many times they want to talk about these problems which range from flying to claim the body of a loved one to dejection over jilting by a lover.

Of all the drunks we've known, none can compete with Mrs. Frazier, a passenger flying to New York from Los Angeles. To begin with, the general run of people boarding airplanes in Los Angeles often leaves something to be desired. Their dress, manners and over-all behavior tend on the whole to rank lower than other cities. But this particular person, Mrs. Frazier, wasn't to be believed.

She was literally carried on the airplane by a Hollywood-looking young man. He was barefooted, had hair down to his shoulders, and wore a T-shirt and chino pants.

"This is my son, Frazier," Mrs. Frazier mumbled as he lowered her into her seat. "I love that name, don't you? Frazier Frazier. Beautiful, isn't it?"

I asked him whether she was fit for the trip.

"Oh yeh, baby. She's just gettin' cool now. A very hip chick, my old lady. Very hip. Even surfs with me once in awhile. Not too good, but A for effort, like."

Frazier Frazier left mommy on the plane. She fell asleep and we crossed our fingers she'd continue in that state until New York. No such luck.

She woke up an hour out of Los Angeles and it was showtime. She was wearing a tight, gold dress when her son carried her on board. The first thing she did was to unzipper the back and take her bra off. Once she accomplished this maneuver, much to the delight of this man sitting next to her, she strolled up the aisle swinging the bra over her head. She also threw in a few bumps and grinds for good measure.

Next came her panties. They were slipped off in her seat and she threw them at a man across the aisle. He caught them and winked at her. We must admit that never once did her dress come off. Her stockings and shoes were discarded, but the dress maintained her decency. She insisted on helping us serve the meals, but we made it very plain that she was to stay in her seat.

"My, my, what efficient girls," she chided. "Just the kind of girls my Frazier needs."

She held hands with the man next to her, poured champagne into her shoe . . . and giggled when it ran out the open toe. She showed us an exercise she used to increase the size of her chest, implying we both could stand enlargement in that department. And she tried to frug with the flight engineer when he came back to replace a bulb in a reading light.

We got so we just couldn't take Mrs. Frazier any longer. She must have had her own secret supply of booze, because she kept getting more zonked as we got closer to New York. We watched with interest as she left the plane. On hand was another young man ready to help her up the ramp. She leaned over his back and together they managed to pass out of our sight.

"Don't ever let me get that drunk, Trudy," Rachel said as we walked together to operations.

"Do me the same favor."

CHAPTER XV

"Baby-Sitters of the Sky"

". . . Well, Miss, the air forces acting on this aircraft are equivalent to both drag backward in the reversed direction of the motion and a lifting force at right angles to the direction of the motion. That is to say . . ."

His mother modestly termed him precocious. To us, he was a seven-year-old genius.

". . . To most learned people, the French Revolution is dated from the states-general convention at Versailles in May of 1789 . . ."

We'd never met a genius before and certainly never expected him to be seven.

". . . absolute Monarchy reigned, of course, from the 16th century until the Revolution . . ."

"He's especially interested in French history," his mother said, as another would of her son's special interest in soccer.

Naturally, we catered to this little fellow with the oversized mind. It was unnerving to talk to him, especially when you tried to think of something to say that might sound reasonably intelligent. You just knew you'd fail.

Before we reached Memphis, we'd learned about frogs, physics, algebra, celestial navigation, selling short on the market, Asian customs of courtship and the future of every major politician in the nation.

"It's the most incredible thing I've ever seen," I told his mother as she gathered up belongings just before descent. "I can't believe it."

"Yes, Craig is bright. Very bright."

We landed and I came over to the mother to say goodbye and see if I could help her with anything. She looked very sheepish.

"Do you have some paper towels?" she whispered.

"Sure. Any problem?"

"Well, it's Craig," she looked at him. His pants were soaked.

"He's been very slow to toilet train," she said with a sigh.

"Oh."

That kind of thing could be a problem for Craig in later life. I've never forgotten him.

COFFEE, TEA OR ME?

We've never forgotten Johnny either, a six-year-old who flew with us from New Orleans to Chicago. Who said there's never been a bad boy? Meet Johnny.

He boarded the plane with his mother, and promptly whipped out a very realistic six-shooter from his belt and said, "Bang, bang," at us. That was cute, except he managed to jam the gun into Rachel's belly while pulling the trigger.

He took all the magazines off the rack before we had a chance to distribute them, and wailed when we asked that he give them back.

"I'll get them from him in a second," his mother said quietly to us, winking to indicate something. She kept her promise, but only after a half hour went by and we came back and asked again. He made an airplane out of the menu and flew it across the aisle. It made a perfect, nose-first landing in the face of a very stuffy lawyer who was trying to get some work done.

He threw up twice.

He spilled his milk all over the seat.

He ran up and down the aisle yelling, "Batman. Batman." An Air Force Major grabbed him by the arm and whispered something in his ear. Johnny returned to his seat.

"What'd you say to him?" I asked the major.

"I told him I was The Penguin in disguise and that I was planning to throw him out of the airplane unless he sat down."

"Very effective. I'll remember that."

Johnny refused to leave the galley when we asked him to do that little thing. "I don't have to," he whined, and stuck his tongue out at us.

Rachel looked around to make sure no one else was watching. Then, she took a knife from a compartment in the buffet and pointed it at Johnny. "Oh yes you do, little boy," she said with a sinister snarl on her face. He took the hint, but not before showing us his tongue on the way out.

Ten minutes later, his mother stormed back into the galley

COFFEE, TEA OR ME?

"My boy said you tried to cut him with a knife."
"Not us, ma'am."
"He never lies."
"I'm sure he doesn't, ma'am."
"I'll report you."
"Yes, ma'am."

Johnny stayed in his seat for the rest of the trip. His mother glared at us all the way to Chicago. As we got close to arrival, we decided it wouldn't be such a good idea to have his mother report us. We felt it might be wise from a practical sense to make amends. We tried, as Johnny and his mother passed by us at the open cabin door.

"It sure was nice having you flying with us today, Johnny," Rachel said happily, leaning over to make sure he heard her.

Johnny answered her. He stood on his tiptoes and whispered in Rachel's ear. His mother grabbed him by the back of the neck and marched him out of the airplane. "You'll hear about this," she threatened. There was no doubt we would.

"What did he say to you?" I asked her after they'd passed out of sight.

"He said, 'I hate you, you stupid doo-doo head.'"
"Oh."

"His father made a great mistake having that boy. Someone ought to send them some birth-control literature."

"Amen," I agreed.

Of course we heard from Johnny's mother. Our supervisor called us in to answer for the mother's letter which had gone to the president. We told her the story.

"Look, I understand," she said, "but no knives, OK?"
"OK."

We've had other little boys and girls on our flights who could have benefited from a few threats, backed up with the blade of a knife. But we'd learned our lesson. We're now more subtle, and tell them things like, "Why don't you play outside awhile?"

As we said, parents are usually to blame when a child

COFFEE, TEA OR ME?

causes trouble on a flight. We realized we were correct in this feeling after taking care of children who were flying unaccompanied. Remove them from mommy and daddy, and they behave beautifully.

If a child is even half-way good on a flight, he or she can be a delight. Children make a lot more sense than many of the adults we've flown with. In fact, not all the passengers who require baby sitting services are children.

It was a night coach from Miami to New York and seemed like a quiet night. But when I went back for a routine check of the seats, I found I was missing two people. I remembered that an older couple had come aboard and I recalled seeing them go into the lavatory. Perhaps they were still there. I checked—they weren't. I counted passengers again. Two short. I told the other stew. She said, "Come off it, Trudy," and began counting with an air of great superiority. She came up two short. Together we checked every cranny of the plane—including the johns and the galley. Nothing.

Finally I went up to the captain "Now, look. Don't say I'm crazy, but two people are missing. They just couldn't have walked off, but we don't know where they are."

The captain walked down the aisle looking at the passengers—some asleep, some reading. Suddenly he let out a yell, "Come here, you'll never believe this."

He was looking up at the rack above the seats where pillows and blankets are kept. There curled up in the overhead rack were our two missing tourists, nicely clothed in pajamas, covered with blankets and sound asleep. I guess they'd always traveled by train before, so they'd figured the racks were berths and just climbed up and turned in. Well, that whole plane broke up. There wasn't anyone on board who wasn't laughing hysterically.

I must remember to tell Aunt Laconia about my sleeping beauties.

CHAPTER XVI

"Even Your Best Friend Won't Tell You"

It was a great party, but hardly worth a thirty-day suspension.

The get-together, an impromptu one, was in honor of a departing stewardess. She was leaving the glamour of the sky for the altar, an event not to be questioned and most certainly to be celebrated.

The celebration began with six of us. It turned into a loud, sloppy ruck within an hour after we toasted our first glass of champagne to the bride-to-be. It ended at three A.M.

Rachel and I stayed until the bitter end despite having to work a 10 A.M. trip the next morning. It flashed through our minds a couple of times how tired we'd be, but it wouldn't be the first time. And we never gave a thought to the rules prohibiting a crew member from drinking twenty-four hours before a flight. That sort of regulation made sense for the men who had to fly the airplane. But it didn't make much sense for stewardesses. A good tooth brushing, breakfast, a few mints and no one would be the wiser. Right?

We were checking in with dispatch when we were handed the note.

"What do we have to report to the supervisor for?" I mumbled as we went to her office.

"Maybe we're going to be commended," was Rachel's suggestion.

"Yeh. Like the first trip we made."

Our supervisor at this period was a pretty good gal. She seemed sincerely regretful as she said, "Sorry girls, but I've got to give you both thirty-dayers."

"What for?" We were just as sincere in our ignorance.

You could almost feel sorry for our supervisor. She hesitated, looked down at her desk and said apologetically, "Drinking within twenty-four hours of a trip.

"The party last night?"

" 'Fraid so."

"Oh, come on. Who the hell sticks that close to that twenty-four ruling? The place was crawling with stews."

"Look, I'm sorry. I didn't make this up. I've got the

word to suspend you for thirty days. And I can't do a thing about it."

The real implications began to sink in at this point. How did they know about the party and the time it broke up?

"How did you know?"

Our supervisor quickly handed us the suspension notices and got up to leave. "I'm sorry." She walked out of her office.

George Kelman savored a crisp piece of sausage pizza as he thought about our tale of woe. It was the first night of our suspension and George, already aware of what happened, arrived with the pizza pies and a sympathetic shoulder.

"Well, now you'll believe me when I talk about stew-spies."

"You think that's what happened to us?" Rachel quizzed.

"No doubt about it."

"Who?"

"Never know." He started on another piece but discarded it for lack of cheese. "Wish they wouldn't skimp on cheese. Cheese is the best part."

"Who's the stew-spy who turned us in?"

"As attuned as I am to the whole stewardess scene, I have to admit ignorance in this matter. I know there are stew-spies but I don't know who they are. But this might be a good time to figure it out. Who was at that party?"

We started to think back and realized most of the people crashed the party. We didn't know eighty per cent of them. We told George this.

"That's a shame. But I'll check into it further. That's a promise." He left our apartment with all the grim determination of a CIA man embarking on a highly dangerous assignment.

"Good luck, George," we yelled after him.

He completed the role he was playing by muttering grimly over his shoulder, "I'll need it."

We got jobs as salesgirls in a department store to tide

us over during our suspension. George wasn't heard from again for two weeks. When he did call us, he was breathless with excitement.

"I've got to see you tonight, Rachel."

He came to the apartment at eleven that night. We'd worked late at the store, and he massaged Rachel's feet as I made drinks. When I served them, he rose from the couch and paced the room, hands behind his back, face furrowed in concentration.

"It's atrocious, girls. Abominable A disgrace on every airline."

I know it was cruel to break his train of thought but my feet hurt, too. "George, how about rubbing my feet."

He beat his fist against his head. "Rub your feet? Really, Trudy. I'm about to unfold a story of deceit and duplicity in front of you and you worry about your aching feet. Really!"

"I'm sorry, George. But we've been standing all night and   ."

"Enough of this. Do you want to know about the stew-spies who were responsible for your suspension?"

"You bet," we screamed in his ear, our sore feet forgotten.

"OK. Now listen." He resumed his pacing. "Would you believe your airline has a dozen girls working as stew-spies?"

We reacted with proper surprise.

"Yes, a dozen. Maybe some are your very best friends. What do you think of that?"

"Horrible. Which one turned us in?"

"I don't know."

We were naturally disappointed. We had expected him to tell us who the culprit was who caused us our thirty-day stint at the department store.

"What are you girls disappointed about?" he snapped at us. "I can't work miracles. Anyway, I did find out how they work. Listen to this. All twelve girls are regular stews and collect their salaries just like you do. But the airline has a contract with a private detective agency in

Chicago. And that agency has the twelve girls on their payroll, too. They collect double and work as spies. Nasty, huh?"

We agreed.

He went on. "Now, I'm going to Chicago and follow up on this whole thing. Maybe I can find out the names of the girls. This whole thing really has me upset. I always knew there were stew-spies but never really saw any damage they'd caused. Now I'm outraged."

George made two trips to Chicago but never found out who the girls were on the double payroll. We finished our month in the toy department of the store and resumed our flying careers. The worst part of the experience was the mistrust it implanted in us. We didn't trust anyone anymore. Every girl we worked with assumed a traitor's mask, each her own stool pigeon in this despicable plot.

However, despite George's failure to uncover the names of the girls, we came up with a prime suspect of our own. Her name was Janis Pool, and she talked too much about stew-spies and how terrible they were. She hated to be questioned about what she knew, but seemed possessed by the subject. We asked George about her.

"I ran down a dossier on Janis Pool," he told us, "and she could be a stew-spy. Very definitely could be. Too much money for just a stew with one income. Lives alone. Always bids Chicago and gets it. Keeps to herself. Loves to talk about stew-spies."

"We've noticed that, too, George. You really think she's one of them?"

"Can't say for sure. But she's a strong possibility. I'll check further."

We didn't wait for later findings by George Kelman. Janis Pool was it, we decided. She had to be.

"Was she at the party?" I asked Rachel.

"I didn't remember her. But I don't remember most of the people, do you?"

"No."

But the girl for whom the party was given did remember Janis Pool showing up. "She came in about midnight and only stayed for a drink or two."

COFFEE, TEA OR ME?

That did it. Janis Pool was our Nathan Hale, and would have to be dealt with.

We began a day-by-day harassment of the suspect. First, on an evening trip, we broke open one of the small ammonia vials used to revive fainting passengers and placed it in the oxygen mask used by us to demonstrate proper technique to passengers before take-off. Janis was all smiles as she held the mask in her hands waiting for me to read the instructions over the PA. I began reading and she placed the mask to her face in accordance with my words. She almost died. She sputtered and coughed, tears carrying make-up down her face, as she plunged into the buffet area.

"Why did you do this to me?" she cried as we stood there in gaping amazement at her condition.

"Do what?"

"Put the ammonia in the mask."

"Janis, don't look at us. Must have been one of those nasty cabin cleaners. That's who must have done it."

"I'll get his ass fired," she threatened through her weeping.

"I'll bet you can, Janis," Rachel said.

"You bet I can," Janis reiterated.

We pulled all sorts of very silly and sophomoric tricks on Janis Pool, each helping us rid ourselves of deep-seated feelings of vindictiveness. Our decision, a kangaroo-court one, was that Janis Pool was a stew-spy, and had turned us in to management. We couldn't see any further. We called her at odd hours and hung up. We took messages from her box and enjoyed her problems when she didn't answer them or take the appropriate action. We even spilled things on her in the buffet, an especially nasty trick because stewardess usually maintain only one uniform.

We're still convinced Janis Pool was the spy. It's never been proven. In retrospect, our actions against her were mean and uncalled for. But we did what we did and felt better for it at the time.

Certain airlines still maintain the stew-spy system. Our

union tries very hard to bring about the end of this big-sister system. So far, they've been unsuccessful.

Of course, we recognize that girls are deceitful creatures at best. There doesn't seem a day goes by without one stewardess stealing away another's boyfriend. We've seen hair-pulling matches between friends of long standing, poison pen notes, vicious gossip and nasty, day-by-day retaliation between the girls. We guess that's the way we are—take it or leave it!

But adopting the "all's fair in love and war" creed is acceptable when only love and war are involved. Our jobs are a different matter of much greater importance than a lost lover. We don't personally know a stew-spy. That's fortunate for them.

CHAPTER XVII

"Have a Merry Mistress"

Charlie Smagg opened the door when we knocked. His head bobbed back and forth like one of those stranger-than-fiction, real-life Christmas dolls. He was drunk. That was obvious.

"Hi, Charlie," we said happily despite the blowing snow swirling around our legs.

" 'Twas the night before Christmas and all through the plane not a creature was stirring not even one li'l ol' bubble in a glass of bubbly champagne." His head bobbed faster.

"Can we come in, Charlie?"

"Why, of course. Course. Come in. Come in."

The motel room was a welcome pocket of warmth. There were maybe a dozen people in the room. A party atmosphere prevailed.

Charlie Smagg, the First Officer on the flight that brought us to Rochester on this Christmas Eve, was obviously the first to arrive at the party. Besides, it was his room, a good running start for anyone.

We weren't supposed to be in Rochester on Christmas Eve. Our schedule called for a return trip to Kennedy Airport late that afternoon. But the unpredictable winter weather of upstate New York held off just long enough for us to land in Rochester at noon. Then, like an overanxious curtain puller at a bad play, the weather swooped in and shrouded the area in a white cloak of snow.

The word that we would not be getting home for Christmas brought sadness to Rachel and me. Neither of us had ever been away from home on Christmas. Our plans were to go back to Kennedy as scheduled, and look for empty seats to Texas and Kentucky. Failing that, we'd at least be able to enjoy the day together in the familiar surroundings of our apartment. But winter wasn't kind.

The whole crew checked into the motel together after a slippery car ride from the airport. The desk clerk, a wizened little man with bad breath and a runny nose set the tone for the evening when he said to the captain, "Have yourself a merry mistress, captain." It did not instill any feeling of ho-ho-ho and glad tidings in us.

COFFEE, TEA OR ME?

We shared our room with Rhonda, the third girl on the trip. Normally on layovers, two girls share a room. But the storm put rooms at a premium. "Well, what'll we do for the night?" Rachel asked as she pulled things out of her suitcase. "Sing Christmas carols?"

"Why not," I agreed. "We might become the Andrews Sisters of Rochester. Ted Mack might hear us and make us famous."

"Right. We could play all the best night spots of Rochester on the same bill with a hacksaw-blade player and a Maltese Santa Claus who does bird calls."

"It makes me so mad," Rhonda said as she pouted in front of the mirror. She was very pretty, with honey hair and fair complexion and an ample figure. Her major problem was she knew it. "My boyfriend and I were going to have dinner and drive up to Connecticut and . . . Well, it was going to be fun. Damn airline. Damn snow."

The phone rang. I answered.

"All right," the voice on the other end said, "get down here." It was Charlie. "We've got some Christmas cheer here for you girls."

"No thanks, Charlie. I'm beat. I'm off to bed."

"Marvelous, Trudy. I'll join you."

"No you won't."

"Is Rachel there?"

"Yup."

"Come on down to the room, Rachel. Little drink for Saint Nick."

"Sorry, chief, but no thanks. I'm falling apart."

"Oh. Where's Rhonda?"

"Right here."

"Put her on."

Rhonda took the phone from Rachel.

"Rhonda, sweetie, how about some Yuletide cheer?"

"Love it. Be right down."

That started the Christmas Eve Party in Rochester. Rachel and I did go to bed as planned, but soon found it impossible to sleep. We got up and went to the party. It was in full swing by the time we arrived. There were four stewardesses from another line who'd met a fate similar to ours. There were three men, not airline types, who happened in on the festivities and were invited to pool their liquor supply with the crew's stock. They evidently had a large supply to offer. Everyone seemed high.

"Hey, a coupl'a more girlies. Yay, yay. Come on in honeys." Our greeter was one of the outsiders, a salesman of heavy construction equipment. He had big bulging eyes and his shirt collar was too tight, its cloth wilted under the folds of his neck. His nose was red and veined. It was the first year he'd missed playing Santa Claus at the office party in Pittsburgh.

The room couldn't stand thirteen people. Smoke threw up a dense screen that gave the scene the feeling of a Fellini film. The radio, one of those quarter-in-the-slot jobs, blared forth with Christmas music between hard-sell commercials, and drippy disc jockey chatter.

"Name's Sidney," the equipment salesman hollered over *White Christmas*. "You from around here?"

"We fly with them," Rachel said, pointing toward the captain reclined in the bed, Rhonda snuggled warmly against him. Charlie Smagg plopped down beside them, a fifth of rye clutched to his chest.

"More stews, huh? Great. Whattaya drink?"

We ordered.

He brought the drinks, handed them to us, and promptly grabbed Rachel by the waist and whirled her around the room in step to *Rudolph the Red-Nosed Reindeer*. He was surprisingly light on his feet for someone that fat. Rachel managed to get free from him and sat on the desk chair. Charlie Smagg got up and handed her his bottle. She gave it back. He tried to sit on her lap but slid off onto the floor. "Greatest stew in the world," he yelled up to everyone over the music and chatter.

Another of the outsiders came over to me. "Hello there. My name is Scranton. Scranton Rigby. So you're a stewardess. So's my daughter."

"No kidding? Who's she fly with?"

"Well, no one right now. Got married Got divorced.

Looking for another stewardess job. Good thing she learned about the little pill before she got divorced from that idiot. Good thing. Kids get hurt, you know. Wouldn't be able to find another stewardess job either, with kids and all that. Good girl. Say, maybe you can help her."

"Gee, I don't think so."

"Well, we can talk about it later. Another drink?"

My glass was still full. "No thanks."

The four stewardesses from the other airline were clustered around the third strange male in the room. He was small, very small. His few long strands of remaining hair were carefully positioned across his head to achieve maximum coverage. His suit was double-breasted, plaid, his shirt a fine check and his tie wide and brilliant with pink roses on a black field. I strolled over and introduced myself to the group.

"Josh is a writer," one of the girls told me after he'd mumbled an introduction to me. "Isn't that interesting?"

"Yes, it certainly is."

"Go ahead and tell us some more," the girls insisted as Josh carefully patted his hairs in place. He was pleased to be asked.

"Well, as I was saying, it's very difficult for me to convey some of the humor of the business to outsiders. You know, show business is a fraternity in itself. I mean, the Broadway crowd I pal with is something else. Something else. There are so many interesting tidbits about the stars and all. Like Sonny Tufts."

"Sonny Tufts?" I chanted with sheer wonder.

"Yes. Sonny Tufts. Did you know he was from a very wealthy family in Boston? Big banking family. And Sonny studied grand opera in Rome and was going to make his debut at the Met. You do know what the Met is, don't you?"

I nodded.

"And I might add that Sonny was quite the society band leader. Did you know that?"

"Noooo."

"See what I mean. It's such an *in* thing. You've just got to look deeper than what you read in the columns."

"Have you ever been in anyone's column?" I asked. I wasn't testing him. I was simply interested.

He chortled a little, admired his polished fingernails, and said, "That's what my press agent is for Keep me out of the columns. Ho, ho, ho."

"Yes."

The others giggled.

"What are you doing in Rochester, of all places?" He didn't like that question either.

"Soaking up local color. I'm doing a play with an upstate setting. I want to feel it, touch it, live it, although it is dreadfully dull, dear hearts. But *being* what I write is important. It really is paramount to meaningful writing."

"What have you written?"

"I've never written for the mass media. You probably have never read or seen my works."

I walked away. Rachel came over and we mixed fresh drinks.

"Who's the little creep?" she asked.

"Playwright, he says. Names's Josh Something."

"No kidding?"

"Yes, I think he's kidding."

"What's he ever written?"

"Something to do with Sonny Tufts. With an upstate New York setting."

Rachel didn't understand. It wasn't important.

The chubby equipment salesman turned the radio up louder. The disc jockey was talking about how the holiday season touched him deeply.

". . . and to all of you out there tonight, wherever you may be and whatever you may be doing, I hope you share with me in all the warmth of this great season. Yes, it's hard to conceive of peace on earth and good will to all men when our boys are away fighting the jungle wars of the world, but irregardless of that . . ."

"Irregardless?" Josh screamed.

Charlie Smagg took a swig.

Then a commercial followed the disc jockey. It was for a local cesspool company with a seasonal special.

"And now here's the big one, the all-time, top-forty

COFFEE, TEA OR ME?

Christmas *favorite—The Christmas Song.*" The DJ's last words were punctuated with an electronic whine that lasted far into Mel Torme's version of his own song. The equipment salesman grabbed Rachel again and swung her around on the carpeted floor. He lost his balance and fell down, vainly reaching for support from Rachel. She let him fall.

There was a knock at the door. Rachel answered. It was the desk clerk. He ignored Rachel and peered past her through the smoke. There was a dirty gleam in his eye as he fixed on the captain and Rhonda. Snowflakes settled on his nose and the wind blew some on Rachel.

"It's cold. What do you want?"

"Oh, yeh. Long distance telephone call for Mr. Josh Pierre. Figured he was here."

Josh came to the door. "Probably my agent," he threw back over his shoulder. "Be right back. I hope Merrick has come to his senses." He left with the desk clerk.

". . . Merry Christmas to you." Mel Torme sang out his tune, the final notes rudely cut off by a station promotion for the local quiz show. Then came a rock-and-roll version of *God Rest Ye Merry Gentlemen.*

"Ba ba doo, ba ba doo, ba ba doo," Charlie Smagg sang as he danced across the room, his bottle clutched tightly to his bosom. "Let's dance, Trudy, my love."

We danced. You could almost feel the smoke brushing up against you as it hung heavy from the ceiling. The smoke, heat, loud noise and drinks were getting to me. I was almost enjoying nutty Charlie Smagg and his two left feet.

". . . tidings of comfort and joy ba ba doo ba ba doo, oooh tidings of comfort and joy ba ba doo ba ba doo YEH!"

Josh came back in the room.

"Just sold another one."

"Another what?"

"Play. Option." He sneered at us.

"I bet it was his mother," I whispered to Rachel.

"Or the keeper at his funny farm," she further speculated.

"You were telling us about Sonny Tufts and that time on Sunset Strip, Josh."

"Right. Right. Now you may wonder why I know so much about Sonny Tufts. Well, it goes way back to . . ."

An hour passed.

"Did you know the Japanese Actor who played King Kong was only five feet tall?" The girls, all drunk now, were still infatuated with Josh Pierre. "And they do the whole thing with mirrors."

The captain and Rhonda were kissing it up pretty good now on the bed. Scranton Rigby was telling me about the bad man his daughter had married and how the poor girl was suffering from the divorce.

"I feel great rapport with you, Trudy," Scranton said, "and I'd like to help you. Like a father. I want to keep you from falling into the pitfalls my daughter has suffered." Then he tried to kiss me and pinched my rear end.

"You're no father."

"I am. I am. Let me tell you . . ."

It was news time on the radio. To the accompaniment of staccato telegraph keys, whistlers, sirens, drums and wind machines, all the world's gruesome headlines were given with breathless excitement.

"We'll be back in a moment with the details."

Then a message from a clothing store with Jingle Bells playing in the background.

"Let me have the key to the room, Trudy." Rhonda stood with her hand out. I gave her the key. She left with the captain. Charlie Smagg laid down on the bed and curled up with the pillow. "This news makes me sad," he said. He switched stations. There was Christmas music everywhere. He settled on the original station. He hummed along with *Hark the Herald Angels Sing*.

"Actually, Sonny Tufts and King Kong are the kings of trivia. Did you know that?" Josh Pierre was still holding court, although one of the girls had left his circle and joined Charlie on the bed.

Every party emits its own particular sense of things to come. You could perceive upon entering Charlie's room a distinct emanation of future wildness. That's fine, in many cases. But the people in Charlie's room weren't right for some unexplainable reason. Scranton Rigby and his paternal line, the waltzing heavy-equipment salesman, little Josh Pierre, the other girls and our own crew didn't seem to mesh. Maybe it was just the time and the place. At any rate, the end result was depressing. The room was terribly hot, the music too loud and the overt advances of the fellows a little too overt. I wanted to get out of there. "Do you want to throw snowballs?" I asked Rachel.

"Hey, gang," Rachel announced. "I've got a great idea. How about a snowball fight?"

The suggestion was met with mixed reactions. But the lack of unanimity didn't deter us. Rachel flung open the door, the blast of cold, wet air causing her to catch her breath.

"Come on," I yelled, "let's go."

No one moved except Rachel and me.

Rachel put on her coat and ran outside. Soon, a large, wet snow-ball came flying through the door and splattered with a dull *sqump* against John Pierre's lapel.

"Let's get 'em," Charlie yelped and raced outside. Others followed. Only Josh remained in the room, a sophisticated sneer on his face showing his contempt for such sophomoric conduct.

The snowball fight was fun until the heavy-equipment salesman pinned me down in the snow and used the spirit of the fight as an excuse to slip his hand under my coat. I let him have it in the face with a solidly packed snowball and slipped out from under him as he sputtered the glaze off his face. Two of the stewardesses were sitting on top of Charlie Smagg and shoving snow down his shirt.

Scranton Rigby, tottering unsteadily on a small snowbank, threw a snowball at me as I ducked behind a bush by the motel's entrance. He missed me, of course, but made a direct hit on the desk clerk who'd ventured out to watch the fight. That brought him into the fray with a great deal of zeal. He tacked Rachel and her screams indicated more than a simple snow fight. Scranton Rigby,

COFFEE, TEA OR ME?

father image that he was, jumped on the desk clerk. The clerk got up, swore at everybody, and went back into the motel. It was only fifteen minutes before the police arrived.

They were nice about asking us to stop the fight and return to our rooms. We all went back to the party room and sat quietly as melting snow formed little puddles on the brown tweed carpet.

Cooled off by the snow and the local policemen, the party resumed with noticeably less gaiety than before the outdoor frolic. Drinking was moderate, chatter was relatively subdued and dancing was formal to the point of stiffness. Charlie Smagg was sober. Josh Pierre was falling asleep in the chair. The heavy-equipment salesman told jokes and Scranton Rigby laughed at them.

The party started to break up at about 2 A.M. The local radio station was still filling the airwaves with Christmas music, the late hour cutting down on the frequency of commercial messages.

"Wake up, Mr. Pierre," I said, gently shaking the little fellow's shoulders.

"Momma, momma," he babbled as he came out of his sleepy slump in the chair. "Oh, here I am. Right. Thanks."

Charlie Smagg was asleep on the bed, the bottle still clutched tightly in his arms. Scranton Rigby reminded me to keep in touch with him.

"If you're ever in Pittsburgh, drop in," were the heavy equipment salesman's parting words.

"We sure will," we answered him.

We were outside before we thought about Rhonda and the captain.

"There isn't anything we can do," I told Rachel as we shivered against the wind. "We'll just knock and tell them we're tired and want to go to bed."

We did that. We were frozen by the time they came to unlock the door. The captain was dressed but Rhonda was in her robe.

"See you tomorrow, girls," he said as he returned to

COFFEE, TEA OR ME?

Charlie's Smagg's room. Rhonda turned down the covers and climbed into bed. "Goodnight," was said all around and sleep came quickly.

The telephone's harsh jangle brought us out of the first hour of sleep. It was the captain.

"Sorry to bother you but I thought you ought to know we dumped one."

It took a minute for his terminology to be understood, but I finally realized he meant our airline had lost an airplane.

"Where?"

"Over Wisconsin. It was on the news just now. Not much detail."

"Any crew names?"

"Not yet. No sense losing sleep over it. We can't do anything. We'll find out all about it in the morning. Say goodnight to Rhonda for me."

"Sure."

Our captain, a twenty-year veteran, could go to sleep; he'd been around before when planes went down. But we hadn't. We turned the radio on and waited impatiently for the next newscast. Then the announcer broke in on the music with a bulletin.

"The plane was believed to be carrying a full load of holiday passengers, but the exact number is not known at this time. Officials of the airline have indicated no known cause for the disaster. Stay tuned to this station for further details."

We tried to stay awake but couldn't. We woke up in the morning to a newscast in which they listed the names of the crew members. We didn't know any of them, except one.

". . . and Miss Sally Lu Johnson."

"You know," Rachel said slowly, "if I had to pick someone from our class at school who would end up like this, I think I'd have picked Sally Lu "

"She was going to quit when Warren bought his own gas station. Looks like he didn't make it quick enough."

I started to cry and so did Rachel. Rhonda didn't know Sally Lu, but she wept, too.

COFFEE, TEA OR ME?

I guess all stewardesses have a true feeling toward the other girls, whether they're close friends or not. We work together in such narrow quarters. We share our after-work lives with each other. We depend on each other. Folded away in the back of each of our heads is the knowledge that danger and death are always out there waiting. We know this. We accept it. I think each of us develops almost the same philosophy: if it's meant to be you, it will happen to you. If it's not your turn, you're OK. And this is the way we would want to go—if it must be.

Rhonda tried to comfort us by telling about her own very bad experience. She'd had a big romance going in New Orleans and wanted to stay on for a few days. When she reported in sick, her roommate took over the flight for her. The plane went down in the Rockies. Her roommate's body was never found. "My first thought was that I'd killed Gerry," Rhonda told us. "I'd sent her to her death. I was torturing myself with guilt. I didn't think I could fly anymore. But after a while I had to accept that this is the way it is. We all have a turn. Sally Lu just didn't make it."

Breakfast with the entire crew was filled with talk of the crash. Each one of us reported what we'd heard on the radio, and the cockpit boys went into their theories about what might have happened.

"Well, how do you feel girls? Ready to make the trip back?" The captain looked us straight in the eye with the question.

"I'm shook a little," I answered him.

"Well, don't be. Did you know that more people are killed at railroad crossings every year than in aircraft accidents?"

"And more people are killed on bicycles," Charlie threw in.

The statistics weren't at all comforting. "I don't think Sally Lu knew about those statistics," I answered

"Well, you'll get over it. You have to."

He was right, of course. And we did. We left the motel for our trip back to Kennedy. We finally got a break in the weather late that afternoon and were at our apartment building at seven that evening.

There was a telegram in the letterbox from Rachel's mother. It read, "CRASH TERRIBLE THING. THINK YOU MUST STOP FLYING. PLEASE. LOVE MOTHER."

"It's funny, Trudy, but I don't feel that way. I don't think I've ever felt more like flying. Know what I mean?"

"Yes, I do."

In front of our apartment door a happy surprise was waiting for us. Chuck was sitting bolt upright against the door, fast asleep. I fell into his arms. "You big goof," I cried, "what are you doing here?"

"I was in Chicago with a forty-eight-hour wait-over when I heard about Sally Lu. I knew you were socked in up there in Rochester. It must be a helluva Christmas for you, so I dropped by and figured I'd wait for you." He looked at his watch. "Come on, I've just got three hours. I'll buy you Christmas dinner."

Rachel suddenly started to remember an appointment with her friends in Great Neck. Chuck grabbed her arm and gave her a bright blue stare with those crazy eyes of his: "No party pooping. It's both of you pigeons for Christmas dinner, or nothing, OK?"

"OK," Rachel said, retrieving her arm. "Do you have your bike outside?"

"This kind of weather I use reindeer," he replied.

"Come on, kids, let's go," I said. We dropped our bags in the apartment and then, each of us clinging to one of his arms, we walked Chuck around the corner to a little French restaurant. I don't know whether Chuck was in exceptionally great spirits or whether he thought he ought to be to cheer us up. Anyway he kept us laughing during the entire meal.

"I'll never get over the things you girls do to each other," he told us at one point. "Remember your chesty friend Betty?"

"Sure, we see her all the time."

"Well, she was hot after the captain on a flight I was on to Phoenix a couple of weeks ago. The junior stew

COFFEE, TEA OR ME?

was a young kid just out of school—a fresh, on-the-make little doll. We all noticed her because she'd hitched her skirt way up to look like a mini."

"How did Betty take that?" Rachel wanted to know.

"I think she called and raised a couple of buttons on her blouse," Chuck answered. "Naturally we drank a lot of coffee that flight and got to know the kid—her name's Gwen—pretty well. By the time we reached Phoenix Gwen was flopping all over the captain from behind, chewing at his ear and saying, 'Tell me about those li'l bitty ol' dials and buttons, honey. What's that one over there?' and she sorta hitched herself over his shoulder to point at the dial, so of course he nestled his head back between her breasts."

"I bet the captain hated that," I said.

"Not the captain—Betty. She came barging in yelling, 'Get your hot pants outta here!' I had to break up the slugfest. It's something to see two dames stage a cat-fight. But that isn't all."

Chuck held up his wine glass for a refill. "On the return flight Betty had Gwen demonstrate the life vest and oxygen mask and . . ."

We didn't let Chuck finish. I said, "Ammonia." Rachel said, "Pepper," The three of us burst into such wild laughter that the waiter thought we'd lost our minds. I was right. Betty put ammonia into the oxygen mask, Gwen took a deep breath to illustrate inhalation technique and the ammonia fumes all but killed her.

"You dames are something," Chuck said with a sigh. "A guy has to be an idiot to get mixed up with any of you."

That was our Christmas dinner. We forgot all about the rotten time in Rochester. For the moment we stopped thinking about Sally Lu. It was just good to be alive and able to laugh. After coffee Rachel said she had to dash. She raced off on an imaginary errand. Chuck and I went back to the apartment. We had very little time but we put it to the best possible use, the very best.

Who says there isn't a Santa Claus?

CHAPTER XVIII

"The Saga of Sandy"

"Where does Sandy get the money to do all the things she does, Trudy?" Rachel asked one night as we were watching *Batman*.

"Beats me. Maybe she has a rich uncle."

"I don't think so."

"How do you know?"

"I just know. I sense it."

"Maybe she takes in washing on the side."

"Yeh. Maybe that's . . . Ouch!" Rachel was reacting to a strong right hand to Batman's head by the Riddler.

The Sandy in question was Sandy Sims, an attractive girl who also flew for our airline. She did seem to get a great deal from life on her stewardess pay. Sandy always vacationed in Europe, an easy feat for stewardesses with cut-rate travel fares. But Sandy stayed in the most elegant hotels while there, and came back with suitcases full of expensive goods. She lived alone in a high-rent brownstone, wore three-hundred-dollar suits, owned a Triumph which she housed in a mid-town parking garage and was never without funds.

There are rich girls working as stewardesses. But Sandy Sims wasn't one of them. People who knew her testified to that. She came from a modest family and wasn't dating any rich playboy as far as anyone knew. In fact, she wasn't known to date anyone. She was a loner, but a pleasant one, who was always ready to pitch in on a flight and lend a hand when needed.

Maybe our questioning was based on jealousy. But a lot of the girls talked about Sandy. Some even said, "Maybe she's hustling on the side." Then we'd laugh. We couldn't believe a stewardess would do that. Prostitutes were girls who came from slums and were forced into lives of vice through bad breaks and unsavory people.

We asked George Kelman about it one night.

"Don't be silly," he said with honest detestation. "What cheap novels have you been reading? There's never been a stewardess hooker and there never will be."

"Yes, sir," we said, saluting.

"Dirty minds," he added.

COFFEE, TEA OR ME?

This made us a little angry. "OK, George, where does she get the money?"

This angered him. "What the hell business is it of yours, anyway? Maybe she just doesn't blow it like you two do. Drop the whole thing. You're just jealous as hell."

His words made sense. We forgot about Sandy Sims and her money until two months later when we received a monthly schedule that included her on most of the legs.

We were flying New York—Dallas, with a layover in the Texas city. As usual, Sandy took a room by herself, saying she had a great deal of reading to do. It cost her above her traveling allowance, but that never bothered her.

Rachel and I were in Room 356C. Sandy was in 365C. It was about eight o'clock. I was settling down for the next juicy chapter of a motion picture actress's best-selling autobiography, while Rachel was doing sitting-up exercises on the floor. The phone rang.

"I'll get it," I said. I picked up the receiver and heard, "Is this Sandy?"

"No, it's not. You have the wrong room."

"Sorry!" He hung up quickly.

"Who was that?" Rachel queried.

"Some guy for Sandy. What room is she in, anyway?"

"Forget. Hey, maybe it's some rich oil man and he's keeping Sandy. Yeh, that's it."

"Oh."

I read further in the book and Rachel turned to push-ups. "It's good for the breasts, you know," she grunted from the floor.

"Tell Betty Big Boobs."

"Up ... down ... up ... down ..."

The phone rang.

"Hello."

"Sandy?"

"This isn't Sandy's room. You've got the wrong one. Check the desk."

He hung up without another word.

Rachel was now on deep breathing exercises.

"In . . . out . . . in . . . out . . ."

"I'll get it," she said when the phone rang again. She picked the receiver up quickly. "Hello . . . No, she's taking a shower. Who's calling?"

The man's voice on the other end hesitated. "Uh, when do you think she'll be finished?"

"Pretty soon," Rachel replied, her voice a strange cooing, sexy sound.

"Oh," the guy said. "Would you tell her Larry called?"

"Sure. But can't I help you?" I was listening closely now, my book relegated to the floor.

"You help me? . . . Well, . . . I didn't know if you . . . I don't think so. Goodbye."

"He hung up," Rachel said, still holding the phone to her ear.

"What was that routine?" I asked. "She's not taking a shower."

"I know. But I wanted him to talk a little. Who are all these guys calling her?"

"Rachel, you are truly jealous. And a busybody to boot."

Rachel turned and looked me straight in the eye. "Aren't you interested, too, Trudy?"

"Yup. Let's figure out what to say to the next call. OK?"

We plotted our action. Rachel would answer and say Sandy had left for an appointment but asked that Rachel substitute for her. The phone rang ten minutes later and our plan was in effect. Only Rachel, as so often happened when I egged her on, became even bolder than we had planned.

"I'm sure you'd like me," I heard her saying and couldn't believe my ears.

"Are you a . . . a stewardess, too?" the man asked.

"Yes, I am. Sandy and I have . . . well, sort of our own private little thing going. Are you coming up?"

"Rachel, you idiot, that's our room. It's one thing to find out about Sandy, but not to have the guy come up here." I wanted to kill her.

"Why not?" Rachel hurried around the apartment

picking up clothing and other personal items. "Might be fun. Ever been on call?"

"Of course not."

"Me either. But I bet we could act like one. I mean two. Now don't get upset. I don't mean we're really going to do what a prostitute does. We can just talk to him and maybe find out more about Sandy."

"But how are we going to get rid of him?" I wanted to know.

Rachel hadn't thought about that. She suddenly paled. "Gee, let's see . . ."

Now it was my turn to improvise. "Suppose we tell him we charge two hundred dollars."

"You're a genius," Rachel assured me. "That'll do it."

But the whole thing had me worried. "You know, Rachel, Sandy will find out about this. She's bound to. He'll tell her about the high price and all."

"He will not. He'll never mention a word. And if he does, we just deny anything. Don't worry about it."

Within minutes, we had our hotel room looking good enough to rival anything Sadie Thompson could have dreamed up on such short notice. One light illuminated the room. The drapes were drawn. We wore our bathrobes (with Bermuda shorts and sweaters underneath). We were beginning to feel the part, and that was a little frightening. We waited for what seemed an eternity before there came a feeble knock on the door.

"Go ahead," I whispered to Rachel.

"You," she countered.

"You started it," I retorted.

"I'm scared," she quavered.

I ran over to her. He knocked again. "Evens," I said. "OK. Odds for me."

"Once, twice, three . . . shoot." I put out one finger and she put out two. Rachel would answer the door. He was knocking louder now.

She slowly opened it and there stood our caller—our first customer. He looked awful.

"Howdy," he said with a broad grin. "Here I am."

"Hi," Rachel managed to say, her voice having obvious trouble getting past her Adam's apple.

"Can I come in? This is the place, isn't it."

Rachel hesitated for a moment. "Sure. Come in."

He walked through the door and stopped dead in his tracks when he saw me.

"Two of you?"

"Yup."

"I'll be damned. Didn't know there was two of you."

"Yup. Two of us," I said, trying to appear at home with the situation.

He rocked back and forth, from one foot to another, as he made up his mind what to say next. He seemed as nervous as we were.

"Sit down," I said to break the silence.

"Name's Bert. What's yours?"

"Roberta," I said, not knowing why that name came into my head.

"I'm Zelda," Rachel threw in.

"Zelda?"

"Zelda."

"Nice name."

"Thanks."

He fidgeted in his chair. He twirled his tie in his fingers and kept blowing his cheeks out.

"Well," he finally managed to say, "I guess we'd better iron things out right now. I mean, about the two of you and all. I mean, about the money. You know?"

Rachel took the initiative. "Sure. The money. We can get to that in a minute. Uh, why don't you take off your shoes. That's a good idea. And loosen your tie."

I was afraid she was overdoing it. Fortunately he didn't want to take his shoes off. He did loosen his tie.

"You from Dallas?" I asked.

"Yup."

"Where'd you meet Sandy?"

"Never did meet her. Another fella told me 'bout her. Didn't know there were others."

"Other what?"

COFFEE, TEA OR ME?

"Well, you know what I mean. Gals like yourselves making a little extra in your spare time."

We evidently looked hurt, or shocked, because he came right back with, "Not that I blame you. Guess you don't make that much workin' for the airline. And guess you figure there's nothin' wrong with it 'cause you're gonna do it anyway. Am I right?"

"Well, yes."

"How'd you get started?" he asked, leaning forward to indicate sincere and deep interest in the subject. This was crazy. He wasn't supposed to interview us.

"Well, it's a long story."

He looked at his watch. "Look, I gotta get home. What do I do. Choose?"

"I guess so," I answered.

"Well, no hard feelings I hope. I'll take you." He pointed directly at me.

For once I was speechless, all my Texas bravado fled. What now?

"You got another room up here?" he asked.

"No. No other room. Just this one."

His eyes began to light up. "Boy, you gonna watch?" he asked Rachel.

"Guess so."

Bert got up and came over to me. He put his arm around me and kissed me on the neck.

"Wait a minute," I said in a panic, pushing him away at the same time.

"Oh, yeh. About that money. My friend said it was thirty-five. OK by me."

Rachel jumped into the discussion. "Thirty-five? You must be kidding."

"Well, that's what he told me. How much is it?"

"Two hundred."

"Two hundred?"

"Sure. We're clean, nice girls. Not like the others who do this. Two hundred."

"Boy, he sure was wrong."

"Sorry. You'd better leave. There are others waiting."

Bert walked out under a cloud of gloom. We'd never

talked about what we'd do if our customer became violent, or if he had the two hundred. Lucky for us, Bert was just sad and poor.

"Well, how about Miss Sandy Sims?" Rachel said with pride that she'd uncovered the plot.

"We know where she gets the money but so what? What do you think we're supposed to do about it?"

"Nothing. I just feel better now that my curiosity can be put to rest."

We decided the evening had been fun. But what a strange feeling to be talking to that strange man about going to bed with him, especially when the money question came up.

"What did you do last night?" we asked Sandy the next morning on the plane.

"Not much. Had a good night's sleep. Say, by the way, the desk clerk had our room numbers mixed up. I got a couple of calls from friends of mine who said they got your room instead. At least I think it was your room. Thanks for setting them straight. I have a lot of relatives in Dallas and it was good to hear from them. You didn't get any other calls for me, did you?"

"No, no, Sandy. Not a one."

"Good. I hate to miss a phone call."

Sandy Sims is the only stewardess we've ever met who made extra money this way. There are a few others we've heard about. But we've never met them. We understand they try to work the charter flights that take a group of men to a convention. That seems sensible to us.

CHAPTER XIX

"What's a Nice Girl Like You Doing in a Plane Like This?"

We talked a little earlier about how a stewardess learns to recognize a married man from the moment he walks on board the aircraft. This developed perception, coupled with the aid of a tell-tale, pale imprint of a hastily removed wedding band, proves extremely valuable in a very practical sense.

But sizing up a male passenger's marital status isn't all we do when things are slow. We also play the game of guessing where he's from and what he does. As stewardesses on the receiving end of perhaps more direct passes than any other group of working girls, we've been able to compare notes on the pitches different men make and how these pitches relate to their nationality and profession. After long and careful study of countless stories by our fellow-stewardesses, together with a normal amount of first-hand experiences, we've been able to come up with our own handbook on the subject. If a given profession or nationality isn't listed, we can only offer the probability that men in that category don't fly, or don't like girls, or both.

GERMANS

German men always do things by the numbers. They seem to base their amorous advances on pages from a strange and misplaced book, a book that will never make the best-seller charts here in America. They try to give you the impression that to accompany them from the airplane and share their bed would be a contribution toward some better, super-world. They usually attack the larger species of stewardesses—the flight's flying Brunhildes.

It is our considered and combined judgment that Germans and actors share honors for being the cheapest dates a stew can accept. Thus, since accepting a date with a German man isn't about to pay off in an evening in the better restaurants, clubs or theatres, you've got to justify your acceptances as accomplishing something for the State. Very few stewardesses accept dates with German passengers.

COFFEE, TEA OR ME?
ITALIANS

Italian men don't pinch stewardesses. True, they use their hands a great deal when talking, but they aren't the grabby kind. What they do is look at you long and hard with eyes that catch hold of a loose thread and unravel all your clothes. They have the ability to *look* your clothes off, a state of affairs possessing almost a hypnotic effect. You *want* to take your clothes off once that spell has been cast.

Rachel was once approached by a rather famous member of Italy's motion picture industry. He cornered her in the galley on a half-empty flight to Los Angeles. He stood with his eyes riveted on the V of her blouse as she poured a cup of coffee for herself. Most of the other passengers were asleep.

"You have a lovely figure, Miss Jones," he purred, never straying his eyes from her bosom.

"I've noticed you've noticed," she answered.

"What is wrong with appreciating the lovely body of a woman?"

"Nothing, now that you mention it."

"I would like to ask you something and feel that you will not take offense, if I may?"

She looked him square in the eye. "Go ahead. I figure I've still got the right to say No." She poured cream in her coffee. "And, I've been asked a lot of silly things before."

He seemed crushed by her use of the word silly. "No, no, no, my dear young lady. There is nothing silly about what I am going to ask. My thoughts are beautiful, pure and on the highest plane of appreciation for what is fine in life. I simply wondered if you would accompany me to my rented villa in Beverly Hills. If you will accept, and I am so confident that you will, I make a solemn oath to you on all that I hold sacred not to even touch your exquisite body with my most unworthy hands. I only wish to look at you as nature intended me to view you, without the harsh cloak of that uniform and those horrible underthings you are forced to wear. I simply wish to fill my eyes with your charm."

Rachel just looked at him. "You're putting me on."

The Italian put his hand to his brow in a supreme gesture of deep and bitter hurt. "Oh, to take such a beautiful and natural wish in so light a vein . . . To think I . . . what is it you say? . . . *put you on?* Oh, no, no, no, no . . . I am simply a lover of living sculpture . . . flesh instead of cold hard marble."

As Rachel tells it, she almost pulled his curly head to her bosom to comfort him, he looked so hurt. She didn't, and left the galley to check on the passengers. She glanced back up the aisle to see him hunched against the wall, his eyes squinting in obvious artistic appreciation of her hip movement, his hand still to his head to help the hurt she had inflicted. He never said another word the rest of the trip.

"I kept passing his seat," she told us over drinks that night, "and I swore each time I was stark naked. I mean, my clothes were *gone*."

AMERICANS

American men always manage to include a hint of humor in their advances to a stewardess. This has to do, I suppose, with the fact that American men never really take sex seriously. They know it's fun, love the obvious pleasures it brings, but just can't make themselves romance a woman. We feel it's the fear of being rebuffed. They seem afraid of attempting too serious an advance. The humiliation of being told No would be too great a blow to their egos.

Maybe it has to do with the need to preserve that rosy-cheeked, Jack Armstrong image American men are stuck with. Whatever it stems from, they manage to come up with the most awkward, clumsy and least effective approaches of all male passengers. It's a shame, really, because of all the potential playmates on a flight, those very same rosy-cheeked Jack Armstrongs are the most appealing. After all, we were brought up sexually with American boys. *But*—as women, we like and need a little bit of the chase, the romancing, the wooing and the intrigue, if only to help us justify to ourselves the final surrender. Of course, we don't want to give the impression that American men never score. We love them. And most of our flings are with them. It's just that they could do a hell of a lot better.

FRENCHMEN

Frenchmen suffer from too lofty a reputation. It's hard to be known as the world's greatest salesman and try to convince someone who's read your clippings that you're not always selling. But despite this knowledge of the French reputation, the aura created still lingers on, especially when a Frenchman can corner you long enough to slide those beautiful sounding syllables off his tongue.

What's fun about accepting an after-flight date with a Frenchman is knowing you won't be rushed. No, the French manner, according to those who have experienced it, is for a lingering, easy evening. Not that we're naïve enough to ignore the eventual goal of our French date. I suppose it's just a matter of enjoying the flight before actually reaching your destination.

We were working a flight with your friend and ours, Betty Big Boobs, when a handsome Frenchman, an architect from Bordeaux, stepped on board for the trip from New York to San Francisco. With all Betty's boasting of the legion of men hot after her body and soul, she never included a Frenchman among her conquests. Maybe she felt she *needed* a Frenchman for her line-up. Anyway, she clamped onto him from the first minute. She rubbed that chest of hers all over him when serving, managed to stretch herself in search of more damned unnamed objects in the overhead rack immediately above him, and, in general, really put on a show.

He, of course, knew it immediately. And he played it beautifully. He played hard-to-get. The more indifferent he became, the bigger and more overt were the advances Betty made to him.

As they left the airplane in San Francisco, Betty whispered to us, "Ah wonder if they're as good as they say—Y'all know, long fuse—short explosion."

You really can't believe anything Betty tells you where men are concerned. She did show up for the next morning's flight, exhausted and beat looking. Her eyes drooped low and dark and her neck showed a series of blotchy, irregular marks. She told us about it in the galley.

"It was so beautiful," she sighed as she counted off the booze lockers. "We danced and he cooed in my ear all those pretty, dirty li'l French words, and he bit my neck and we drank and rubbed noses and all like that. And then when we finally ended up in his room, ah was so damned tired ah didn't know if he was French or Eskimo. Ah guess he enjoyed it, though. He made a lotta noise."

SPANIARDS

It seems that every Spanish gentleman traveling on our flights considers us a collection of young, fighting bulls, despite the obvious conflict in gender. And, a Spaniard loves to wave a red cape of promise in our eyes every mile of the flight.

He's convinced that all women run to red, especially when the matador is dark, mysterious and renowned in matters of love. In effect, he dangles *himself* in front of us, hoping one of his flight's bulls will tire and succumb to the inevitable thrust a bull is subject to at the end of the battle. I myself have tired and lost on one occasion. I've always been kookie over red.

Spaniards like to board the aircraft with their ties off, their shirts unbuttoned three or four from the top and their pants indecently tight. This seems to apply to all men of Spanish origin, regardless of their financial standing. Admitting a slight amount of prejudice, I vote for Spaniards as the world's greatest lovers. I know other girls who agree. The only ones we know who were disenchanted after a fling with a Spaniard were those who took their advances seriously. Spaniards are never looking for anything that even smacks of permanence. They're like married men in that respect. They're simply after an exhilarating and challenging afternoon and evening in the ring with a new, healthy and spirited bull. It's fun to try the sport on occasion, and unlike the case of the real bull, you don't get killed in the end.

ENGLISHMEN

Men from England are effective simply because they ignore you. The trick is not to misread their intentions. They have on their mind what any other male passenger has on his mind. They rely on a passive technique, however, one that goes with the universal impression of the British gentleman.

We've never been able to figure out why the British are considered cold and aloof where physical love is concerned. From what we've heard, some of the gayest, hottest and most unusual bedroom scenes have resulted from a stewardess accepting the stiff and proper advance of a Britisher. They sit in their seats, splendid in tweedy tweeds, sipping the tea you've served them, their curved pipes close by at their sides. Immediately, you project yourself into a future that finds you rubbing toes in front of a roaring fire in the drawing room of an English manor house. A shaggy Collie sleeps at your side and you listen attentively as the master relates how the down-trend on the London Sugar Exchange is playing all sorts of havoc in New York.

"Yes, sir," you answer and promptly ready yourself for the Mrs. Minniver role.

It's all so marvelous dreaming these dreams as you smile at the tweedy gentleman in seat 5A.

But after hearing stories from girls who've tried to play out that dream, you come to realize that men from England are not only as hot blooded as their southern counterparts, but their intentions aren't nearly as honorable as their attitude would suggest.

COFFEE, TEA OR ME?

But you must admire their technique. They actually ward off any advances a stewardess might make, all for the sake of implanting the needed trust in the girl's mind.

ARABS

One of our captains, a guy with at least thirty outside business interests and the money to prove their success, did business of one sort or another with an Arab firm. We were flying with him from St. Louis when he asked us about our plans for that night.

"Look, here's the situation," he said as we passed over Columbus, Ohio. "These two very wealthy Arab businessmen are in New York for a few days and I've arranged a party for them at the Waldorf. It'll be at their suite of rooms and they're pretty damned important to me. I thought you might like to come, enjoy the food and drinks, and rub elbows with all that oil money."

We arrived at 8:30 dressed in our best and were ushered into the suite by a tiny fellow with white turban and gold teeth.

The suite was large and beautiful with many rooms off the main living room. About twenty people were chatting over drinks. There was a heavy smell of lamb in the air and this spicy fragrance mixed with the heavy, sweet odor of some sort of pipe tobacco, brought on a strange feeling of menace.

Our captain introduced us to Elkim al Salim, a sinister-looking man with a big, pock-marked face, heavy brows and a set of gold teeth. It was a little unnerving to see him look us up and down, turn to the captain and smile and nod his head in indication of acceptance, then look at us again. It was like being on the open slave market.

We mixed with some other people for about an hour. The captain brought us fresh drinks and we asked him about the guests most of whom were women.

"Well, don't get shook, but there are quite a few call-girls here tonight. You know how it is. These big shots from other countries like to swing with something different when they get here."

COFFEE, TEA OR ME?

"It must cost him a fortune," Rachel offered.

"It costs me a fortune," the captain answered.

"You?"

"Sure. It's good business to keep him happy. A couple of broads a night and he's good for more business with me."

We never figured our captain for a pimp. We never expected the next line either.

"Look, now don't take me wrong, but he really has his eye on you two. He said something about sweet, unspoiled girls. You both could pick up a bundle here tonight. And you wouldn't be the first stewardesses to moonlight."

Without a word Rachel and I walked away from the captain and went into one of the other rooms to look for our coats. We had just found them on a bed when our Arabian oil mogul with the flashing mouth appeared in the doorway and closed the door behind him.

"I didn't expect you to be ready so soon," he said hoarsely. "But I'm pleased."

We started past him but he barred the way.

"There's no need to go anywhere. Right here is fine. My staff will see that we are not disturbed. I trust the two of you won't become too loud."

"Get out of the way, you pig," Rachel screamed at him. It didn't upset him. In fact, it made him smile.

"I think that's good that you want to fight a little. I like that. Warren said you might struggle a little and I told him that makes it all the more pleasurable for me. Would a little smoke of hashish help?"

"Get your ass out of our way," Rachel piped, "or you'll go back to your harem with my foot still there."

He lunged at me but I stepped aside. Rachel opened the door and I followed her out of the room. We knocked over some drinks on the way through the main room, took a second to upset our captain's drink down the front of his suit, and got out of there on the run.

We were going to report the captain but didn't. He resigned from the airline the next month to take care of his other interests.

Naturally, we've told this story many times to many people. The telling and reactions we get have given us some insight into the whole Arab thing when it comes to sex.

A friend of ours who spent six years in Arabia with The Arabian-American Oil Company explains it this way. Arab men are all sexually unhappy, no matter how large their harem. Women of Saudi Arabia are not attractive by any stretch of the imagination. So, when an Arab has the chance to get out of the world's biggest sand box, he tries to cram as much action as possible into his sex life. It's the same with booze. He can't drink in his own country and consequently can't get enough when he's away. His sex life is actually so unsatisfactory that many Arab men prefer clean, fair-skinned boys to their own women, a problem facing every military and oil man assigned to Arabia.

SCANDINAVIANS

Let's face it. When the women of your country are held in the highest esteem for beauty and love-making, you've got a tough time trying to escape their long shadow. That's the way it is with Scandinavian men. They approach you as if it's the result of maximum and directed effort, and that's a feeling that no woman has ever appreciated. Someday, when the eyes of the male world shift from the Nordic beauties to perhaps Yugoslavian or Congolese women, then Scandinavian men will have a chance. As it is now, they usually ask if you like to ski and if you answer in the affirmative, and you are a true ski nut, things might work out between you. It's also true that Scandinavian men are quiet and seldom make passes. This makes identifying them for game purposes difficult. Generally, they're blond, which is somewhere to start.

IRISHMEN

No matter how an Irishman tries to escape it, he's

COFFEE, TEA OR ME?

bound to be heavy laden by the Cross. This makes giving a stewardess a line difficult because the Irishman, all his professed charm and wit notwithstanding, fumbles in his attempts as he looks over his shoulder for ghosts and spooks and the like. Still, despite the handicap, Irishmen try hard.

This talk of the heavy yoke of religion is not confined to the old-world Irishman. Even a member of the young, "God is dead," generation is tightly bound by ever-present fears of spending an eternity in Hell for one night with a stewardess. He usually will make the decision to act on his physical motivation, but he's rarely able to shake the feeling that he's being watched.

We know a West Coast stewardess who was quite serious about a young Irish accountant but finally gave up.

"That business of crossing yourself everytime gave me the creeps," she confesses. "I kept getting the feeling he was praying for me to perform good. Like a baseball player."

Actually, a stewardess probably would be happiest with a Unitarian. You have a clearer conscience when you know everything will be all right the next day if you find a little old lady to help across the street.

SCOTSMEN

Never believe all that jazz about a Scotsman being cheap. We've found them to be free spenders, a finding that rates them high on our list of prospective companions. They'll spend every cent they have in pursuit of a particular girl, usually with substantial results.

A Scot is moody, proud, unpredictable and difficult to get along with in many instances, but once he's interested enough to commit himself, you can do a pretty effective job of making things run your way.

RUSSIANS

We seldom have any trouble with Russian men. Our requirements are such that we must keep a reasonably trim figure. Russians can't seem to see women except on the end of a plow, and it's obvious we don't have the necessary pulling power. Russian passengers usually just watch the movie or listen to Russian classics on stereo.

JAPANESE

Miniaturization just doesn't seem to have an advantage where sex is concerned. TV sets and radios, yes—but never sex.

* * *

Once the nationality of the men on our flight is established, we turn our attention, after serving drinks, dinner, wine and strawberry parfait, to an analysis of their field of work.

There are sure and certain tip-offs, of course. The style of his brief case, a football helmet over the arm, a copy of *Method Acting* clutched to the breast, a uniform, a typewriter, a stethoscope, a storyboard, a picture of Earl Warren or a button reading "Black Power"—all are clues to what the man does. When such obvious aids are evident, we take off three points.

We should also preface the next section by admitting that good or bad personal experiences with a certain man in a certain profession will tend to taint these comments slightly. The same holds true for the previous section on nationalities. You'll just have to accept our opinions as presented and react in your own way.

PUBLIC RELATIONS MEN

Men engaged in this dubious profession are usually confused about their work. And it shows in their approach to us. After striking up an idle conversation about the altitude, weather or ETA, they'll tell you about their job as image builders, management consultants, marketing executives or community relations experts. They never will admit to being flacks unless they function in

COFFEE, TEA OR ME?

the show-business area. If they are of the theatrical type, you can count on being told, "I can make you a star, baby." And sometimes they can.

PR men rank high on our date list. They always dress nicely and have huge expense accounts. Those with gray hair have larger expense accounts than others. A typical opening from a PR man might start with, "Say, honey, I've got an idea you might be interested in. We're opening a new bottle plant in Tempe, Arizona, and you'd make a perfect queen of the ceremony. You know, cut the ribbon and pose for the local press and that jazz. How about it?"

"Oh, are you a public relations man?"

"No, I'm a management consultant. I double in community relations."

"Gee, would I get paid?"

"Hard to tell how much at this time, but I swing a lot of weight with JB . . . He's chairman now. Good exposure for you. Never know about those things."

If you've been flying long enough and have been involved in your own airline's press activities you'll turn him down cold.

There is a sure-fire way to make *your* approach to a PR man if he looks interesting to you. One of our fellow stewardesses from Los Angeles always used this line:

"Well, that's just wonderful that you're in marketing and community relations. Doesn't that involve trying to place stories in newspapers and on TV?"

"Yes. That's just part of the over-all team effort of the marketing management deck. We've all got to be pretty good writers, you know."

Our friend would let enough time elapse and then throw in the clincher.

"Funny thing I should meet a marketing man. My brother is managing editor of the *Los Angeles Times*. I guess he's the one who says what goes in the paper. I really don't know too much about these things."

He's hooked. He'll spend every dime he has wining and dining you, his motives double-edged. He figures he can either take you to bed, get a story in the *LA Times,* or maybe both.

It does help if your brother really *is* in a high capacity in the news media.

ENGINEERS

Gravely lacking any background, academic or practical, in the arts or humanities, engineers will try to make chit-chat about the aircraft's performance characteristics or outer space or why the ball always comes down after it goes up. It's best to feign ignorance if you're interested; engineers hate anyone to know anything about their sphere of knowledge.

Occasionally, an engineer will have the brains to realize that a stewardess isn't interested in all that mechanical routine. This type of individual will say something like, "Have you read *Moby Dick* lately?" You've got to give him credit for trying.

"No. I always wait for the paperback on these new best-sellers. The prices they get are ridiculous."

Now that he's impressed us with his deep love for literature, he springs the big question.

"How about *The Carpetbaggers*?" Oh, that leer, that twisted grin and those raised eyebrows. "Pretty blue stuff, huh?"

Again, it depends on whether you want to continue the relationship. If you do, you come back with, "Well, times have changed and I think we all have a looser, more realistic view of these things. At least, I do."

I personally can't stand engineers. One actually took the dinner check in Cleveland and figured the mark-up of the food we ate with his slide rule right at the table. Rachel dated one who damned near gouged her chest out with a pocket full of pencils, pens, slide rule, ruler, pipe and fingernail file.

But they make good, solid husbands, if you can stand a lifetime of excerpts from *Moby Dick*.

ACTORS

Actors usually try very hard to appear humble. They

COFFEE, TEA OR ME?

expect this unexpected humility to completely sweep a girl off her feet, or at least result in an autograph request or a quickie in the jump seat.

Actors will yawn frequently when they talk to you. They like to use vulgar, four-letter words in their speech, to show their non-comformity with us run-of-the-mill folk. They love to end their sentences, especially those containing many four-letter words, with an ever-so-slight lowering of the voice to indicate sophistication.

Actors are make-believe people. They usually ask you to meet them in some delightful female impersonation spot on *The Strip,* or a delicious little stretch of sandy beach where so and so film was photographed on location, or on a terrace in the Hollywood Hills where that darling old actress met with that absolutely dreadful fall.

Every stewardess accepts a date with an actor at least once in her flying career. It's a necessity if you're to go back home and answer all the questions about your newfound career of glamour and excitement.

My only intimate experience with an actor came on my eighteenth month with the airline. The girls on the flight presented me with a cupcake decorated with one and a half candles, right after we served the meal on a New York-Los Angeles trip. This little ceremony seemed to interest a fairly well-known leading man who'd fallen asleep the minute he boarded the aircraft and slept all through dinner. I was naturally flattered when he called me over to his seat and wished me many years of happy flying.

"I think you ought to have a little more celebration than that cupcake," he told me in a voice that was deep and familiar. "I'd like to provide it for you when we reach Los Angeles."

I was tingling with excitement. I searched my mind for things I had read about this star's marital status. I remembered he had recently married a starlet after divorcing wife number three or four. But that didn't make one bit of difference with me. This was my big chance to go out with a movie star, a man who left millions of women drooling in their popcorn in theaters across the nation.

COFFEE, TEA OR ME?

His starlet would just have to do without him for one night.

"That sounds wonderful. I'd love to," I told him.

"Fine. Here's the address of an apartment in Beverly Hills. It belongs to a friend of mine. Come up as soon as you can and I'll have the staff prepare dinner for us. I can't stand all that nightclub rat race in Hollywood. I'll even get our own live music. After all, a girl doesn't survive a year and a half in these damn airplanes everyday, does she?"

"She sure doesn't," I said breathlessly. "I'll be there."

I was the talk of the galley all the rest of the trip. And I was sworn to make a full detailed report the next morning.

I watched him leave the airport, carefully noting whether his newest wife was on hand to greet him. The only person I could see was a Chinese driver in a black uniform.

After I rushed through my post-flight routine, I took a cab to the address he had given me. It was hardly to be called an apartment, at least not by my standards. It was a large house set back behind an even larger house. The long driveway was dark and I made my way carefully along exquisite shrubbery that formed a clean-cut silhouette in the moonlight.

I went to ring the bell, but the door opened before my finger reached the button. It was the same Chinese man who'd picked up the movie star—*my* movie star. (I think I'll call him Robert for the rest of the story.)

The chauffeur-butler led me up a long stairway to a massive room that spanned the entire length of the house. It was simply gorgeous. I sank ankle-deep into the white carpet. My host came across the room to join me, his hands outstretched, his eyes indicating pleasure in seeing me. I felt silly in my wrinkled uniform and cursed myself for not having changed before coming. I had a dress in my bag downstairs and wanted desperately to run down and get it.

"You look simply beautiful, my dear," he said as he took my hands.

"You're very sweet, but I have a dress in my bag downstairs and I think I ought to change."

"By all means, if that's what you'd like to do. But why a dress? Why not be comfortable?"

"I have slacks . . . and a sweater, if that would be all right."

"That would be wonderful." He laughed that same wicked laugh that always sent me to the powder room when I saw him in the movies. "I'm a nudist at heart. But I won't put you through that kind of embarrassment . . . yet. Go change while I make you a drink."

I ran downstairs, grabbed my bag, and followed the butler to a powder room. I pictured Robert upstairs swishing gin around in a crystal pitcher as I fumbled with the bottons on the uniform. The slacks I had with me were the tightest I owned, and the sweater wasn't any looser. I came out of the bathroom and went back upstairs to join Robert.

He handed me my drink, toasted me, and we both took a healthy sip. I had just brought the glass down from my lips when he grabbed me and planted the biggest, wettest kiss on my lips I'd ever experienced.

"You're very lovely, you know," he crooned. I wanted to look around for the cameras and microphones. He said it just as he'd said it to all those glamorous actresses in films. I grabbed him and returned the kiss.

"Easy, easy, my dear. The night is ours. We'll make it ours."

I know that kind of dialogue sounds corny. But who was I to argue with his script writer? Besides, here I was with my reason for flying—my glamour, my excitement, my romance. Who would believe this back in Amarillo?

He kissed me again and moved away. "Now a superb dinner," he said, "the perfect wine and music for the soul and for the two of us." I was totally under his spell as he spoke those words to me. He pushed a button and two servants entered carrying large, elaborate trays. They seated us at a table in front of the floor-to-ceiling picture window, and served dinner with expert care. The steak was delicious and the wine cool and dry. I couldn't take

COFFEE, TEA OR ME?

my eyes from his as he deftly consumed his food, sipped his wine and talked about a picture he'd just made in Spain. I knew my reactions were those of a silly school girl but I didn't care. It was just that simple—I didn't care.

The piano player arrived as we were starting on dessert. He apologized to Robert for being late and immediately sat down and tinkled familiar melodies on the grand piano in the corner. Imagine having your own piano player on call for last-minute dinner dates! You bet I was impressed.

We finished playing out the dinner scene from our script and proceeded to the next stage, the conquest.

Robert picked me up and carried me, like a bride, across the room to the biggest couch I'd ever seen. It ran at least twelve feet long, was easily five feet wide, and was covered with what seemed to be duck feathers, all soft and warm and fleecy. He placed me gently on the couch and slipped his hands under my sweater. It came off easily, and he unzipped my slacks. Soon, we were both on the couch nude. It's a funny thing to think of at a moment like that, but I noticed he didn't seem as husky and tan as he did on the silver screen. It was a disappointment, but a mild one. We made love there, smooth, satisfying love during which Robert whispered marvelous endearments.

Afterwards we fell back exhausted. Then, like an explosion, a door flew open and someone started clapping with great gusto. "Bravo, bravo," a female voice yelled. I leaped up from the couch to see a young, shapely blonde coming towards the couch. Robert got up slowly and bowed to her from his naked waist.

He introduced us.

"Miss Baker, my wife, Marcia. Marcia, Trudy Baker."

"You've outdone yourself, Robert," his wife said as she looked me over from head to toe. "The whole scene was marvelous." Then she started to slip out of her tight shift. The piano player who had discreetly vanished a little earlier came back into the room.

"Wait a minute," I shrieked. "What's going on here?"

"She's sweet, Robert," Marcia said, now as nude as we were. "Hurry up, Louis," she scolded the piano player who was hanging his pants over the chair I'd sat in during dinner.

"Oh no," I said as I quickly got back into my bra, pants, sweater and slacks. "I'm not the orgy type. Thanks for dinner."

I ran down the stairs, grabbed my bag and raced along the winding drive. I must have walked for an hour before finding a cab to take me to the hotel.

I told the story to Rachel the next morning with great embarrassment.

"What are you upset about, hon?" she asked. "Chalk it up as something to tell your grandchildren."

I think my night with a leading man was the beginning of a new phase in my flying career. The yen for glamour seemed to be gone. I had no further interest in actors after Robert and his troupe. Well, except Marlon Brando. I still wanted to meet him. You know how it is.

ATHLETES

Most athletes like to sit and flex before dinner. We've all read about those college whiz kids who plow through the opposition on the gridiron every Saturday afternoon, and still breeze through advanced bacterial science with straight honor grades. Sorry, but we've never met one. All the athletes we've met have been rather slow and ponderous in their attempts to converse with us, unless they're complete pigs and just grab (linebackers tend toward this approach).

Of course, the nature of the sport they're engaged in determines somewhat their mental standing. Golf pros, tennis pros, swimming champs and badminton winners tend to be a little more intelligent, at least in the way they present themselves to their stewardesses.

But no matter what sport the man is engaged in, one dominant and salient fact stands out: Athletes are the cheapest guys around.

Rachel dated a professional baseball player once. Their date consisted of one line of bowling, a game of skeet ball at the local penny arcade, and a shared pizza.

Never let it be said that stewardesses look only to a man for how much money he'll spend. That's not at all true. But when a guy is making forty thousand a year and starts reaching for a feel ten minutes after you've gotten into his car, he's got to come up with something better than skeet ball.

There is some advantage in dating an athlete if you're a sports fan yourself. He usually can come up with free tickets for you. He's sold most of his free ones to people like his sister, mother and brother, but he should have a few left over. Naturally these tickets always come with strings attached. For our money, or lack of it, we'd prefer to watch the game on TV with a date who just bought us dinner at "21".

WRITERS

Most writers, even the very successful ones, never acquire a public name. Consequently, when you find out he's a writer, don't ask which novel he's written. He probably hasn't, but will say he's working on one.

Writers are the most quiet and reserved men on an airplane. They remain introspective and withdrawn, devoting most of their energy to obtaining an extra drink above the two-drink maximum.

The classic approach for a writer is to say he's researching a book or movie about stewardesses and would like to spend a few hours asking some questions. We usually accept, after convincing ourselves he really is a writer. Why not accept? You either become the underlying source of inspiration for a great novel or end up reading all your little idiosyncrasies in another best-seller, usually a very dirty one. Either way, you've become a Lady of Letters. The only possible trouble you can encounter is when you marry and your husband reads about all your little idiosyncrasies in someone else's book.

COFFEE, TEA OR ME?

Stewardesses who majored in English in college are fair game for writers traveling on their flights. The writer can succeed with the girl as long as she envisions him writing the great American novel or Oscar-winning screen play. As soon as she finds out he's only a junior editor of the *Montana Coal, Iron and Cobalt Quarterly,* she loses interest.

Between us, Rachel and I can count eleven different men who approached us with the line, "I'm writing a book on stewardesses and would love to be able to talk with you."

What we're planning on doing next is a book on millionaires. We intend to approach men of great wealth and say, "We're doing a book on millionaires and would love to be able to talk with you."

It's called reverse seduction.

DOCTORS

Doctors are rich. Having so much money gives a doctor a sense of total power, except over those patients he's always dunning for a late bill. He also picks up a false sense of security in having to sound so cocksure in front of every patient, despite the fact he's never seen this disease before. We grow up thinking doctors can do no wrong. Then we discover how silly this is, especially when you're their patient—or stewardess.

The stewardess consensus is that doctors usually make their pitch via a note placed on their tray after dinner. Usually, it will contain something terribly clever like, "I am a doctor. I'm staying at the Mark Hopkins. My room number is 2030. Nine o'clock."

If you're pregnant, getting one of these notes could be construed as a good deal. If you're not, but maybe have a headache, it might also make sense to trudge up to his room. But remember—all doctors are married. You must have this firmly in mind before making any decision. And if you do decide to go, be on time. Doctors hate to be kept waiting.

COFFEE, TEA OR ME?

POLITICIANS

We feel sorry for politicians. They must, out of deference to their constitutents, be at all times above-board and pure. They never are, of course, but they must make it look that way. Lately though, with the apparent acceptance of sin, misuse of funds, blackmail and pay-offs by our nation's leaders, politicians seem to be a little more relaxed, more pliable and more willing to accept the fact they're the same as other men.

If a politician is about to make a play for you, he'll test you for signs of a loose tongue.

"Well, young lady, just what part of this fair nation of ours produced that charming accent?" he'll start.

"Texas, sir." Good answer.

"Well, how about that. You folks sure are going to benefit from that new dam. You know, I voted for it."

"What new dam?"

"Ho, ho, ho, got a sense of humor, too, huh?"

"Yes, sir."

"Well, no sense in a pretty young thing like you worrying about dams and things like that. That's for people like me to worry about, ho, ho, ho."

"That's certainly a lot to worry about."

"That's my job."

"Ho, ho, ho."

"By the way, young lady, you don't happen to know Sammy Jim Bowie, do you? Fine young Texas Congressman."

"Sammy? I went to high school with Sammy He sure was a creep. Guess he's changed."

That kills it. Had I extolled Sammy's virtues, or at least remained noncommittal about him, it might have gone further. But politicians hate to be talked about behind their backs. They do it too much themselves.

If the politician happens to be from your own home territory, there is no chance to play with him. Politicians always play far away from home and their voters Puerto Rico or Alaska are safer than the local motel.

COFFEE, TEA OR ME?

If you do become entwined with a politician, you can count on a secret, over-the-shoulder romance that must be carried on between votes on poverty programs and fund-raising appearances with his wife. It's better in the long run to stay away from politicians unless you figure they're going to lose in their next election and return to private life. When that happens, they're likely to divorce their wives for losing the election for them, and might even consider taking you on as a permanent addition to their new household and career.

NEWSPAPER MEN

Newspaper men are usually traveling free, courtesy of your airline's public relations department. They're on your airplane with your airline's hope that someday, somehow, somewhere they'll say something nice about your airline. Before they board, they're fed, boozed-up and taken to the airport in a long, black Carey limousine. They're already drunk when they get on the plane, and you've been instructed by the airport public relations man to forget about the two-drink rule where this elite member of the press is concerned.

Obviously, newspapermen are spoiled by your public relations department. In fact, they're spoiled and drunk enough to think *you* come with booze, food, limousine and free ticket.

Their approach is often direct, clumsy, distasteful, arrogant, lewd and highly annoying.

All of this poses a dilemma for the stewardess. Just how much does she want to endear herself to her airline, its management and stockholders? Do you go out of your way to be nice to the slob with the pencil behind his ear in 3B, or do you follow your natural inclinations and spill hot coffee on him? There is no answer, at least not in the manual.

MILITARY MEN

Military men are generally polite in their advances to

COFFEE, TEA OR ME?

us. Whether this results from their rigid military training or is inborn is unanswered in our minds. But they'll approach us nicely, directly and without great fuss.

Unfortunately, men in uniform assume a second-class paranoia because they're flying at half-fare. It's a shame they feel this way because we look at their half-fare status as something that should be done for our men in the armed services.

If a military man does make a pitch to a stewardess, and if she does accept, you can count on a pleasant evening with the best bars and restaurants included. Once a man gets away from the grim confines of his club at the military installation, he likes to enjoy the good life. And we do, too.

ADVERTISING MEN

Advertising men are insecure. Their need to conform to every little whim of fashion indicates this. And because they're insecure, they approach us as they would a potential account, anxious to get all they can *now* because tomorrow we might sign up with another agency. Actually, their attitude in this respect is probably a realistic one.

But their insecurity poses even greater problems where a girl is concerned.

We know a stewardess who entered into a prolonged relationship with one of these three-button boys (they only button the top two on their jackets). He worked for one of the largest agencies in New York.

This stewardess, forgetting her loop or pill or whatever it was she was using, became pregnant by the Madison Avenue flash. She told him about her condition on a Friday night.

"Give me a few days to run this thing around the track, honey," he said thoughtfully. "Let's swish it around a little before we drink it."

She hadn't heard from him by Wednesday of the next week so tried to call him at the agency. She was told he no longer worked there but could be found at another agency.

She called the other agency and was told he had never started there because the account never materialized. But they thought he was with a pharmaceutical agency. She tried there and found he was out of town.

She tried him again the following week but he was no longer employed by the pharmaceutical agency. They didn't know where he was.

The gal had her condition taken care of, a course of action always under great debate when we get together, and finally ran into her ad-hero at Friday's, a bar on First Avenue. She let him know just how furious she was.

"Well, sweetie, you know how it is. I wasn't running from you. This agency business is a tough sell, tough sell. Run all the time. By the way, I just put in a new $597.95 amplifier in my pad. Let's go up and have a drink and talk about old times."

"Let's not rush into things," she replied. "Why not run some juice through your friggin' $597.95 amplifier and see if it blows up."

Assuming you don't misplace your loop, ad men can be good for a fast night on the town. We find that ad men make more pitches to us than any other group of men. They all have a strange attraction to stewardesses which is part of their insecurity. An ad man never dates just *a girl*. She has to have a handle, an image for him to date. That's why ad men, when recounting past dates, will always say she was a stewardess, a model, an artist, a bunny, a writer, an actress, a director or an heiress. It's kind of sad, really. A *girl* just won't do.

Their insecurity shows up in other ways, too. Everything they own has a price tag on it. They have a $597.95 amplifier, a $200 chair, a $107.25 watch or a $210 suit. And until you get on to this dribble, you tend to be as impressed as they are. But then again ad men are impressed easily. So are their bosses and clients who prefer their underlings to look right rather than think right.

But there are worse dates.

CIVIL SERVANTS

Asking a civil servant what he'd like to drink is like

COFFEE, TEA OR ME?

trying to get service from one when you're renewing your driver's license. He'll chit-chat with his seat partner, look out the window, clean his nails and light a cigar After you've asked him for the fourth time, he'll look at you and say, "What do you want?"

Civil servants are a small part of our life. They aren't inclined to make a pitch and the few that do try fail mightily. But identifying them correctly helps build up our point score.

LAWYERS

A stewardess usually takes the first step in her own seduction where a lawyer is concerned. Everyone in the world has a legal problem of one sort or another and wants free legal advice.

Consequently, all a lawyer need do is announce his profession at the earliest part of the flight. This takes him out of the running as far as the identification game is concerned, but puts him strongly in the running as far as the evening is concerned.

"I have a silly question and I'll bet you're tired of being asked silly questions but would you mind being asked another?" the stewardess will ask at an opportune moment.

"Go right ahead," replies the lawyer.

"Well, you see, three of us have this rent-controlled apartment in New York and the lease is up soon and we want to know whether the landlord can raise our rent now."

"Well, there are many factors to be considered here This kind of a situation can be long and costly where the courts are concerned. That is to say, deeming your stand legal, in view of the validity of the elements heretofore contained in the lease instrument, might as well be construed as a *de facto* admission. See?"

"I think so."

"But I think it would be silly to spend all the legal fees required over this situation. Look, I'll call you when I come back to New York and we'll set a date when I can come up, look at the apartment and check the lease "

"You have to actually look at the apartment?"

"Of course. That is to say, if, in fact, there is evidence of landlord neglect in certain vulnerable areas, we may be able to ascertain the validity of the entire clause in the lease instrument, as opposed to a part or portion thereof as might effect the entire agreement."

"Here's my number. And bless you."

MUSICIANS

It's hard to tell a musician unless he's carrying a bass fiddle. When he does carry one, you're in for trouble.

Most airlines will sell a bass fiddle a seat at half the usual fare. This instrument is large and fragile, and its owner must carry his bass fiddle in this manner. Putting it in the cargo area of the plane would be certain disaster.

We had a jazz bass player on a flight to Los Angeles where he was to appear at the Monterey Jazz Festival. He carried his wooden seat companion, strapped it in with great care and settled back for the flight. The fiddle caused no trouble until mealtime.

"Hey chick, where's the meat for my friend?" he asked.

"That's funny, sir. But obviously we can't give a meal to a bass fiddle."

"You're puttin' me on, chick. Like I bought a seat for my friend and he should get a meal, like."

"That is so funny. But we can't."

"Oh, like, I'm gonna flip baby all over this big eagle."

"All right. I'll get your friend a meal."

"Hey, wait a minute. Like, you forgot to serve him his juice, too."

"His juice."

"Yeh, like, his goon-water, you know. His *booze*."

"Absolutely not. Food, yes. But I know you're just going to drink his two drinks and that's against the rules."

"The rules? The rules? To be broken, baby, to be broken. One seat's worth two drinks, right?"

"I'll check the captain."

"No, no, no, swinger. Don't upset our fly-boy. I'm like

shook enough already. Just bring my friend two gins on the rocks. No peel."

We were tempted to pour the drinks into the monster strapped next to the musician. But we didn't. Better a drunk bass fiddle than an upset musician.

Generally, musicians are good passengers. And their approach can always be counted on to be funny, different and unobtrusive.

TEACHERS

Teachers have managed to con the world for too long a time. The general conception we all have about teachers is that they represent purity of mind and body, a dedicated group of men and women interested only in educating the nation's youth.

But they're not that way. If you've been around at all you know that female teachers rank among the world's greatest swingers. Put a knowledgeable guy in a bar loaded with women of different backgrounds and he'll head for the teacher. He knows.

The same goes for the masculine version of the teaching profession. Both sexes are weary of being looked at constantly by their boards of education for any violation of the highest code of personal conduct. Put them on an airplane where there isn't likely to be that scrutiny and you've got a man or woman on the prowl.

Married men working as teachers are even more prone to swing. They have both the school board and their wives on their back, and succeeding in accomplishing a little action on the side is as welcome as a pay increase.

The specific approach a teacher will make depends a great deal on what he teaches. If he teaches business law, he'll take the lawyer's tack. Math teachers will go after you à la engineer. And so on.

SALESMEN

All the traveling salesmen jokes are true, at least based

COFFEE, TEA OR ME?

on what we've observed. The unique thing about a salesman is that he isn't at all concerned whether he scores with you or not. He has plenty of girls in the cities he visits, and his interest in you reflects his need to keep his stable fully stocked.

There is very little we can add to all the stories about salesmen. It seems the majority of our passengers are salesmen and consequently we're on the receiving end quite often. We suppose salesmen have become "old hat." Other men now have expense accounts and are good talkers. The day of the traveling salesman knocking over girls like bowling pins is gone.

Salesmen are generous to stewardesses. Very few flights go by on which we don't receive some sample from some salesman. His samples don't buy us but they're nice to receive.

SUMMATION

Everyone has his own special pitch and to attempt to be all-inclusive in this chapter would be impossible. We'd end up covering such professions as undertakers, the clergy, mailmen, grape pickers and male secretaries.

Despite the many bad thoughts we have about many men, we usually end up marrying one. That's the way it's supposed to go, and we wouldn't have it any other way.

Should we be asked to divulge what we consider the perfect pitch a man can make to us, we'd both agree that a courteous, reserved man with a sense of humor and a respect for the difficult job we perform would rank at the top of the list. Of course, climbing aboard our airplane with a copy of this book in hand will surely elicit some conversation from any stewardess. You might even end by checking the validity of what we've said.

CHAPTER XX

"Should We Strike?"

We belong to a union. It seems a good idea. As stewardesses, we're subject to an incredible number of company policies and rulings that can make life miserable. Our union tries to make our lives easier. It gives us the comfort of numbers, in a group with common problems and goals. Rachel and I have never been involved in a strike by our own stewardess union. But we've been affected by strikes by other unions within the airline.

We remember one strike when all the maintenance men walked out. They wanted their mother's birthday off or some such holiday. Naturally, without these people to fix the airplanes when they got sick, the airline couldn't operate. They immediately put all employees on half-pay, threatening that if the strike wasn't settled within fifteen days, we'd all go on no-pay. It wasn't a happy thought.

On the sixteenth day of the strike, money stopped coming. That meant a scramble for rent, food and cosmetics funds. It was at this gray point in our lives that we realized the value of having a steady beau, preferably one with a well-paying job. The girls who did enjoy such a situation made out pretty well.

The strike also gave the hoarders the last laugh on those of us who had scorned them for their frugality. A fringe benefit of being a stewardess is the chance to walk off a flight occasionally with a couple of filets, a lobster tail or two, miniature packages of cigarettes and whatever bottles of booze the first-class passengers didn't drink. Usually when we'd come home with an unusually good haul, we'd throw a party. Not so with the stockpilers. Their food would be carefully wrapped in foil, labeled with their name and placed in the freezer for their own use. The miniature bottles would find a secure place in a locked drawer and the cigarettes would nestle alongside the bottles. Most of us think of this kind of Hooverism as distasteful and even anti-social. Except during a no-pay period.

We managed though, with the nurturing of the stew-bums who gladly seized this opportunity to further entrench themselves in our minds and hearts. Stew-bums have saved many a stewardess during a strike. There were rent parties, too, to which we invited everyone we knew. Each guest brought a bottle and five dollars for the cause —our cause. It was all marvelous fun and the take from such a party often far exceeded the rent needs.

In retrospect, some strikes were fun times. But others weren't, especially when the strikes were on other airlines. As soon as another airline which flies routes also served by our line goes on strike, we beef up service to those cities. This is all very neighborly. But it puts a severe strain on stews and crew to deliver the extra service.

Once in a true picture of management ingenuity, the airline brought back ex-stewardesses to fly during such a strike. Rachel spotted one of these re-hired stewardesses in the terminal as we walked toward our flight.

"The uniform looks funny with the white hair," she commented casually.

I saw what she meant. "It's not white hair, Rachel. Just sort of gray."

"It's white, Trudy. She must be at least forty."

Rachel was right. The stewardess in question had obviously been away from the airline for more than just a few years. To our surprise she was flying our trip with us. She was very pleasant, smiled a lot and seemed willing to help.

We were off the ground and ready to bring the meals out of the galley when we realized our white-haired stewardess wasn't around. We looked for her in the cabin and found her chatting with a businessman.

"I used to be a stewardess, you know," she was telling him. "I'm married now and have four children. It's fun to be back helping."

If only she would help.

"I don't think I should actually serve meals, girls," she said. "I've been away too long and you two are expert at it. I'll keep everyone happy so you won't have to bother with that."

Today, in the jet era, the only way to keep passengers happy, to the extent they can be happy is to give them what they're supposed to have, and give it fast. Our forty-year-old good-will merchant went up and down the aisle smiling at everyone and telling them how much fun it was to be back flying and so on and so on. In the meantime, the two of us struggled to get the drinks and meals served, a chore that's hard enough to accomplish with three girls working at it.

We managed, despite our returning angel of the skies. Then she got sick. Fortunately, she made it to the lavatory.

Close to arrival time she came into the galley as we frantically tried to clean up. She said, "I know this may sound silly to you, but I'd love to make the PA announcement when we arrive. For old time's sake, you know. I think the people in the cabin would appreciate it, too. After all, they remember when I was flying the line."

"Why not?" Rachel answered.

We landed, and our *senior* stew got on the microphone.

"Ladies and gentlemen, this is . . . This is *Miss* Caleb. It wasn't so long ago that I was flying to cities such as this on a regular basis. In fact, many of you might even remember me. Well, anyway, coming back to serve aviation and everyone of you dear passengers is something I was most willing to do when asked by my airline's management."

Rachel shoved the standard arrival announcement sheet under her nose. She ignored it.

"Of course, all this new meal service has me a little befuddled. But the training we received in how to make a passenger feel comfortable in his flight never leaves one. A stewardess never forgets her dedication."

"Read this," Rachel said in a hard whisper, pointing to the announcement form.

"So, ladies and gentlemen, I say it is a vast pleasure to be back serving . . ."

Rachel cut the PA system, took the mike from our matronly partner and gave the usual arrival pitch. The ex-stewardess seemed hurt, but smiled through it all.

We didn't even bother trying to say goodbye to the passengers as they deplaned. Our retread was right there shaking hands and laughing and cocking her head in hu-

COFFEE, TEA OR ME?

mility at their words of encouragement. She came back to the galley after everyone had departed, fluffed her hair and stated, "Imagine that. One of the gentlemen asked me for a date. Once a stewardess, always a stewardess, huh?"

"Sure," I said.

We flew with her again. She still managed not to do anything physical; we didn't allow her near the PA. After the strike we asked her why she'd called herself Miss on that one PA announcement she'd made.

"Well, I think the male passengers would prefer the illusion that we're all single. It makes them feel they might have a chance with *us*, silly boys." And this after passing around snapshots of her four children.

Want to know some of our gripes? Here they are:

Thefts: Our complaint is not about having things stolen from us. What does upset us is to have a supervisor grab us after a flight and say, "All right girls, empty your purse and coat pockets on the seat." She's come on the aircraft secure she'll find a filet in each pocket, a dozen miniature bottles of bourbon in the purse and a frayed copy of *Field & Stream* under our girdle. The maddening thing is that these supervisors stole the airline blind during their flying days. Now, with a new-found sense of morality, they've turned private eye, their targets the girls who report to them.

Being fired: It was easy for a stewardess to be fired, until the union decided to show a little of its feminine muscle. There's no doubt, as many a seasoned traveler will testify, that a few girls do deserve to lose their jobs. What bothers us are the good stewardesses who, for one reason or another, make one small slip in performance or regulation, then receive a lay-off or even the pink slip.

There was one rather famous case in which a girl was fired for being caught in the lap of the flight engineer. What had happened was this: the girl went to the flight deck to serve coffee and was pulled into the fellow's lap in a silly little gesture of playfulness. At the precise moment she landed, a supervisor, working the trip undetected, entered the cockpit. She immediately suspended the girl.

The union fought back. And won. The girl is still flying the line.

Certainly, there have been firings that appear warranted. Annual physicals will occasionally turn up a girl who is virtually blind. Or one who is pregnant. Also, certain girls will find themselves fed up with flying and, rather than resign, direct their change of attitude against any passenger who happens to be near.

Bad letters: It's appalling how many airline passengers write letters of complaint about stewardesses. Again, to indicate a rational view of this situation, we must admit that some letters are justified. But most really aren't.

Drinking or smoking on the job: Have you ever been on an airplane when the heating system decided to stop working? We have, and a quick shot of bourbon can do wonders for the human heating system of the stewardess. But we don't try it, even if our hands turn blue. It's against the rules. Same goes for smoking. We can't smoke when working a trip, even in the confines of the galley. Actually, the no drinking and smoking rules are sensible ones. But as with any rule, exceptions should be allowed when conditions warrant them.

Weight: Every airline watches its stewardesses with the eye of a carnival weight-guesser. They feel that even a pound over your listed weight is a pound to be lost. They make it easy for you to lose that pound. They suspend you. You sit home worrying about that pound and you eat to stave off the frustration. It's a losing battle. It's our belief that every girl can look attractive within a range of weights. Sure, some girls do become *fat,* and that shouldn't be allowed. But Rachel looks better when she's about five pounds over her listed weight. That's what should count.

Age: Every airline has its own rulings about when a girl becomes too old to fly. Never has a ruling caused so much controversy as with those airlines which retire girls at thirty-two. True, they insure us ground jobs if we've stayed around that long. But most of us can't think of

COFFEE, TEA OR ME?

anything more distasteful than working as a stewardess supervisor. Of course, there's always the chance to teach at the stewardess college under the guidance of Big Momma. No thanks. If we haven't hooked a man before age thirty-two, we'd just as soon keep flying.

Many men believe a woman really isn't in her prime, both physically and emotionally, until she's in her thirties. But some airlines have decided we're over the hill at thirty. We're certainly not advocating white-haired stewardesses. We recognize the value to the airline of pretty young stewardesses. But thirty-two? Over the hill? Too old?

How about an age limit on stewardess supervisors? They all think young until they become supervisors. Then they adopt older ideas, believing their supervisor's role calls for a mother's approach to a daughter. OK. Let's have a minimum age for supervisors of sixty-two. That way they can justify their actions and stay out of trouble with vice presidents at the same time.

Marriage: Some airlines allow their girls to fly even after they're married. This seems reasonable, especially in light of their desire that we don't play around with the male passengers on our trips. Airlines that make you stop flying after marriage do it because they want men passengers to envision conquest after conquest when they travel. These airlines also say a married girl will find it difficult to make her marriage work without interfering with her stewardess schedule. That might be. Let us get married and when our performance slips, fire us. But let us get married—if we've found someone to ask us.

Anti-marriage rules force many girls to hide the fact they're married. This is a tricky feat to pull off and produces dialog like this:

"You devil, you. I just found out you've moved and are married."

"I'm not married."

"But what about Harry, the man in your apartment?"

"Oh, Harry. I just live with him."

A stewardess who is married and hiding the fact must always have two telephones in the apartment so a man

COFFEE, TEA OR ME?

won't answer. A secretly married stewardess must also conceal the fact from her parents. This can be difficult when they come to visit. Hubby goes to the YMCA and is introduced as a friend.

"He seems very nice," says your mother. "He'd make a good husband, I bet."

"I don't know, mom. He might turn out to be mean."

Of course, there's no way to continue the pretense when you become pregnant. They've got you there.

"It was quite a honeymoon," she says to her supervisor. "Got pregnant right away." The supervisor knows she was married long before and doesn't buy her story.

Change of address notification: We must notify the airline of any change of address within twenty-four hours of the change. Good rule. Makes sense. Except where Betty Elkin was concerned.

Betty came down with appendicitis one night and her roommate rushed her to the hospital. "Don't forget to call the airline and tell them," Betty said as they wheeled her to the operating room. Her roommate promised, but forgot. Betty was on a four-day break.

The roommate was out the next day when the airline called to ask Betty to come off her four-day and work a trip. There was no answer. So, they called the landlord of the two-family house where the two girls lived upstairs.

"Betty's not here," the owner informed the airline. "She's in the hospital."

A simple situation. It obviously was, except in the mind of Betty's supervisor, who promptly wrote her up for not notifying the airline of her *change of address*. The airline reviewed the case and didn't bring any punishment against Betty.

Conduct unbecoming a stewardess: Now here's bit of vague, ill-defined and questionable double-talk. Under this heading, we can be fired for almost anything. Naturally, the interpretation of this clause varies with the airline involved. Each airline chooses its girls for different reasons. Each airline likes a certain type of girl, and betraying her "type" would be construed as conduct unbecoming a stewardess.

COFFEE, TEA OR ME?

American seems to prefer the all-American girl. They judge her conduct accordingly. It becomes difficult to ascertain what is an all-American girl. Hugh Hefner claims the girls in his centerfold are all-American girls, like the ones you find next door. We don't think American has this in mind.

TWA evidently interprets stewardess conduct as that of a Vassar or Wellesley graduate. TWA girls have that air about them, and to violate that vague, questionable image would not be prudent for a TWA hostess.

Braniff, from what we've observed, considers a large, full bosom necessary when judging stewardess conduct and appearance. Betty O'Riley's impressive overhang would not have violated the Braniff image. Her conduct is another matter.

United has average girls, in every sense of the word. This is good, because you can then apply average, middle-of-the-road criteria to a United girl's performance. Average usually has a negative meaning. Not so with United. It just means their girls aren't far out one way or the other, and usually wear medium-cup bras.

Why do National Airline stewardesses have that hard look? They're sexy, but it's a knowing look of sex, too knowing for most other airlines. Stew-bums say you almost expect a National girl to set an alarm clock next to her bed when entertaining a gentleman. We're sure that isn't true, but it is a graphic way of stating it.

PSA, that California airline, has what are probably the pick of American womanhood. Take everything good about all other stewardesses, lump it together in one package, and you have a USA stewardess. Amazing for a smaller airline.

Air Canada naturally likes plump, British-looking girls. Their standards of stewardess conduct must be based on the British system, one that many men seem to prefer.

Eastern's girls are improving.

Delta's girls are southern.

Pan Am's girls are primarily the snobby, jet-set type. Unfortunately, many of them only strive to be this way. They don't make it too much of the time.

COFFEE, TEA OR ME?

Other airlines have their own standards. And as a stewardess you live up to those standards—or else.

One of the most exasperating jobs is that of a union leader in your city. We have a good friend who has held this job for over a year, and her life is a series of middle-of-the-night telephone calls from girls in trouble.

"I'm pregnant."

"They caught me stealing a lobster tail."

"I just got married."

"I've been raped."

"This V.P. is after me to go to bed with him. He says I'll lose my job. What should I do?"

"I told a passenger he was a pain in the you know what and I'm sure he's going to write."

"The captain's wife knows."

"My husband knows."

"The supervisor knows."

"I know."

And so on.

Also included in the union leader's life are the pleas for money by a broke stewardess, confessions of an alcoholic, dope runner, aborted mother, and just plain homesick gal. It's a tough job.

As a group, we're reasonably happy with our pay, even though it isn't great. Girls now start at about $345 a month. That sounds low, but the company pays for life insurance, medical bills, dry cleaning and our hotels, meals and cabs when we're away from home. Because we're home so little, we don't really need elaborate housing or a fancy car. Then there are the fringe benefits—the $40 weekends in Europe, the mere $312 to go around the world, the hotel passes and all the other extras. How can we really complain?

CHAPTER XXI

"A Layover Is Not What You Think"

Every job and every industry boasts its own peculiar set of terms and phrases. Being a stewardess for an airline is no different. We have our own jargon that we communicate with effectively. Some of it is as follows:

Actual flying time: The time from the moment the blocks are removed from the wheels of the aircraft at the point of departure, to when they're replaced at point of arrival.

ATC: Air Travel Card. We give you credit for a little status when we know you have such a card. We credit you with similar status when you flash a membership card to an airline's VIP club. It doesn't always mean you deserve status. Some of our greatest disappointments are card holders. But it's a reference point with which to begin.

Belly: Underneath the plane where the baggage is carried.

Bid Sheets: Each month, every stewardess receives a bid sheet on which she bids for certain trips the following month. Naturally, the longer you've been flying, the more preference you're given. It takes at least a year before you've achieved enough seniority to get what you bid. This can fluctuate according to how rapidly the girls are finding men and leaving the job for marriage. In a good year, when romance is running wild, you can climb up the seniority ladder more quickly.

Booze report: How many bottles of liquor were served on any given flight? That question, and its answer, will determine how many bottles must be returned after the flight. It's all on the beverage report. By the way, we don't get away with as many bottles as the airline believes we do. It's not easy.

Bumped: We're going to Phoenix for a glorious weekend vacation. We're flying on a free pass. We get as far as Chicago and keep our fingers crossed. We're told it looks good—there are two open seats and we can have them. And then you come running down to catch that Phoenix flight at the last minute. You bump us off the trip. We

COFFEE, TEA OR ME?

spend the weekend drinking in Chicago to keep warm. Thanks.

CAT: This is not a term to describe a new counter-espionage group. It stands for Clear Air Turbulence, that mysterious and undefinable rough air you hit when flying on a clear, beautiful day. It causes many problems, usually because seat belts are unfastened when we hit it. CAT never shows up on aircraft radar.

Cattle Car: Tourist-class aircraft or the tourist section of a two-class airplane.

Cockpit key: Our government frowns on passengers entering the flight deck and hi-jacking the airplane. Thus, we have a Federal Regulation that dictates that the cockpit door will be closed and locked at all times. We each carry a key under our jacket.

Credit time: If any crew member is away from his home base for too long a time, the pay scale is adjusted accordingly to a higher rate. We then are paid for our credit time.

Crew sched: These are the men who schedule stewardess trips and check us in and out. They're located in operations and, for the most part, are pretty good guys.

CTO agent: City ticket agent who works behind the counter in the city.

Dead head: It could mean you're dull. But more often it means a crew member is returning to his home base as a passenger. He or she has worked a trip to some city and must return home without a flight to work.

Demo O2 mask: The oxygen mask we use to demonstrate procedure before take-off. Black pepper in it is a marvelous way to reap revenge on a naughty girl.

Ferry: Bringing an aircraft or crew back from somewhere to another point. Passengers never fly on ferry flights.

Flag stop: A special stop to pick up passengers left stranded through the fault of the airline. Especially prevalent during bad weather in certain sections of the country or during strikes by other airlines.

Flight deck: Airline's fancy term for what you've always called the cockpit. This change in nomenclature is designed to dispense with the World War I image of pilot with silk scarf around neck and wind in face, goggles, etc. Call it what you will, but we must call it flight deck. OK?

Flight pay log: All crew members keep records of their flying time for pay purposes on this sheet, which is kept in the cockpit.

FTO agent: Field ticket agent who works behind the counter at the airport.

Galley: Where we cook up all the goodies you enjoy on your flight. Also called the buffet area, when someone wants to add class to the conversation. In reality, it's a kitchen, no cleaner or dirtier than yours at home and designed for the same functions. It's also the only solitary place on an airplane where a stewardess can retreat and lick her wounds. Please take note that we *hate* people to poke their heads in the galley when the drapes are closed.

Jump seat: An extra seat on an airplane where the stewardess sits on take-off and landing.

Layover: Our moment of complete collapse. We lay over after working a trip to a destination away from home base. We stay there for a period of time and then return home on the return leg of the trip. If you're laying over somewhere too, and would like to "bump into" a stewardess, you might try the following hotels:

NEW YORK
    Lexington
    St. Moritz
    International Inn
    Commodore

MIAMI
    Skyways
    Miami International Inn

ATLANTA
    Air Host Inn
    International Inn
    Holiday Inn
    Hilton Inn

COFFEE, TEA OR ME?

ST. LOUIS
　The Chase Hotel

CHICAGO
　Palmer House
　Various airport motels

DENVER
　Cosmopolitan

SEATTLE
　Olympia

WASHINGTON, D.C.
　Burlington
　Shoreham
　Conrad's
　Mayflower

SALT LAKE CITY
　Newhouse

BOISE
　Boisean (Didn't know you could find a stewardess in Boise, did you?)

DALLAS
　Hilton Inn

NEW ORLEANS
　Hilton Inn

BOSTON
　Hilton Inn
　Copley Square

LOS ANGELES
　International Inn
　Airport Marina
　Miramar
　Santa Monica

COFFEE, TEA OR ME?

SAN FRANCISCO
 Hyatt House
 Holiday Inn
 Downtown Hilton

MEXICO CITY
 Vista Hermosa
 Maria Isabel

ACAPULCO
 Hotel Caleta

PHOENIX
 Adams

NEWARK
 Robert Treat

TORONTO
 Skyline

CLEVELAND
 Sheraton Cleveland

Mechanical: Trouble with the equipment on a flight that causes delay or cancellation.

Milk run: Those puddle-jumping flights that stop at many places before reaching their final destination. We just pray when working them that we won't develop aircraft trouble and be forced to spend the night in one of the intermediate cities.

Mis-connect: Our airline has booked you on the wrong flight or we were late and you missed your next trip. You're a mis-connect and we're sorry.

O.L.P.: We call you this when you've made your reservation through one airline for passage on another. You're an off-line passenger.

O.S.B.: Actually means Other Stations Boarding. You've made your reservations in one city but board in another. You're an O.S.B. Talk nasty to us and we shift the letters.

COFFEE, TEA OR ME?

Over-water pay: Flying trips over water bring extra pay for stewardesses.

PA check: Our supervisor sneaks on board the plane before take-off and checks us for all necessary items. Gloves, flashlight, grease pencil, etc. Naturally, we're never one hundred percent right, and as passengers, you should be happy supervisors conduct these PA checks. There's no telling what we'd forget without them.

Pass rider: An employee riding free on a pass. All such passengers fly space available, and are only there because the plane did not have a full load of paying passengers. Airline employees are instructed not to tell other passengers they're traveling free. There's no sense upsetting the guy next to you who has just paid $200 for his ticket.

PSR: Passenger service representative. His job with any airline is to try and soothe you when your feathers are ruffled. It's a very difficult job and you really can't blame any of these people for turning to the bottle later in their lives.

Reserve: When we're on reserve, it simply means we're on call to cover any trip that is short of a stewardess. Being on reserve is usually the plight of junior girls who can't win bids. You'll also find senior girls flying reserve because they didn't bother bidding for a particular month or turned their bid sheet in past the deadline. One thing is certain: Fostering a love interest is damned tough when you're on reserve.

Seat chart: The chart on which we record your names and destinations; that is, when we can spell your name. You might try helping us once in a while.

Senior pay: The senior stew on a trip receives extra pay for the paperwork she's responsible for.

CHAPTER XXII

"An Unhappy Landing"

I got on the 707 bound for San Francisco low in spirit. My gloomy mood was a combination of many things. I still had a bad taste in my mouth from my ugly experience with the Hollywood star. I couldn't get Sally Lu completely out of my mind. A kind of general lethargy had set in—I didn't have my old pep and zoom. I no longer bounced out of bed in the morning, eager to get on a plane, meet the day's passengers, wrestle with the flight's problems. The routine seemed monotonous. The problems were boring. I'd already met all the passengers. Clearly I was in the doldrums.

The Chuck situation bothered me, too. He was the greatest guy I'd ever met. Everything was marvelous between us. The fact that I didn't see him very often kept the level of excitement high. It was like a holiday when he turned up. He'd made it pretty clear that he might be interested in marrying me someday, some remotely future day when I'd gotten all the flying and the chasing after glamour out of my system. I was sick of flying as of right now. Did that mean I was ready to marry Chuck?

My thoughts sped round and round like little animals in a cage. I was really in a poisonous mood as I passed out the second round of drinks on the San Francisco flight. Suddenly I felt a tap on my fanny. I spun around. It was Mr. Shackwood in the last row of first-class seats. He was a man with one of those tight expressionless little faces and a hairline mustache. I never like that type. I waggled my index finger in front of his nose. "That's a no-no. Mustn't touch." That was my automatic answer to tappers and pinchers.

He beckoned me closer to him. "Lean over. I want to tell you something."

There was nothing to do but lean over and hope he wouldn't start crawling down the front of my blouse. "How about when we get to San Francisco," he said, "I buy you a dinner and then we go to my hotel and screw."

That was precisely the invitation I needed at that moment in my life. And from this vile little creep. "I guess you mean tonight," I snarled at him.

He grinned broadly, "That's right."

"That's what I thought." I walked away from him in utter disdain. Rachel was getting the dinner trays ready in the galley. "If Shackwood rings in the back of this section, you take him. I'm likely to toss him out a window."

"Sure, Trudy." He rang at that moment.

Rachel trotted off and was back a few minutes later.

"Trudy, did you know that one out of every ten girls will accept a direct pitch from a guy? Did you know that a magazine article suggested that a man simply stand on a street corner and say to the first ten girls who pass, 'How about going to bed with me?' The magazine says one out of the ten will accept. How about that?"

"I never heard of such a thing. It's ridiculous."

Rachel looked me squarely in the eye. She squinted a little and kept looking at me. Finally, she cleared her throat and said, "Well, Trudy, old friend and confidant, you'll be pleased to know that you're number ten."

"What are you talking about?"

"Shackwood back there. His theory. He told me all about it, and said he tried it on you. And he's bragging it worked. Tell me, did you accept a date with him tonight in San Fran? Did you agree to go to bed with him? Just like that?"

"Rachel, he's out of his nasty mind. I never agreed to any such thing."

"Did he pinch you?"

"He tapped me on the rear end."

"He tried with me, too. But they don't call me ol' swivel hips for nothing. Come on, Trudy, let's have it. What did you tell him?"

"Rachel, stop it. You know I never accepted anything from that . . . that cretin."

"Save your breath. It's him you'd better convince."

I avoided Shackwood as much as possible. Rachel took over that side of the airplane. He sat there leering at me, his tongue going back and forth over his lips. He hissed at me a couple of times and tried to motion me over to him with his head. I looked the other way and served my passengers.

"Ladies and gentlemen, we now proudly present a feature-length motion picture for your enjoyment." Rachel was reading the standard announcement for show time on the 707. She went through the instructions about dialing the volume tuning, the music channels and using the headphones. Everyone settled back to enjoy second drinks and the film. It was a brand new Hollywood release, a Grade-B thriller with go-go girls, good guys and bad guys, a sinister plot to steal sinister secret papers, wild chases in automobiles over sheer mountain cliffs, through sleepy little peasant towns and in airplanes that seemed to crash every twenty frames. All this frantic action completely captured the passengers, and I used the short lull to freshen up in one of the two vacant lavatories.

I latched the door behind me, drew a deep breath, and took a long look at myself in the mirror. I smiled at myself and myself smiled back. The smile took an effort. "Come out of it, girl," I scolded. "What's happened to the old Trudy?" I was reaching for the door latch when I heard knocking on the wall. It came from the next lavatory. I put my ear to the wall.

"Hi there," I heard faintly through the partition. It was Shackwood. "Clever, clever," he said. "Great way to be able to talk to me without anyone else listening. You're a clever one, sweetie pie. A-OK in my book. A-OK."

I should have pulled my ear away but I listened from sheer outrage.

"You know what, pumpkin? You've got great pectorals."

Suddenly I was back in Amarillo, and standing behind that wall in the next lavatory was Henry, my pre-med boyfriend with the Braille approach to necking. Two years of escape and this is how I ended up. I almost started to cry.

Shackwood laughed a deep, dirty laugh.

"Tits. Boobs. You've got great ones."

I opened the door and stepped out into the aisle. So did he. I tried to walk past him but he managed to say, "Meet me in the one you just left in twenty minutes. A little quickie, huh?" He sat down with an air of conquest.

COFFEE, TEA OR ME?

I debated whether to tell the captain. It hardly seemed worth the trouble. I was a veteran stewardess, not a green kid fresh out of school. I could handle an overbearing nut like Shackwood myself.

People were just finishing their molded kumquat dessert with whipped cream and almonds, the bad guy was about to run an ice pick through the head of the good guy, and Shackwood was dozing off when it happened.

POP! EEEEEAAAAAAAH!!! ZIP! ZIP! ZAP! S-T-T-T-T-T

Everyone leaped out of his seat at once. The dissonant, screeching sounds had rushed through all the earphones into everyone's inner ear. Passengers frantically tore the phones from their heads. The picture went black. And smoke started seeping from the entertainment control panel at the front of the aircraft.

Everyone started yelling at us at once.

"Something's wrong with the sound, miss."

"I was listening to a beautiful thing by Ravel when it happened. Terrible. Simply terrible."

"Man, they was just gettin' inta somethin' when everything like went to a minor chord."

"Booooooooooo," someone yelled from the couch section.

Rachel did a quick PA as I went forward to inform the captain of the problem. The flight engineer came back and opened the control panel. He touched a wire and sparks started flying.

"Goddamn it," he drawled, "I always said movies don't have any place on an airplane." He pulled a couple of wires loose and the smoke stopped.

"That's all I can do 'til we arrive. Better tell 'em they'll have to go to their local theatre to see the end of the movie."

Rachel apologized on the PA and I started up the aisle to flash a stewardess smile at the disgruntled folks. I hadn't taken three steps when what never happens, happened. All together, in unison, all the oxygen masks dropped from their storage compartments above each seat. Down they came, orange face masks on white plastic ethers. They bobbed up and down in everyone's face. Most of the faces turned white. No one listens when the stewardess goes through the oxygen mask procedure prior to each flight. It's silly to worry about that. You'll never need them.

People started grabbing masks. Some, aware of the stated procedure, clamped them to their faces and started breathing quickly into them. Some yanked them right out of the ceiling slots. Five or six stood up, masks in hand, and yelled at Rachel and me for help. We showed them what to do. Then we grabbed our masks and started breathing.

It took us a few minutes before we began wondering why one of the cockpit crew hadn't come back to check on things. It was also strange we hadn't begun descending to a lower altitude. We continued to sit there breathing into the masks. Finally, the cockpit door opened and the First Officer stepped into the passenger cabin. He looked around at the emergency scene, looked at us, and looked back again at the passengers.

"What the hell's going on here?" he asked Rachel.

She gingerly took the mask from her face and told him about the emergency situation in the cabin. "The masks dropped and that means cabin pressure has changed. You know that . . . sir."

"There's nothing wrong with the pressure in this plane."

"So why'd the masks drop . . . sir?"

"How do I know? Tell these people to get those damn masks off their faces. There's nothing wrong."

"Yes, sir."

We did a PA in which we said the problem had been corrected and that all was well. A few didn't believe us and kept on breathing into their masks. We almost had to pry the mask away from the woman who loved Ravel.

We walked up the aisle checking each passenger. No one seemed any worse for the experience, except Mr. Shackwood. Unfortunately, I'd forgotten about him and made the mistake of checking his side of the cabin.

He was sitting limply in his seat, his collar open,

face white and wet. He rolled his eyes up at me and groaned.

"Are we going to die?" he asked weakly.

I couldn't resist it. "Yup."

His eyes really rolled now, and his lips quivered.

"Miss," he pleaded.

"Yes?"

"I'm sorry."

"For what?"

"For saying those things to you."

"You should be."

"If there was a priest here, I'd tell him that, too."

"I didn't know you were a religious man, Mr. Shackwood."

"Oh, yes. Eight kids, too. Forgive me."

"You're forgiven. Go in peace."

He looked relieved.

After much cockpit speculation about what had caused the masks to pop, it was decided that the short circuit in the entertainment system had also shorted out another circuit that controlled the masks.

"Do you know that more people are killed riding bicycles every year than on commercial airplanes, Trudy?" Rachel asked as we cleaned up the galley.

"I've been told."

"And that more people are killed at railroad crossings, too?"

"Those statistics must have come out before in-flight entertainment. I have the feeling this multi-million-dollar bird is about to fall out from under us."

"Let's not worry about it, Trudy. You're just generally jumpy anyway. You've been like a caged cat the past few weeks."

I tried not to worry anymore. I didn't have long not to worry because we had another mishap in five minutes. This time it was nothing as complicated as short circuits in the movies. It wasn't even as dramatic as the oxygen masks dropping by mistake. All it involved was Number three engine quitting. You couldn't even see it, an ob-

298

vious advantage a jet has over the easily observed prop engine. We didn't know it until our captain told us.

"Number Three quit," he said flatly.

"Figures," I mumbled.

"Huh?"

"I said it's good we have three more."

"Let's hope they don't quit."

"Could they?"

"Never know."

I smiled. "Two years is too long."

"What, Trudy?" The captain was in no mood for games.

"I said two years is too long. To be a stew. Don't you agree?"

"Oh, sure. Too long."

"That's what I said."

No one in the passenger cabin knew anything else had happened to the jet. And we weren't about to tell them, even though regulations state that passengers should be alerted to any malfunction that might possibly cause injury, no matter how remote the possibility. The loss of one engine was in no way a major threat to anyone's safety. But, if we went by the book, we'd tell them. We decided the book was for reading, not necessarily aloud. We skipped any announcement.

We started our let-down for the San Francisco approach when the cockpit signaled we were wanted up front.

"Small problem, girls."

My heart came up in my throat and stuck there. I swallowed it back down to where it belonged and listened as the captain explained the next foul-up in an already less-than-perfect trip.

"That little light says the gear won't go down. Doesn't mean it won't. But then again, you hate to turn your back on that little light. If it's right, no wheels. If it's wrong, wheels. That simple. Just like they told you in school." He laughed.

"We didn't tell them about the engine. We'd better tell them about this. What's procedure?"

COFFEE, TEA OR ME?

"The usual. Crash position for everybody. Make sure they realize it might be just a foul-up in the bulb. But maybe not. You two have been around enough time. You know what to say."

"Two years."

"Oh yeh. I remember. Happy anniversary."

Rachel did the PA. I gave no sign of fear, although my heart was galloping. Shackwood flailed his arms around in the air for me to come.

"What's it feel like?" he asked with trembling lips.

"What's what feel like?"

"When you hit. You know, when you . . . hit. What's it like?"

"I haven't any idea. Don't worry. You'll be OK." I'd forgiven him. You can't bear a grudge in a plane with one engine out and maybe no landing gear.

A pass over the airport showed the wheels down in proper position. But that was no assurance they were locked in place. We dumped all excess fuel, had all passengers take the emergency position of head down between the knees, pillow on lap, eyeglasses off, high heels under seats, and seat belts securely fastened. We braced ourselves along with them as the big jet settled down onto the concrete ribbon at San Francisco. The wheels touched the ground, lost contact for a moment, touched again and stayed there, firmly and securely locked under everyone.

I had just gotten out my deep sigh of very sincere relief when the captain's voice came over the PA. He had applied reverse thrust on the engines, the three of them that were functioning, and the plane was slowing down for the turn-off onto a taxi strip.

"Ah, ladies and gentlemen, a light in the flight deck indicates a fire condition somewhere on the aircraft. Please make ready for emergency evacuation through the emergency exits as marked. Please wait for your stewardesses to lead the way on the inflated chutes. This is purely a precaution in case fire is present."

Click. Off went his voice and a few shrieks came from the cabin. Rachel grabbed my arm and we blew out the emergency exits and popped the long, limp emergency

COFFEE, TEA OR ME?

chutes that dangled from the doorways to the concrete below. Fire vehicles were racing across the field, their sirens screaming loudly.

The chutes were supposed to inflate, providing a smooth trough for each passenger to slide down to the safety of the ground. But these chutes are famous for not fully inflating. Ours were no exception. They stiffened up halfway and quit.

Rachel helped the first passenger out the door, and we watched her bounce down, make it almost to the ground, and then roll off the edge. She landed with a resounding thud on the concrete. Rachel, realizing she should be down there to help clear the bottom, went next. She landed hard on her rear end, her skirt sliding up around her hips.

One little kid enjoyed the ride down. The Ravel lover refused at first. Then, after I insisted, she made the plunge. She went off the side almost immediately and landed on her shoulder, obviously hurt. Two ambulance attendants worked over her.

The cabin emptied out fast. Finally, only two people remained; Shackwood and me.

"No, no. After you." He'd suddenly gained some sense of courage and valor.

"*Now*, Mr. Shackwood."

"You first."

"Please, Mr. Shackwood. Quickly."

I wasn't about to argue with him. I grabbed the edges of the door and slid myself onto the chute. I no sooner touched the chute than I felt Shackwood jump on behind me, his legs hugging around my hips, his hands securely fastened on my chest.

"Wheeeee," he screamed as we down. We both went off the edge. Shackwood landed on top of me, his hands still holding onto my breasts as though they were handles.

I ached all over, but managed to scramble out from under his dead weight. "You . . . you . . . you dirty, filthy sex fiend," I screamed at him. Then I swung and my fist caught his jaw. It sent him back two or three steps.

COFFEE, TEA OR ME?

Rachel grabbed me from behind and pulled me away. Shackwood started screaming to anyone who would listen about how he'd have me fired. I tried to go after him again but Rachel hung on tight. I finally just broke down and cried.

There had been no fire in the aircraft. It was just another one of those lousy little lights that decided to light up at the wrong time. Shackwood's complaint against me was dismissed after Rachel told my supervisor about his actions on-board. Even with her testimony, the airline was a little reluctant to take the word of a stewardess over that of a paying customer, especially a religious family man with eight potential travelers for the future.

I was pretty well bruised, but nothing serious. I rubbed my aches and pains for a week while on sick leave, and soon the black, blue and purple spots disappeared. But the depression didn't.

Rachel tried everything, we dated every good-looking fellow we could entice. We partied, drank, told funny stories, saw funny movies and kept every minute filled with some sort of gay activity. But it really wasn't very effective.

I told my supervisor about my feelings, and she appeared sympathetic—to a point.

"You know, Trudy, we can't have an unhappy, unsmiling stewardess serving our valued travelers, can we?"

That seemed logical.

"One must always remember, Trudy, that one paying to travel our airline expects the finest and most pleasant service from our girls."

"Yes."

"But one also knows that occasionally, one becomes upset over certain situations."

"Yes."

"You've contributed two valuable years to service Trudy. We recognize that. Now it's up to you. We can't have you flying the line in the frame of mind you obviously have developed recently. One can understand that, can't one?"

COFFEE, TEA OR ME?

"Yes." Who was this One she kept talking about?

"I'd like to suggest a course of action, Trudy, that might prove valuable to you . . . and the airline. We can recommend a good psychiatrist who might help you become once again the happy, smiling stewardess you were. How do you feel about that?"

"Yes. I mean fine. Why not? One must do these things at times, mustn't one?"

"Guess what, Rachel?" I said with more enthusiasm than I'd been able to summon for weeks.

"Shackwood apologized, he's divorcing his wife and you're marrying him."

"Right."

"Which goes to prove that one out of two girls will accept a marriage proposal from a perfect stranger."

"I'm going to a psychiatrist, Rachel."

"Why?"

"Our super thinks I should. And maybe she's right. Anyway, I kind of think it's that or stop flying. And I really don't want to quit."

"What doc are you going to?"

"She gave me a name. I think he's an old guy from Vienna with a beard."

"Take notes and tell me what he says," Rachel said. "And I'll split the bill with you. That way he can shrink two heads for the price of one."

Remember, I told you way back at the beginning that we only had one head between us?

CHAPTER XXIII

"We'll Give It One More Year, Okay?"

It turned out the psychiatrist was a *young* man from Vienna with a beard.

"Take the chair by the window, Trudy. You'll be more comfortable." The doctor tactfully waved me away from the couch, a heavily tufted black leather monster that looked slippery and uninviting. He seated himself behind his desk and shuffled papers for a few minutes. I noticed he wasn't wearing a wedding ring, and my keen stewardess eyes could detect no pale, fleshy ring of a band hastily removed. An unmarried, I thought, and a doctor to boot. Unusual—very unusual.

"Now, Trudy, let's talk a bit. Let's see if we can't find out a few things about Trudy Baker."

"What's to find out? I feel rotten. Totally rotten."

"Totally?"

"Yes."

"Physically?"

"Headaches."

"That's all physically?"

"Yes."

He smiled and stroked his beard. "But I'm not a headache doctor, Trudy. You know that."

"But if my headache is psychosomatic, and I'm internalizing and reverting back to mother problems, my headache would certainly fall into your area of specialization. Wouldn't it?"

He sat up straight. I noticed for the first time a nervous tick in his left eye. If I didn't know better, I'd have thought he was winking at me.

He got up from behind his desk and walked to a table on the far side of the room. He poured a drink of water from a silver and teak executive pitcher and drank slowly.

"Could I have a drink, doctor?"

It startled him. "Oh, of course, Miss Baker." He couldn't find another glass and had to ring for his nurse. She brought one.

He sat down again behind the desk, his eye going at thirty winks a minute.

"Do you think you *do* have a mother problem, Trudy? Do you think you *are* internalizing?"

"How should I know? I just read a little before I came here. How should I know what's the matter with me? I just know I'm not the same Trudy everyone knows. I'm depressed and blue and itchy and jumpy. Thinking of climbing on another airplane gives me the creeps. And I want to keep on working as a stewardess."

He stroked his beard and said, "hmmmmmmmmm."

I felt a surge of vocal energy.

"You see, doctor, you fly long enough and you meet so many different people that sometimes you lose faith in the human race. Rachel says . . ."

"Who's Rachel?"

"Oh, she's my very best friend. We're very close."

"Hmmmmmmmmmmm."

"Why do you say hmmmmmmmmmmm, doctor?"

"Just how close are you and Rachel?"

"You couldn't get any closer."

"Hmmmmmmmm. Has there ever been any intimacy between you?"

"Oh sure. We share the closest secrets. Why . . ." It dawned on me what he was getting at.

"Absolutely not, doctor. Rachel and I are normal, heterosexual young ladies."

He almost seemed disappointed. There was a long period of silence.

"Doctor, do you mind if I take notes?"

"Take notes? Why?"

"Oh, just for the fun of it."

"Well, I've never had this occur before with any patient. Do you always take notes?"

"I've never been to a headshrink . . . Ah, psychiatrist before."

He seemed to be searching back into his textbook past for a proper answer. His eye went faster.

"If taking notes will make you feel better, please feel free to take notes."

"Thank you." I pulled out a steno pad and pencil and sat poised in the chair. Neither of us spoke. The doctor kept his eyes on the desk top. I looked straight at him.

He swiveled around in his chair and coughed and winked and cleared his throat.

"Now, Miss Baker, suppose we begin."

"OK."

Silence.

"Ah, let's see doctor. I was born in a small town and had a boyfriend named Henry."

"Henry, huh? Did you have a normal sexual relationship with this young man?"

"Well, we always did things in Braille."

"What?"

"Braille. He liked to touch me."

"I see. And you didn't like to be touched."

"Oh, no. I loved it. Especially my popliteal."

"What's that?"

I giggled. "I thought all psychiatrists had to become medical doctors before psychiatrists."

I think he got mad. He snorted.

"That's the back of the knee, doctor." I took note in my steno pad of his facial reaction. He didn't like being exposed as not knowing something.

"What did you just write there, Miss Baker?" he asked angrily.

"I wrote you got mad because I knew something you didn't know."

"I wasn't mad," he said with a mad voice. "You can't expect me to remember every term from medical school."

"Henry went to medical school. He's still going."

"Who's Henry?"

"My boyfriend. The one with the Braille."

"I think you're trying to make fun of me, Miss Baker."

I hadn't been really. And I felt sorry for the doctor feeling that way.

"Oh, don't feel that way, doctor. I wouldn't make fun of you. Honest."

He seemed slightly relieved.

"You have to realize, Miss Baker, that being a doctor on a retainer fee from a company places certain strains on that doctor. Most of my income is derived from the air-

309

line and I'd hate to think of you going back and maki[ng] fun of me. It could cost me this job." He was sorry he said this. But I looked very understanding and tried [to] comfort him.

"Oh, doctor, I understand fully. It's very hard feeli[ng] secure these days in any company. I know." I took a fe[w] notes in my pad.

"What are you writing now?"

"That you're a nice guy."

"Oh, that's nice. Thank you."

"I guess being single is a problem for you, too." [I] couldn't help it. It just came out.

"Yes, a little bit . . . You see . . . Now wait a minut[e.] We're getting off the track here."

"I sure don't want to do that."

"Good." Forty winks a minute now. "Let's talk abo[ut] your recent experiences on the airplane that left yo[u] shaken."

I told him about Mr. Lippingdone and Mr. Shac[kel]wood. I told him about the drunks and pinchers and ki[ds] and captains. He said nothing. He just looked at his des[k] top and went "hmmmmm" a few times. I talked until [I] heard the tiny tinkle of an alarm bell ring from his des[k] drawer. It startled him more than it did me. He sat u[p] straight and turned on a very large smile for me.

"I think we're getting somewhere now, Miss Baker. O[r] may I call you Trudy?"

"By all means."

"That ends our first hour together. See my secretary o[n] the way out for an appointment next week."

I got up, stuffed my steno pad back in my purse, an[d] walked to the door. He stopped me by saying, "This i[s] just the beginning, Trudy. We have a long way to go. A long way. Perhaps in a few months I'll be able to recommend to the airline that you go back on the flying line. O[f] course, we'll continue to work together for at least a year. Maybe longer."

"Oh that'll be nice, doctor. And don't worry about [any]thing. I won't say anything that might upset the airlin[e] about you. In fact, I really like you."

COFFEE, TEA OR ME?

He beamed. "That's good, Trudy. It's important for the patient to like his or her psychiatrist."

"In fact," I continued, "I know a great girl for you. Would you like me to fix you up?"

"O no, Oh, no, no, no, no, no. I'll just see you next week."

I nodded my head and left. I didn't make an appointment with the secretary. I just walked straight home, singing, happy and gay for the first time in weeks. Rachel was at the apartment when I arrived.

"How was it?" she asked, never looking up from her copy of *The High and the Mighty*. (It was her tenth reading of it.)

"Great. He has problems. That's for sure. I think it might have something to do with his father never having taken him fishing. Or something like that."

"Idiot. He was supposed to help *you*. And me!"

"Who needs help? I feel the same as I always did . . ."

"Wow. This doc must be the best. What did he feed you? LSD?"

"He didn't feed me anything. I just feel better knowing someone else has more problems than I do. The blues have gone to someone else and I'm squared away."

"That's great, Trudy," Rachel said with much enthusiasm in her voice. "Great!"

I smiled.

"We'll give it one more year, OK? Then we'll both have found our respective knights on the white horses and we can move into houses next door to each other and write a book about it all over coffee."

"It's a deal, Rachel. One more year . . . By the way, do you think Betty Big Boobs would be interested in a young psychiatrist with a beard?"

We laughed.

We shook hands.

And had a mushroom pizza with extra cheese.

BANTAM BEST SELLERS

MILLIONS OF COPIES SOLD AT TOP PRICES!
NOW READ THEM
FOR JUST PENNIES!

Look over the list and order the ones you missed, at just a fraction of the price paid by millions for the same bestsellers in hardcover editions. Bantam's popular paperbacks are available at newsstands everywhere, or mail this page with check or money order directly to the publisher.

- [ ] REPORT OF THE NATIONAL ADVISORY COMMISSION ON CIVIL DISORDERS. What happened? Why did it happen? What can be done? (QZ4273—$1.25)

- [ ] A SEARCH FOR THE TRUTH. Ruth (A GIFT OF PROPHECY) Montgomery's startling personal experiences in the psychic world. (N3725—95¢)

- [ ] BY-LINE: ERNEST HEMINGWAY. Papa's behind-the-scenes news stories that served as the background for THE SUN ALSO RISES, A FAREWELL TO ARMS and FOR WHOM THE BELL TOLLS. (Q3788—$1.25)

- [ ] A GIFT OF PROPHECY. The startling story of the phenomenal Jeane Dixon, the woman who predicted Kennedy's assassination. (N4223—95¢)

- [ ] ANYONE CAN MAKE A MILLION by Morton Shulman. The man who turned $400.00 into a fortune tells all. (N3369—95¢)

- [ ] EDGAR CAYCE: THE SLEEPING PROPHET by Jess Stearn. Only paperback edition of the phenomenal national bestseller. (N3654—95¢)

- [ ] THE PASSOVER PLOT. A fascinating new interpretation of the life and death of Jesus by Dr. Hugh J. Schonfield. (N3341—95¢)

- [ ] THE MEDIUM IS THE MASSAGE by Marshall McLuhan and Quentin Fiore. This is the book that pictorially explains McLuhan's provocative philosophy—that electronic media are changing our daily lives. (R3348—$1.45)

AVAILABLE AT NEWSSTANDS EVERYWHERE

**BANTAM BOOKS, INC., Dept. GA1, Room 300,
271 Madison Ave., N. Y., N. Y. 10016**

Please mail me the Bantam Bestsellers checked above. I am enclosing $——————(Chck or money order—no currency, no C.O.D.'s please. If less than 5 books, add 10¢ per book for postage and handling.)

Name————————————————————————

Address——————————————————————

City——————————State——————Zip——————

Allow two to three weeks for delivery